Books by Jude Deveraux

The Velvet Promise
Highland Velvet
Velvet Song
Velvet Angel
Sweetbriar
Counterfeit Lady
Lost Lady
River Lady
Twin of Ice
Twin of Fire
The Temptress
The Raider
The Princess
The Awakening
The Maiden
The Taming
The Conquest
A Knight in Shining Armor
Wishes
Mountain Laurel
The Duchess
Eternity

Published by POCKET BOOKS

JUDE DEVERAUX

ETERNITY

POCKET STAR BOOKS
New York   London   Toronto   Sydney   Tokyo   Singapore

An *Original* Publication of POCKET BOOKS

A Pocket Star Book published by
POCKET BOOKS, a division of Simon & Schuster Inc.
1230 Avenue of the Americas, New York, NY 10020

Cover art by Hermine Brindak

Printed in the U.S.A.

Pocket Books
Proudly Announces

Jude Deveraux
SWEET LIAR

Coming in Hardcover
September 1992

The following is a preview
of *Sweet Liar* . . .

SWEET LIAR

Fifteen minutes after Samantha Elliot landed in New York City, her wallet was stolen. She knew it was her own fault because she'd reached inside her purse to get a tissue and forgotten to close the zipper, so all the thief had to do was slip his—her—hand inside and remove her wallet. One Master Card, one American Express gone, as well as most of her money. She'd had sense enough to put a hundred and fifty dollars in her carry-on so at least she wasn't destitute.

By the time she'd reported the theft, canceled her credit cards and gotten her suitcase, her carry-on slung over her shoulder, she was shaking with exhaustion and frustration.

Now all she had to do was get a taxi, the first taxi she had ridden in in her life, and get into the city.

Thirty minutes later she was inside the dirtiest automobile she had ever seen in her life. It stunk of cigarette smoke so strongly she thought she might be sick, but when she tried to roll down the window, she found that both of the inside handles of the doors were missing. She would have spoken to the driver but his name on the paper under the meter seemed to be spelled mostly of x's and k's and he didn't speak much English.

Looking out the dirty window of the cab, trying not to breathe, she tried not to think of anything at all, not where she was, why she was there, or how long she was going to have to stay.

The cab drove under a bridge that looked as though it should have been condemned, then down streets filled on both sides with tiny, dirty-windowed shops. When the driver asked for the address for the third time, Samantha gave it to him yet again, trying not to relay her frustration to him. The paper her father's attorney had given her said the apartment was in a brownstone, located in the east sixties, between Park and Lexington.

As the driver slowed, looking for the address, she saw she was on a street that seemed quieter and less cluttered than most areas she had seen. When the cab stopped she paid the driver, quickly tried to calculate the tip, then removed her two bags, without his help, from the floor of the car.

Looking up at the building in front of her, she saw a narrow five-story house—quite a pretty house actually—with a number of steps leading up to a front door. A wisteria vine growing up the left side of the house all the way to the roof was covered with purple buds just about to burst into bloom.

Samantha pushed the doorbell then waited. There was no answer. Even after three rings and fifteen minutes, there still was no answer.

"Of course," she said, sitting down on her suitcase. What had she expected? That the landlord would be there to give her a key? Just because she had written him and informed him of her arrival time didn't mean he should bother himself to be there to open the door for her. What did it matter to him that she wanted a shower and to sit down on something that wasn't moving?

As she sat on her suitcase waiting for her landlord, wondering if he was going to show up at all, she speculated about what she would do in a city the size of New York with no place to stay. Could she take a taxi to a hotel and spend the night there? Could she get her father's attorney to wire her more money until she could open a bank account in New York?

Several more minutes went by, but no one came, nor did most of the passersby seem to notice her. A couple of men smiled at her, but she pointedly looked away.

After a while Samantha noticed that down at ground level was another door into the house. Maybe that was the front door of the house and she was to knock there.

Not knowing whether it was safe or not to leave her bags up on the stoop, she decided to leave them and pray they weren't stolen. She walked down the steps and around a pretty, wrought-iron, spike-tipped fence before reaching the ground floor door, which she knocked on several times. There was no answer.

Taking a deep breath, her fists clenched, she looked back up at her suitcases sitting safely at the top of the stairs. Beside the ground floor door was a box of red geraniums and the sight of the flowers made her smile. At least the flowers seemed happy: they were well cared for, not a dead leaf on them, the soil moist but not wet, and the flowers were heavy with bloom.

Still smiling, she started toward the stairs, but just as she rounded the corner, a football came whizzing so close over her head that she ducked. When the flying football was followed by what looked like a couple hundred pounds of male clad in denim shorts and a sweat shirt with both armholes torn out to the waist, Samantha slammed herself flat against the wall of the stairs.

At least she tried to get out of the way of the man, but she wasn't fast enough. He caught the football as it sailed over her head, then, startled, he saw her just as he was about to land on her. At the same time that he released the ball, he reached out to catch Samantha before she fell against the spikes of the fence.

Giving a little gasp as she nearly fell, he caught her and pulled her to him in a protective way.

For a moment she stood encircled by his arms. He was taller than her five foot four, probably just at six feet, but the protective way he bent toward her, put them almost at eye level with each other. They were nearly isolated, with the tall stairs behind them, the next house's stairs not far in front of them, the fence and flower box nearby. Samantha started to say thank you to the man, but as she looked at him, she forgot what she was going to say.

He was an extraordinarily good-looking man, with black, curling hair, heavy black brows, and dark eyes with eyelashes any female would kill for, all atop a full-lipped mouth that looked as though it belonged on a sculpture by Michelangelo. He might have looked feminine if his nose hadn't been broken a couple of times and he didn't have three days' growth of black whiskers on his chin—and if his finely sculpted head weren't sitting on top of a body that bulged muscle. No, he didn't look feminine. All the eyelashes in the world couldn't make this man look less than one-hundred-percent male. In fact, maleness oozed from him, making Samantha feel small and helpless, as though she were wearing yards of lavender lace. He even smelled masculine: not like an artificial smell that could be purchased in a store; this man smelled of pure male sweat, a little beer, and acres of bronzed skin warmed by sun and exercise.

But it was the man's mouth that fascinated her the most. He

had the most beautiful mouth she'd ever seen on a human being. It was full and sculpted, looking both hard and soft at the same time, and she couldn't take her eyes off of it, and when she saw those lips moving toward her own, she didn't move away. He placed his lips on hers, softly at first, as though asking permission. Samantha, reacting to instinct and need and to something even more basic, opened her mouth slightly under his and he pressed closer. Had her life depended on it, she couldn't have moved her lips away from his warm, sweet mouth, but when she put her hand up in halfhearted protest, she came in contact with his shoulder. It had been a long while since she had felt male skin near her own. And she had never felt a shoulder such as this one. Hard, firm, round muscle rounded over the top of his arm—and Samantha's hand curved over the muscle, her fingers digging into the resilient flesh.

When her hand closed over his arm, he leaned closer to her, his big, hard, heavy body pressing against hers, pinning her close to the wall. Samantha's hand slipped to his back, slipped under his open-sided shirt and met with the contours of the muscle on his back.

A moan escaping her lips, her body began to sink into his.

Putting one big hand behind her head, he turned her to the side and began to kiss her with all the passion she had missed in her life. He kissed her the way she had always wanted to be kissed, had dreamed of being kissed, kissed her the way fairy tales are supposed to end, the way all the books say a kiss should feel—the way no one had ever kissed her before.

As he moved one of his big, muscular thighs between her much smaller ones, Samantha's arms went fully around his neck, pulling him closer, pulling him as close as he could come to her.

Moving his mouth away from hers, he kissed her neck, kissed her ear lobe as his hands moved down her back. Cupping her buttocks in his hands, he moved her so most of her weight was on his thigh, then ran one hand down the length of her leg and lifted it, settling her ankle about his waist.

"Hey, Mike, you're drawin' a crowd."

At first Samantha didn't hear the voice, didn't hear anything; she only felt.

It was the man who broke away. Pulling his lips from her skin, he put his hand to her cheek, caressing her cheek with his thumb while looking into her eyes, smiling at her.

"Hey, Mike, this your long-lost cousin or somebody you picked up on the street?"

Leaning forward, the man gave Samantha one more soft kiss then took her ankle from his waist and held her hand.

It was when he moved away from her that Samantha began to think again. And the first emotion she felt was horror, absolute, sheer horror at what she had done. She tried to snatch her hand from the man's grasp but he held her fast.

There were three sweaty men, men who looked as though they wore their cigarettes rolled up in their tee-shirt sleeves and drank beer for breakfast, standing in front of them, all with leers on their faces, all with smirking expressions, as though they knew something they weren't supposed to know. "You gonna introduce us or not?"

"Sure," the man said, holding onto Samantha's hand in spite of her tugs as he pulled her forward. "I'd like you to meet . . ." Turning, he looked at her in question.

Samantha looked away from him; she didn't want to look in his face again. No mirror was needed to tell her that her own face was brilliant red with embarrassment. "Samantha Elliot," she managed to whisper.

"Oh yeah?" the man holding her hand said, then looked back at the three men, who were now nudging each other at this new knowledge that Mike didn't know the woman he had moments before been kissing as though he meant to swallow her whole.

"I'd like you to meet my tenant," the man said with a grin. "She's going to be living in my house with me." The pride and delight in his voice came through clearly.

Giving a sharp jerk on her hand, Samantha freed herself from his grip. She would have thought her incredulity could not deepen, but at the realization of who this man was, it did. Horror, humiliation, panic, revulsion, were all emotions that crowded into her, and she wanted to flee. Or die. Or, preferably both.

"Some roommate!" Laughing in a vulgar way, one of the men looked her up and down.

"You wanna live with me, baby, just let me know," the second man said.

"With you *and* your wife," the third man said, hitting the second one in the ribs. "Honey, I'm not married. I'll take real good care of you. Better than Mike would—or could."

"Get out of here!" Mike yelled back good-naturedly, no animosity in his voice, just good humor as he picked up the football and tossed it to them.

One of the men caught the ball and the three of them went off down the street, punching each other and laughing as they walked.

The man turned to her. "I'm Mike." Putting out his hand to shake, he didn't seem to understand when Samantha only stared at him. "Michael Taggert." When she still didn't respond, he began to explain. "Your landlord. You wrote me a letter, remember?"

Not saying a word, Samantha walked past him, careful not to touch him, and went up the stairs. Her luggage was in her hands before he was beside her.

"Wait a minute while I open the door. I hope the apartment's all right for you. I had a crew come in and clean the place and put clean sheets on your bed. I'm sorry I wasn't here when you arrived but I lost track of the time and— Hey! where are you going?"

A suitcase in each hand, Samantha had gone down the stairs and was three houses down the block by the time he got the door unlocked.

Bounding down the stairs two at a time, Mike came to a stop in front of her, and reached out to take her bags. She jerked them away from him, trying to walk around him, but he wouldn't let her pass.

"You're not mad because I was late, are you?"

Giving him a quick, hard glare, Samantha again tried to move around him. After three pivots, all of which he blocked, she turned and started walking in the other direction, but he blocked her in that way too. Finally, she stopped and glared at him. "Would you please let me pass?"

"I don't understand," he said. "Where are you going?"

Still glaring at him, she said, "Mr. Taggert, I am going to find a hotel."

"A hotel? But I have your apartment all ready for you. You haven't even seen it yet so you can't dislike it. It's not me, is it? I told you I was sorry I was late. I'm not usually late but my watch got wet last week and it's in the shop and I couldn't tell what time it was. And those bozos I was with probably couldn't tell time if they had a watch and could figure out how to buckle it on."

Giving him a look that was meant to wither him on the spot, Samantha moved around him.

But he wasn't to be put off so easily as he stepped back in front of her and started walking backward. "It's the guys, isn't it? Pretty crude, aren't they? I apologize for them. I only see them when I want to toss a ball around with someone, and I see them at the gym. I mean, I don't see them socially, if that's what's worrying you. You won't have to see them in our house. I promise."

Halting for a moment, Samantha had to marvel at the man. How could he be so very beautiful and understand so very little? She forced herself to look away from him. It was his beauty that had gotten her into trouble in the first place.

When she started walking again, he was beside her. "If it's not that I was late and it's not the guys, then what's the problem?" he asked.

At the corner of the block, she stopped. Now what should she do? she wondered. She had no idea where she was or where she was going, but she saw lots of yellow-painted taxis driving by. In the movies people hailed taxis by standing on the curb and lifting their arms, so she hoisted her tote bag onto her shoulder and raised her arm. Within seconds a taxi came to a halt in front of her. Acting as though this was something she'd done a thousand times, she put her hand on the car door.

"Wait a minute!" Mike said as she started to open the door to the cab. "You can't leave. You've never been in the city before, and you don't know where you're going."

"I am going as far away from you as I can get," she answered, not looking at him.

Mike's face was the embodiment of surprise. "But I thought you liked me."

With a gasp of exasperation, Samantha started to get into the cab.

But Mike stopped her by taking her suitcase, then her arm, both of which he held firmly. "You're not leaving," he said. Then, glancing into the cab at the driver, he said, "Beat it."

The driver took one look at Mike, at the muscles bulging on his body, most of them exposed by the skimpy clothing he was wearing, and asked no questions, not even waiting for Mike to slam the door before he sped away.

"All right," Mike said quietly, as though talking to a skittish horse. "I don't know what's going on, but we're going to talk about it."

"Where? In your house? The house where I'm supposed to live with you?" Samantha asked angrily.

"Is that what this is all about? You're mad at me because I kissed you?" Giving her a slow, soft smile, his voice lowered significantly. "I rather thought you liked my kissing you," he said, stepping closer to her.

"Get away from me." She took a step backward. "I know this is a city that's not supposed to care, but I imagine someone will pay attention if I start screaming."

At that Mike stepped back and looked at her. She was dressed in a prim little "outfit"—that's the only word he could think of to describe what she had on—of navy blue. It was a very plain dress with a skirt that reached below her knees and a jacket with a white collar and cuffs, and, somehow, that boring little dress managed to completely hide every curve of her body. If Mike hadn't just had his hands all over her and hadn't felt for himself what an incredible body she had, he would have thought she was straight as a stick. When he'd kissed her he'd found his hand at the small of her back, atop what seemed to be a rather deliciously curved fanny, and he'd run his hand down the length of her, over the lovely curve of her bottom, down firm, perfect thighs, down to her ankle and her slim, little foot. He would have taken odds on it being impossible to hide a body like hers under any amount of clothing, but somehow she had done it.

Looking at her face, he saw that she was a cross between pretty and cute, but she wore very little makeup, as though she meant to detract from her prettiness, rather than enhance it, and her hair was pulled tightly back from her face. He could tell her hair was long and the way she wore it made it look absolutely straight, but a wisp had escaped from the band at the back and the stray strand curled along her cheek. Remembering his thumb pulling that strand loose, Mike now wished he could touch it again.

But looking at her now, it was difficult to believe that this was the woman he'd kissed, for there was no sexiness in her face or her body. Actually, in her prim little dress, her blonde hair pulled back in a neat and utterly tidy bun, he would have thought she was the mother of a couple of children and taught Sunday School, and if he'd passed her on the street, he wouldn't have looked twice at her. But he remembered vividly that he'd seen her looking very different a few minutes ago. The lusty, desirable, hungry beauty who'd kissed him was in there somewhere.

When he'd leaped around the stairs to catch the football, he'd nearly trampled her, and out of instinct, he had caught her before she fell against the spikes of the railing. He'd opened his mouth to ask if she was all right, but when he'd looked into her eyes, he'd not been able to say a word, for she was looking at him as though she thought he was the best looking, sexiest, most desirable man in the world. Mike had known since he was a kid that he was attractive to girls and he'd used his looks whenever possible, but no woman had looked at him as this one had.

Of course he had to concede that maybe he had been looking at her in much the same way. Her big, soft blue eyes had been filled with surprise and desire, looking at him from over a small, pert nose that was set atop a mouth so full and lush that he thought he might die from wanting it so much.

He'd kissed her, at first not sure if he should since he didn't want to do anything to scare her away, but the moment his lips touched hers, he knew he couldn't stop himself, knew he couldn't hold back. No woman had ever kissed him as this one did. It wasn't just desire he felt coming from her, but hunger. She kissed him as though she'd been locked in a prison for the last ten years and now that she'd been released, he was the man she most wanted in the world.

But right now Mike didn't understand what was going on with her. How could she kiss him like that and ten minutes later look at him as though she detested him? For that matter how could this proper little lady be the same enchantress who'd wrapped her leg around his waist?

Mike didn't have answers, nor did he understand anything that was going on, but he knew one thing for certain: he couldn't let her get away from him. He'd like to pick her up and carry her back to his house and keep her there, maybe forever. But if she wanted something from him first, like maybe for him to climb to the heavens, pick up a dozen or so stars, string them together and hang them in her bedroom, he thought he'd like to know so he could start tying ladders together.

"I apologize for whatever I did to offend you," he said, although he didn't mean a word of it. All he could remember was her ankle on his waist.

Samantha narrowed her eyes at him. "Is that supposed to make me believe you?" Taking a deep, cleansing breath, she tried to recover herself, for she was aware that they were beginning to draw the attention of the people on the street.

"Couldn't we go somewhere and talk about this?" he asked.

"Your house maybe?"

Missing the sarcasm in her voice, Mike thought that was a fine idea but didn't say so.

"There's nothing to talk about."

This time there was no missing her insinuation that she believed his house to be a den of sin. Mike took a deep breath. "We'll go back to the house, sit on the stoop—in plain sight of all of New York—and talk about whatever the problem is. Later, if you still want to leave, I'll help you find a hotel."

Samantha knew she shouldn't listen to him, knew she should hail another cab and find somewhere to spend the night.

"Look, you don't even know where you're going, do you? You can't get into a cab and say, 'Take me to a hotel.' Not anymore. You don't know where you'll end up, so at least let me call and make a reservation for you."

Seeing her hesitation, Mike took the opportunity to start walking toward his house, hoping she'd follow with her suitcase and totebag. Not wanting to press his luck with the headway he'd made with her, he didn't say any more as he walked, moving slowly, but stopping now and then to make sure she was following him.

When he reached the townhouse, he carried her bags to the top of the stairs, set them down and turned to her. "Now, you want to tell me what's wrong?"

Looking down at her hands, Samantha knew that she was very tired from the long, exhausting, traumatic day. For that matter it had been a long, exhausting year. "I think the problem is obvious," she said, trying not to look at him because he had on so very little clothing. While he stood there leaning against the rail, he reached inside the old, sideless sweat shirt he wore to scratch his chest, and Samantha saw a stomach covered with washboard muscle. When he said nothing, she spoke again, this time intending to make herself very clear. "I do not plan to live in the same house with a man who will spend his time chasing me all over the place. I am in mourning for my father, I have just ended my marriage and I do not want more complications."

Perhaps Mike shouldn't have taken offense at her words, but she made him sound like a dirty old man who couldn't keep his hands off the luscious young girl. Resisting the temptation to point out that he had by no means forced himself on her, he was also tempted to tell her that all they had shared was a kiss, nothing more, yet she was acting as though he were a convicted rapist who'd just tried to molest her.

"All right," he said in a cold tone. "What are the rules?"

"I have no idea what you're talking about."

"Oh yes you do. Anybody who dresses as you do must live by rules, lots of them. Now tell me what your rules are."

At that Samantha picked up her totebag and reached for her suitcase, but, putting his hand on it, he wouldn't let her have it.

"All right," he said again, this time with a sigh of defeat. "I apologize again. Couldn't we start over?"

"No," she said. "It's not possible. Would you please release my bag so I can leave?"

Mike wasn't going to let her leave. Beside the fact that he wanted her so badly there was sweat running down his chest even though it was a cool day, there was the promise he'd made to her father before he'd died. Mike was aware that she knew nothing about how close he had been with her father, that Dave and Mike had spent quite a bit of time together until Dave had told him Samantha was coming home. After that announcement Dave had confined their friendship to calls and letters, because, for some reason, Dave hadn't wanted Mike and Samantha to meet, at least not while Dave was alive. Then, two days before Dave died, he'd called Mike, although by then Dave had been too weak for Mike to hear all of what he had to say, but Mike had understood the essence of it. Dave had said he was sending Samantha to him in New York and he'd asked Mike to take care of her. At the time Mike hadn't felt he'd had any other choice, so he'd given his word that he'd protect her and watch out for her. But so far, Mike didn't think these last few minutes were what Dave had in mind.

Mike looked down at Samantha's two bags. "Which one has your overnight things in it?"

Samantha thought that was a very odd question but then the last few minutes had been the oddest of her life.

Not waiting for her answer, he picked up her totebag and opened the door to the house. "Five minutes, that's all I ask. Give me five minutes, then ring the bell."

"Would you please give me back my bag?"

"What time is it now?"

"Quarter after four," she answered automatically after a glance at her watch.

"Okay, at twenty after ring the bell."

Shutting the door behind him, he left Samantha standing alone on the stoop, half of her luggage missing, and when she pressed the doorbell, there was no answer. She was tempted to take her large case and leave, but the fact that her remaining money was hidden in her totebag made her sit down on her suitcase and wait.

Trying not to think of her father, trying not to ask herself why he had done this to her, and especially trying not to think of her husband—correction, ex-husband—she forced herself to look at the sidewalks and the street before her, forced herself to look at the people, at the men dressed in jeans, and the women in outrageously short skirts. Even in New York the air seemed to be full of the laziness of a Sunday afternoon.

This man, this Michael Taggert, had said he wanted to start over, she thought. If she could she'd like to start her life over, like to start from the morning of the day her mother died, because after that day nothing in her life had ever been the same, and today, having to be here, was part of all the pain and trauma that had started that day.

Looking at her watch again, her first thought was that maybe she could pawn it, but the watch had cost thirty dollars new so she doubted that she could get much for it. Noticing that it was twenty-five after four, she thought that maybe, if she rang the bell now, that man would answer, and maybe he'd give her back her bag so she could find a place to stay. The sooner she got started on this year-long sentence the sooner she could get out of this dreadful city.

Taking a deep breath, smoothing her skirt, making sure her hair was tightly in place, she put her finger on the doorbell.

When the man opened the door promptly at Samantha's ring, she stood for a moment blinking at the change in him. He was wearing a clean blue dress shirt, partly unbuttoned but still neat, a loosened silk tie, dark blue tropical weight wool trousers and perfectly polished loafers. His thick growth of black whiskers was gone and the black curls of his hair had been tamed into a conservative, neat, parted style. Within minutes he had gone from looking like the sexy, rather dangerous leader of a gang of hoodlums to looking like a prosperous young banker on his day off.

"Hello, you must be Miss Elliot," he said, extending his hand. "I'm Michael Taggert. Welcome to New York."

"Please give me back my bag." She ignored his outstretched hand. "I want to leave."

Smiling, acting as though she hadn't spoken, Mike stepped aside. "Won't you please come in? Your apartment is ready for you."

Samantha did not want to enter this man's house. For one thing, she found it disconcerting that he could change his looks so quickly and so completely, that within minutes he could go from looking like a muscle-bound jock who'd never done anything more intellectual than memorize a few football plays to looking like a young professor. If she had met this man first, before the other one, she wouldn't have guessed what he was really like. As it was now, she wasn't sure which man was the real one.

When Samantha saw her totebag at the foot of the stairs, she stepped inside the house to get it, but as her hand touched the handle of the case, she heard the door close behind her. Turning toward him in anger, her lips were tight, but he didn't meet her eyes.

"Would you like to see the house first or just your apartment?"

She didn't want to see either, but he was standing in front of the door, blocking her exit, as big as a boulder in front of a cave entrance. "I want to get out of here. I want—"

"The house it is, then," he said cheerfully, as though she'd answered positively. "The house was built in the twenties, I don't know the exact year, but you can see that the rooms have all the original moldings."

Refusing to move away from her bag, she stood where she was.

But Mike forced her to participate, however reluctantly, as he put his hand on her elbow and began to half pull, half push her out of the foyer, propelling her toward the living room. She saw a large room, with big, comfortable-looking black leather chairs and a couch strewn about, a rough, handwoven carpet on the floor, folk art from all over the world tastefully scattered about the room, as well as two enormous palm trees in the corners by the windows. Several masks hung on the walls, as well as Chinese tapestries and Balinese paintings. It was a man's room, with dark colors, leather and wooden objects—the room of a man of taste and discrimination.

The room didn't look much like a bordello as she would have thought from her first impression of him. In fact, the man beside her, the one wearing the banker's clothes, looked more at home in this room than the jock she had first met.

Aware that Mike was looking at her face, she sensed that he seemed to be pleased with what he saw because the pressure on her arm lessened. Reluctantly, but with less anger, she followed him from room to room, seeing a dining room with a large table from India and a magnificent cinnabar screen against one wall, then a powder room papered with Edwardian caricatures.

Relaxing more every minute, she was shown a library paneled in oak, with floor to ceiling shelves filled with books. She was impressed by the sheer number of books until she saw that, as far as she could tell, all the books dealt with American gangsters: their origins, biographies, even books on the economics of being a gangster.

Michael led her upstairs, and showed her two bedrooms, both of them decorated with art from around the world, one of them furnished with wicker chairs covered with pillows printed with ivy vines.

"You like it?" he asked, not attempting to control the eagerness in his voice.

Samantha smiled before she caught herself. "I do like it."

When he grinned in response to her assertion, Samantha almost felt her breath leave her. He was even better looking when he smiled like that, such a smile of pleasure, untainted by any other emotion. Feeling that it had suddenly become very, very hot in the room, she started toward the door.

"Want to see your apartment now?"

Looking away from him, looking at anything but him, she nodded.

She followed him up the stairs to the third floor and when Michael opened the door to the first room, Samantha forgot all about New York and this man who unsettled her, for she could feel her father in this room. Her father had always said that if he had to start from scratch he'd decorate the place in green and burgundy—and this living room had been made for her father. A dark green couch had been placed at an angle to a green marble fireplace, with two big, comfortable-looking green-striped chairs across from the couch, all of them set on an Oriental rug handwoven in colors of green and cream. Around the room were pieces of dark mahogany furniture, not one piece having spindly legs that would make it easy for a man to knock over.

Walking to the mantel, Samantha saw several framed photos of her family: her mother, her parents together, her paternal grandfather, and herself from infancy to one year ago. Tentatively, she picked up a silver-framed photograph of her mother and, holding it, she looked about, closing her eyes for a moment. The presence of her father was so strong in the room she almost expected to turn and see him.

Instead, when she turned, she saw a stranger standing in the doorway—and he was frowning at her.

"You don't like it," Mike said. "This room's not right for you."

"It's perfect for me," Samantha said softly. "I can feel my father here."

Mike frowned harder. "You can, can't you?" As he spoke, he looked at the room with new eyes, seeing that it wasn't a room for a pretty blonde female. This was a man's room. Specifically, it was David Elliot's room.

"The bedroom's through here." As Mike walked behind Samantha, he saw all the rooms through different eyes. His sister had decorated these rooms as well as the ones downstairs and at the time Mike had bragged to Dave that all you had to do was tell his sister what you wanted the finished product to look like and she could do it. Dave had said he wanted his apartment to look like an English gentleman's club and that's what it looked like. But now Samantha looked as out of place amid the dark colors as she would have in an all male club.

In the bedroom the walls were painted dark green and the windows leading onto a balcony were hung with curtains of green-and-maroon-striped heavy cotton velvet. The bed was a four-poster with no canopy and the linens were printed with plaids and sporting dogs. Watching, he saw Samantha lovingly run her hand over the comforter. "Did my father ever stay here?"

"No," Mike said. "He did everything by mail and telephone. He was planning to come here but—"

"I know," she said, looking at the dog prints on the wall. Being in this room was almost as though her father weren't dead, almost as though he were still alive.

Mike showed her more rooms, two bathrooms done in dark green marble, a sitting room with red and green plaid chairs, and book shelves filled with the biographies her father loved. There was a guest bedroom, and on the fourth floor was a study with a heavy oak desk and French doors opening onto a balcony. Opening the doors, she stepped out and saw the garden below.

She had not expected a garden in New York—certainly not a garden such as this one. In fact, looking at the lush green lawn and the two tall trees, looking at the shrubs about to burst into bloom and the beds of newly-set annuals, she could almost forget she was in a city.

Turning back to look at Mike, her happiness showing on her face, she didn't notice his frown. "Who takes care of the garden?"

"I do."

"May I help? I mean, if I were to stay here, I'd like to help in the garden."

His frown gave way to a slight smile. "I would be honored," he said, and should have been pleased by her words, but, for the life of him he couldn't figure out what was bothering him. He wanted her to stay, but now he was almost wishing she wouldn't, and his yes/no feeling had something to do with the way she moved about the rooms—Dave's rooms. Something about the way she was still gripping that photo of her mother to her breast made him want to tell her to leave.

"Would you like to see the kitchen?"

When Samantha nodded, he went to the west side of the room and opened a door, exposing a narrow, dark stairway leading downward. "It's the servants' stairs," he explained. "The house hasn't been remodeled into apartments so you and I will have to share a kitchen."

She looked at him sharply.

"You don't have to worry about me," he said, annoyed that

once again he was defending himself. Maybe he should give her a police statement that swore to his clean record, swore he wasn't a rapist, a murderer or had ever had so much as a speeding ticket. "I know less about kitchens than I do about computers so you won't be running into me in there very often. I can work a refrigerator and that's about it. Even toasters confuse me."

Saying nothing, she continued to look at him, letting him know that she was far from convinced of his good intentions.

"Look, Sam, maybe the two of us got off on the wrong foot, but I can assure you that I'm not a . . . a, whatever you seem to think I am. You'll be perfectly safe here with me. Safe from me, that is. All your doors have good, sturdy locks on them and I don't have keys to the locks. Your father had the only set. As for sharing the kitchen, if you want we can set a schedule for use. We can arrange our whole lives around a schedule if you want, so we don't have to see each other at all. Your father paid me a year's rent in advance so I think you should stay here, and, besides, I've already spent the rent money, so I wouldn't be able to refund your money."

She wasn't sure what to answer, whether to say she'd stay or not. Of course she shouldn't stay, not after the way they'd met, but right now she could feel her father's presence more strongly than she could remember this man's touches. Maybe she shouldn't stay here with him, but could she leave the second home her father had created? She had lost her home in Louisville, had lost all those memories, all those ghosts, but here she could feel the beginning of new memories.

Reluctantly, she put the photo of her mother down and started walking down the stairs, all the way to the ground floor where the kitchen was. For all that this man said he knew nothing about cooking, someone did, for the pretty, spacious, blue and white kitchen looked to be well equipped and highly usable.

She started to ask questions but then she looked toward the end of the kitchen, across a charming little breakfast room, and saw the glass double doors leading into the garden. Turning away from him, leaving the kitchen behind, she went out the doors and into the garden. As backyards go, the space wasn't very large, but it was surrounded by an eight-foot-tall solid wooden fence so the yard was private and secluded. Upon closer inspection, she could see that the garden was prettier than it had seemed from the fourth-floor balcony, with pink climbing roses growing over the fence. They were the old-fashioned, full-blown, fragrant roses that she had always loved, not the tight, scentless modern roses.

Turning, she smiled at Mike. "You have done a beautiful job."

"Thank you," he said, seeming to be truly pleased by her praise.

As she inhaled the fragrance of the roses and thought about the rooms upstairs—her father's rooms—she whispered, "I'll stay."

"Good. Maybe tomorrow I could show you a few places to buy furniture as I'm sure you'll want to change the rooms since they're not exactly what a female would want. My sister is an interior designer and I can get things wholesale through her so—"

Turning toward him, her face was stern. "Mr. Taggert, thank you so much for your offer, but I want to make myself clear from the start. I am not looking for a friend, a lover, or a tour guide. I have a job to do in this city and when it's finished I'm leaving, and between now and then I have no desire to . . . start anything. Do you understand?"

Looking at her with one eyebrow raised, he let her know he did indeed understand. "I understand perfectly. You don't want anything to do with me. Fine. Your keys are on the kitchen countertop, one for the front door, another for the deadbolts inside your apartment. Your father wanted the locks in his apartment keyed alike so he'd have only one key to bother with."

"Thank you," she said, walking past him toward the kitchen.

"Samantha," he said as she passed him. "I have a request."

She didn't turn around. "What is it?" she asked, bracing herself.

"We're going to be seeing each other now and then in passing, especially in the kitchen, and I'd like to ask you . . ." His voice lowered. "If you should come downstairs at night or early in the morning, don't wear one of those white lacy things. You know, the kind that floats around you. Red or black is okay, I can handle red or black, and blue would be easy, but I could not deal with white lace."

Without a backward glance, Samantha ran into the house, grabbed the keys and ran up the stairs.

Chapter One

Warbrooke, Maine
1865

As Jamie Montgomery walked through the long house, he didn't so much as glance about him, for he had grown up in the house and knew it well. Had anyone else seen the cozy comfort of the house, they would not have guessed the wealth of the family that owned it. Only an art student would have been aware of the significance of the signatures on the paintings that hung from the plaster walls, or of the names on the bronze statues, and only a connoisseur would have recognized the value of the carpets that were worn and stained from years of use by dogs and children.

The furniture had not been selected for its worth but for the needs of a family that had occupied the house for a couple of hundred years. An antiquarian would have seen that the old cabinet against one wall was actually Queen Anne, the little gold chairs were Russian Imperialist, and the porcelains in the cabinet in the corner were Chinese and too old for the comprehension of the young American mind.

The house was filled with pictures and furniture and fabrics from all over the world, the accumulated haul of generations of Montgomery men and women's travels. There were souvenirs from every corner of the globe, ranging from exotic items from the tiny islands of the world to paintings by Italian masters.

Walking swiftly, with a long-legged stride, Jamie went from one room of the enormous house to the other. Twice he patted the little flannel sack that was carefully tucked under his arm, smiling each time he touched it.

At last he came to a door and, with only a soft knock that wasn't meant to be heard, he entered the darkened bedroom. For all that the rest of the house wore a tattered opulence, this room showed every cent of the Montgomery wealth.

Even in the dark, he could see the gleam of the silk bed hangings, draping the huge, four-poster bed that had been carved in Venice, the bedposts fairly dripping with carved and gilded angels. From the top of the bed hung hundreds of yards of pale blue silk, and the walls of the room were upholstered with a darker blue damask that had been woven in Italy and brought back to America on a Montgomery ship.

Looking down at the bed, Jamie smiled, for he could see a blonde head just above the silk-covered, down-filled coverlet. He walked to the windows, threw back the heavy velvet curtains to let sunlight into the room, then watched as the head snuggled deeper into the covers.

Smiling, he went to the bed and looked down at its occupant, but all he could see was one golden curl clinging to the sheet; the rest of her had disappeared beneath the covers.

Lifting the bag from under his arm, Jamie opened the drawstring and withdrew a tiny dog that weighed no more than eight pounds; what body it had could hardly be seen for the long, silky white hair that covered it. The dog was a Maltese, and he'd brought it all the way from China as a gift for his baby sister.

Slowly lifting the coverlet, Jamie put the little dog in the bed with his sister, then grinning in anticipation, he took a chair and watched as the animal began to move about and lick its bedmate.

Slowly, and with great reluctance, Carrie came awake. She always hated to leave the warm cocoon of her bed and put it off as long as she could. Now, she moved a bit, her eyes still closed as she flung the covers down about her shoulders. At the first lick of the little dog, she smiled, then smiled again at the second lick. Only at the tiny bark did she open her eyes, looked into the face of the creature, then sat up, startled, her hand to her throat. Leaning back against the headboard, a carved angel's wing tip poking her in the back, she looked at the dog, blinking in wonder.

It was the laugh of her brother that made her turn her head, and even then it took her a moment to understand what was going on. When the understanding came to her that her beloved brother had at last come home from the sea, she gave a squeal of delight, then launched herself at him, dragging silk coverlet and cashmere blankets with her.

Catching her in his strong sun-browned arms, Jamie whirled her about, while on the bed behind them the little dog yapped excitedly.

"You weren't due in until next week," Carrie said, smiling and kissing her brother's cheeks and neck and whatever she could reach of him.

Jamie, trying to act as though he weren't reveling in his sister's enthusiastic greeting, held her at arms' length, her feet off the floor. "And you would have been down at the wharf to greet me, no doubt, if you'd known when I was going to arrive. Even if I'd come in at four in the morning."

"Of course," she said, smiling at him, then, a concerned look on her face, she put her hand on his cheek. "You've lost weight."

"And you haven't grown an inch." Looking her up and down, he tried to put an older-brother expression on his face, but it wasn't easy to be stern when looking at Carrie's tiny exquisiteness. Carrie was five feet even, yet all her brothers were over six feet. "I was hoping you'd have grown until you at least reached my waist. How did Mother and Dad produce such a runt as you?"

"Luck," she said happily as she turned to look at the little dog, which was now standing on the bed, its pink tongue hanging out. "Is this my present?"

"What makes you think I brought you a present?" he asked reproachfully. "I'm not sure you deserve one. Did you know that it's ten o'clock in the morning and here you are still sleeping."

She wriggled her shoulders to make her brother put her down. Carrie's interest, now that she had seen that he was home and well, was in the pretty little dog. When her feet were once again on the floor, she went to the bed, and when she slid back into it, the dog at once came to her to be petted.

While Carrie's attention was on the dog, Jamie looked about the room, noting what had been added since the last time he had been home. "Where did this come from?" He held up a foot-tall ivory carving of an Oriental lady, beautiful and intricate.

"Ranleigh," Carrie answered, speaking of another of her brothers.

"And this?" Jamie nodded toward an oil painting framed in gold.

"Lachlan."

Looking up from the dog, Carrie smiled at her brother as

though she had no idea what was causing him to frown. She had seven brothers, all of them older than she, all of them travelers, and every time they left the country they brought her back a present—each gift more flawlessly beautiful than the one another brother had brought her. It was almost as though they competed with each other to see who could bring their little sister the most marvelous gift.

"And these?" Jamie asked, picking up a string of pearls from Carrie's dressing table. His voice was sounding downright prim.

Smiling enigmatically, Carrie picked up the little dog and hugged it, burying her face in its soft fur. "This is by far the nicest present I have ever received in my life."

"Did you tell Ranleigh that when he gave you the lady?" Jamie was sounding almost jealous.

As a matter of fact, she had told Ranleigh that his gift was the best, but she wasn't going to tell Jamie that. "What's his name?" she asked, speaking of the tiny dog and doing her best to change the subject.

"That's for you to decide."

As Carrie stroked the dog, it sneezed. "Oh, Jamie, he really is the very nicest gift I ever have received. He's so very alive."

When Jamie came back to his chair by the bed, she could tell by his face that he was somewhat mollified by her assertions that his gift was indeed the best. Smiling at her, he watched the way the sunlight touched her thick mass of dark blonde hair and the way her blue eyes glinted with pleasure as she played with the dog, and knew that she was quite the prettiest thing he'd seen in a long while. She was as small as her brothers were large, as sweet tempered as they were irascible, and as full of laughter as they were of anger. And she was as used to luxury as they were to work. Carrie was the spoiled, adored, darling baby of the large family, and any of her brothers would have killed anyone who even thought of harming her.

Jamie leaned back in his chair, for he was glad to be at home, glad to be no longer on a rolling ship. "What have you and the Ugly Horde been up to lately?"

"Don't call them that!" Carrie said, but without any real animosity. "They aren't ugly."

When Jamie grunted at that, Carrie smiled. "Not *too* ugly anyway, and, besides, what do looks matter?"

He grinned at that. "Nineteen years old and already a philosopher."

"I'll be twenty soon."

"My, my, such a great age."

Carrie didn't mind his teasing, for, to her, there was little that her brothers could say or do that was wrong. "Whatever our appearance"—she generously included herself with the "Uglies"—"the girls and I are involved in a very important project."

"I'm sure of it." Jamie's tone was patronizing, but adoring at the same time. "As important as saving the frogs from the giggers? Or making poor Mr. Coffin give his geese free running space?"

"Those projects were in the past. Now we're involved in—" She broke off as the dog sneezed twice in succession. "You don't think he's catching cold, do you?"

"More likely he's reacting to all this silk. This place looks like a harem."

"What's that?"

"Something I'm not going to tell you about."

Carrie's lower lip protruded a bit. "If you ever want to give me a really spectacular gift, you could tell me, in detail, all that you've done on a voyage."

At the thought of what such a revelation would entail, Jamie looked a bit pale, and it took a moment before his color returned. Smiling, he said, "That's one gift you're not likely to receive from any of us. Now tell me what you and the Uglies have been doing."

"We're marrying people," Carrie said proudly then was pleased to see her brother's jaw drop in astonishment.

"You got someone to *marry* those ugly girlfriends of yours?"

She gave him a look of exasperation. "They aren't so ugly and you know it. And every one of them is as nice as can be. It's just that you think all women should be utterly and totally beautiful."

"Like my dear little sister," he said, and there was honesty in his voice as well as love in his eyes.

Blushing with pleasure, Carrie said, "You'll turn my head."

At that impossibility, Jamie whooped with laughter, causing the dog to start barking, then sneezing. "Turn your head," he said. "As if you didn't already know that you're the most beautiful thing in five states."

Carrie gave a mock look of deep, deep hurt. "Ranleigh said six states."

Jamie laughed again. "Then I'll say seven."

"Much better," Carrie said, laughing. "I'd hate to lose a state. The seventh isn't Rhode Island, is it?"

"Texas," Jamie answered, and they smiled at each other.

As Carrie leaned forward, holding the little dog, Jamie thought that she and the animal already looked as though they belonged together, just as he knew they would when he'd purchased the puppy he could hold curled in one palm.

"Jamie, we really are marrying people to each other," she said earnestly, her face serious. "Since the War Between the States, there have been so many women who have lost their husbands, and in the West there are a great many men who need wives. We match them with each other. It's been very interesting work."

Blinking at her for a moment, trying to understand what she was telling him, Jamie sat there staring at her. Sometimes it seemed to him that of all the family, sweet, adorable Carrie was the most stubborn. When she decided to do something, she had tunnel vision: Nothing on earth could stop her. Thank heaven that, so far, all her causes had been worthy ones. "How do you find these people?"

"The women we have already, quite a few of them from here in Warbrooke, although we've had to let people in the rest of Maine know that we're providing this service, but the men have been found through newspaper advertisements."

"Mail-order brides," he said softly, his voice rising with each word. "You're doing mail-order brides, like in China. You've stuck your nose into other people's personal lives."

"I don't think it's nosiness exactly, more that we're providing a service."

"Matchmaking, that's what you're doing. Does Dad know you're doing this?"

"Of course."

"And he doesn't object?" Before Carrie could answer, Jamie spoke again. "Of course he has no objection. He's always allowed you to do whatever you wanted to do since the day you were born."

Stroking the tiny dog, Carrie smiled sweetly at her brother and fluttered her lashes a bit. "You aren't going to make any complaints, are you? Ranleigh didn't."

"*He* spoils you," Jamie said, looking stern, but Carrie was still smiling at him, and he couldn't retain the look of severity on his face. "All right," he said with a sigh, knowing he'd lost his attempt at being strict, "so tell me more about this non-nosy matchmaking."

Carrie's delicate face brightened with eagerness. "Oh, Jamie, it's just lovely. We've had such a good time. I mean, we do enjoy ourselves while we perform this much-needed service, that is. We put advertisements in papers out West and say that if the men will send us a photograph of themselves—we won't send anyone out unless we've seen the man, since a photograph tells so very much about a person—and a letter explaining what they want in a wife, then we will try to match them up with a lady."

"And what are the women required to do?"

"They must come to us to be interviewed. We make cards listing their qualifications and then match them with a man." She gave a dreamy smile. "We make people very happy."

"How do these women get to the men?"

"Stagecoach, usually," she said, looking down at the dog. When Jamie didn't say another word, she looked back at him, her little chin set at a defiant angle. "All right, yes, Montgomery money pays their way, but it's for a good cause. These people are lonely, and they need each other so much. Jamie, you should read some of the letters from these men. They live all alone in places that no one has ever heard of, and they need company so much."

"Not to mention a good strong back to help work the farm as well as someone in their bed," he said, trying to interject a note of realism into her dreams of everlasting love.

"Well, the women need that too!" Carrie snapped.

"And what do you know of such things?"

He was teasing her, and she couldn't help being annoyed at his attitude. Most of the time she loved being pampered by her big brothers, but sometimes they could be a pain. "More than you and the others think that I do," she shot back at him. "In case you haven't noticed, I'm not a little girl any more. I'm a grown woman."

Sitting there in the tumble of silken bed clothes, her thick hair down about her shoulders, snuggling with the toylike animal, she didn't look over ten years old. "Yes," he said softly, "a grand old lady."

Carrie sighed. As much as she loved her brothers, she also knew them, and not one of them, or her father, wanted her to grow up. They wanted her to stay their adoring little sister whose only thoughts were for them.

"*You* aren't trying to find a husband, are you?" Jamie asked, and there was alarm in his voice.

"No, of course not." She knew better than to tell any of the men in her family that she was someday planning to get married, for they all thought she was little more than a toddler. "I have all the men I want here."

Jamie narrowed his eyes. "Just what is that supposed to mean? 'All the men you want'? Since when have 'men' been part of your life?"

Since the day I was born, Carrie wanted to say. Since I was fifteen minutes old and looked up from my cradle and saw seven of the most handsome boys on earth peering down at me, a mother and a sister in the background. Since I took my first steps holding onto a man's hand, since men taught me how to ride, sail, tie knots, curse, climb trees, and flirt to get whatever I want. "Why don't you come downtown with me? We're using the old Johnson place as our headquarters. You can see what we're doing." She gave him her best, most seductive, through-the-eyelashes look that she hoped was persuasive.

Jamie paled at her invitation. "Willingly walk into that bunch of ugly women?"

Carrie bit her lips to restrain her smile. She knew that what actually scared Jamie was the way her friends fell all over themselves at the sight of one of her unmarried brothers. Carrie thought that she should speak to her girlfriends about their behavior, but it was so amusing to see her handsome brothers ill at ease that she couldn't resist presenting them to her friends.

"Ranleigh went with me," Carrie said, looking down, her lower lip protruding just a bit. "But then Ranleigh isn't afraid of anything. Maybe you're afraid because you're my second-most handsome brother, and, too, maybe Ranleigh has more self-confidence than you do. Maybe Ranleigh—"

"You win," Jamie said, throwing up his hands in defeat. "I'll go, but only if you swear you'll not try to match me up with one of your unwanted women."

"I wouldn't dream of it," she said as though appalled at the very idea. "Besides, who'd want you after they'd seen Ranleigh?"

Jamie grinned wickedly. "About half of China," he said, leaning forward to cluck her under the chin, then looked down at the dog when it sneezed again. "What are you going to name him?"

"Choo-choo," Carrie answered brightly, making Jamie groan at the infantile name, just as she knew he would.

"Give him a name with a little dignity."

"Tell me about the women in China and I'll call him Duke," she said eagerly.

Pulling out his pocket watch and looking at it, he said, "I will give you one hour to dress and for every ten minutes of that hour that you don't make me wait for you, I'll tell you a story about China."

Carrie grimaced. "About the scenery? About the roads and the storms at sea?"

"About the girls who danced for the emperor." He lowered his voice. "And . . . they danced for me. In private."

In a flurry of silk and flying pillows, Carrie was out of the bed in a flash. "Thirty minutes. If I can get dressed in thirty minutes, how many stories will that earn me?"

"Three."

"They'd better be good stories and worth all the rush," she said in warning, "because if they're boring, I'll invite Euphonia to dinner every night you're home."

"Cruel. You are cruel." Again looking at his pocket watch, he said, "Time starts . . . NOW!"

Running from the bedroom, Carrie made a dash for her dressing room, Choo-choo in her arms.

"Thirty minutes," Jamie said, half in anger, half in exasperation. "You said you'd be ready within thirty minutes. Not an *hour* and thirty minutes, but thirty minutes flat."

Carrie yawned, not in the least disturbed by his tone. Jamie was all bark and no bite. "I was sleepy. Now tell me another story. You owe me two more."

As he flicked the reins of the horse harnessed to the little carriage, Jamie looked down at her. He knew that he complained to his brothers about how they spoiled their little sister, and he knew that now he should be firm and deny her the promised stories, but then he saw the way she looked up at him, with her big blue eyes full of love and adoration, and he cursed under his breath. There wasn't a member of his family who could deny her anything. "Maybe just one more story," he said. "But you don't deserve it."

Smiling, she hugged his arm. "You know, I think that as you get older you get better looking, and in another year or two, you might surpass Ranleigh in looks."

Jamie tried to hide his smile then gave up and grinned. "Imp!" he said and winked at her. "Like the dog, do you?"

She hugged Choo-choo. "By far my favorite present," she said, and this time she was sincere. "Now tell me more about the dancing girls."

When Carrie, with the little white dog tucked under her arm, walked into the parlor of the old house on her brother's arm, the entire room came to a halt. All six of the young women, who had been Carrie's friends for all of her life, looked up in unison. At first they merely halted their actions, then their eyes widened, then they gave a sigh that came from deep within each woman. For all that Carrie teased her brother that he wasn't as good-looking as her brother Ranleigh, Jamie was handsome enough to cause women to make genuine fools of themselves.

Smiling in pride as she looked at the women who were frozen like statues, Carrie bent a bit and blew out the match that Euphonia had just lit before it burned her fingers.

"All of you know my brother, Jamie, don't you?" Carrie said, acting as though she hadn't noticed the women's standstill. Glancing up at Jamie, she saw that, even though he was pretending he was embarrassed, she knew him well enough to see that he was actually flattered by the reaction of the young women.

Taking his arm possessively in hers, she pulled him forward. Their movement made the women come to life as they began to clear their throats and try to cover their awkwardness.

"How was your voyage, Captain Montgomery?" Helen tried to sound normal, but her voice came out in a rather curious-sounding squeak.

"Fine," Jamie half snapped, wishing he hadn't agreed to accompany his sister.

Carrie pulled him toward the far wall of the room where twenty-five photographs of men were pinned. The men ranged in age from a boy who didn't look much more than about fourteen to an old geezer with a gray beard halfway down the middle of his chest. "These are the men," Carrie said unnecessarily.

Nervously running his finger around his collar, Jamie looked at the board, but didn't see much. All the women were behind him now, and he could feel their eyes upon him, maybe even feel their collective hot breaths on his neck.

"Have there been any new arrivals today?" Carrie asked as she turned away from the board. She turned rather quickly, just in time to see Helen do something rather odd: She slipped something under a book lying on a table. Carrie pretended she had seen nothing.

"A few," one of the women answered. "But nothing promising. We have about twice as many men as women. You wouldn't like to put your picture on the board, would you, Captain?" She was doing her best to sound nonchalant, but there was just a touch of desperation and yearning in her voice.

Jamie gave the woman a weak smile. "Carrie, my love, I think I'd better go. I have to—" He couldn't think of what he needed to do except get out of there because the women were making him feel like something in a zoo. After giving his sister a quick kiss on the cheek and a look that said, I'll get you for this, he was gone.

For a moment the room was silent, then the women emitted a second combined sigh before turning back to their stacks of letters and photographs. Carrie stood where she was for a moment, then set Choo-choo to the floor, pointed him toward Helen, and gave him a little push.

"Catch him!" Carrie cried to Helen. "He'll run away."

Helen began to chase the little dog, leaving the table she had been standing by as though guarding it. Choo-choo decided he didn't want to be caught and within seconds all the women in the room were chasing him—all of them except Carrie, that is. She used the commotion to cover her movements as she went to Helen's table, lifted the book, and took what was hidden from under it.

Carrie pulled what was, by now, a very familiar-looking envelope from under the book. It was the type of envelope that held the photograph and letter from a man desiring a bride.

While the others were busy chasing the dog about the room, Carrie opened the letter, pulled out the photo, and looked at it. The picture was of a young man standing behind two badly dressed children, and it was the children Carrie examined first. There was a tall boy of about nine or ten and a girl of four or five. The clothes the children wore were clean but fitted them badly, as though they had been given whatever the local charity office had without consideration for fit.

But far more important than their clothes was the sadness in the eyes of the children, a kind of sad loneliness that said that there was very little laughter in their lives.

When Carrie looked up from the faces of the children, she gasped, for she saw the face of what she thought was the handsomest man in the world. Oh, maybe he wasn't actually as good-looking as her brothers, for there was an altogether different look about him, and this man had a look of melancholy about him that no Montgomery had ever had.

Helen snatched the photograph from Carrie. "That wasn't very nice of you to snoop like that. This is mine."

Carrie didn't answer but sat down on a nearby chair, feeling as though the wind had been knocked from her. The moment she sat down, Choo-choo ran and jumped onto her lap, and unconsciously, she hugged the warm little animal.

"Who is he?" Carrie whispered.

"For your information, he's the man I'm going to marry," Helen said proudly. "I have made up my mind and no one is going to change it."

"Who is he?" Carrie repeated.

Snatching the photo from Helen, Euphonia turned it over. "It says on the back that his name is Joshua Greene, and the children are named Tem and Dallas. What an odd name for a girl, or is the girl named Tem? Look, he misspells Tim."

As the women passed the photo around, they looked at it. The little group was a handsome family, in spite of the children's clothes, and the man was certainly handsome in a dark sort of way, but they had all seen better-looking men before. Not one of them could understand why Helen would hide the photo or why Carrie was looking as though she'd seen a ghost.

"I liked the man we saw last week better. What was his name? Logan something or something Logan, wasn't it? *He* didn't have two children already. If I were going to marry a man I'd never met, I'd want one without children so I could have my own."

The other women nodded in agreement.

Helen snatched the photo away from the women. "I don't care what you think. I'm going to marry him and that's that. I like him."

Euphonia, who had been reading Joshua Greene's letter during this, began to laugh. "He won't want you because he says he wants someone who knows how to work. He wants a woman with a great deal of farm experience, one who can run a farm if she has to, and he says he doesn't mind a woman who is older than he is—he's only twenty-eight—and he doesn't mind a widow. He'll even take on more children. What's important to him is that she knows all there is to know about farming." Smugly, she looked up at Helen. "You know so little about farming that you probably think the way to get milk is to pump the cow's tail."

Helen grabbed the letter away from her. "I don't care what he *says* he wants. I know what he's going to get."

As Helen grabbed the letter, the photo fell from her hands to the floor and Carrie picked it up. Looking at it again, she decided that it was the eyes of the man that called to her. His eyes were filled with hurt and longing and need. They were the eyes of a man who was crying out for help. My help, she thought. He needs *my* help.

Standing, she tucked Choo-choo under her arm, smoothed her blue silk skirt, and handed the photo back to Helen. "You can't marry him," she said softly, "for *I* am going to marry him."

There were a few seconds of stunned silence before the women began to laugh. "You?" they laughed. "What do you know about farming?"

Carrie was not laughing. "I don't know anything about farming, but I know a great deal about that man. He needs me. Now," she said regally, "if you'll excuse me, I have some preparations to make."

Chapter Two

Never before in her life had Carrie had to do anything in secret. She had never needed to hide anything from her family or friends, but now she had to work entirely in secret.

It had been easy to silence her friends. Since they had been children and had formed their circle of seven, Carrie had always been the leader of the group, with the others following Carrie into whatever she decided to do. They had sometimes been appalled or even afraid when one of Carrie's crusades threatened to get them into trouble, but they had always been obedient to her wishes. Carrie's oldest brother said that this was why Carrie had them for friends, because she could make them do what she wanted to do.

And now here was something that Carrie wanted more than she had ever wanted anything in her life before.

After that first day, the day Jamie came home, the day she first saw the man's photograph, she was a woman obsessed. It had been rather easy to defeat Helen and "take" Joshua Greene away from her. Carrie felt a little bad about taking him away from her friend, but Helen had to understand that Josh—as Carrie was already calling him—belonged to Carrie. Josh was hers and hers alone.

That first day she left the old Johnson house, the photograph and letter in one hand, her dog in the other, she went to the old Montgomery boathouse that was rarely used any longer. She wanted to be alone to sit and think and look at the man and his children.

She seemed to have some sense left, for she repeatedly told

herself that she was being ridiculous, that this man was no different from a hundred others who had sent in their pictures. She had seen them all, but none of the pictures had ever affected her. Not at all. She had never thought of leaving her home and her family to go out West to marry one of the men from the photographs. But this man was different; this *family* was different. This family was hers and they needed her.

She spent the day in the boathouse, sometimes sitting on a dusty old rug in a canoe, sometimes pacing, sometimes just staring at the photo. After pinning it to the wall, she looked at it and tried to analyze what it was that she liked about the man and his children. She tried to think in cold, hard terms, but try as she might, she couldn't come up with any answers.

Twice she told herself that she should forget about the man, that maybe the look in his eyes was just a trick of the light. Maybe there was another reason for the sadness she thought she saw. Perhaps the children's dog had died that morning, and that was why all of them looked so lost and alone.

At about four, when Choo-choo was getting restless and Carrie was beginning to feel her own hunger, one of the old men who worked in the chandlery came into the boathouse.

"Beggin' your pardon, miss. Oh, it's you, Miss Carrie."

Carrie nodded to him then motioned for him to come to her. "Look at that picture," she said, pointing to where she'd pinned the photo on the wall. "What do you see in that picture?"

The man studied the picture, squinting at it. Carrie took it down from the wall, so the old man could take it to the window to look at it in the light. She could see that he was taking her question very seriously. When he finally looked back at her, he said, "Handsome family."

"Anything else?" she urged.

The man looked confused. "Not that I could see. They don't look rich, but maybe they've fallen on hard times."

Carrie frowned. "They don't look, well . . . sad to you?"

The man looked surprised. "Sad? But all of them's smilin'."

It was Carrie's turn to look surprised. Taking the photo from him, she looked at it again. She would have thought there was nothing new in it for her to discover, but now she saw it in a new light. All three of the people in the picture were indeed smiling. If they were smiling, how could she have thought they were sad?

The little boy had his arm around the girl, and the father had a hand on each child's shoulder. How could they be lonely if they had each other?

Carrie looked back at the old man. "Not sad and not lonely?"

"They look particular happy to me, but then what do I know?" He smiled at her. "If you want them to be sad, Miss Carrie, then I guess they can be."

Carrie smiled back at the man as he tugged at the brim of his cap, then left the boathouse.

Not sad or lonely, Carrie thought. Other people saw a happy, smiling family, but that's not what Carrie saw, and for the life of her she couldn't figure out why she saw them as sad or what it was about the family that appealed to her. Cried out to her, actually.

She stayed in the boathouse another few minutes, then picked up Choo-choo and went back to her own house. That night there was a celebration dinner in honor of Jamie's return, and all their Montgomery and Taggert relatives were there, which meant that the house was filled with so many people that no one noticed that Carrie was unusually quiet.

For the next three days Carrie was quiet. She went about her daily life, went to the old Johnson house every day and looked at the photographs the men sent, interviewed the women who wanted husbands, and tried to pretend that her mind was on something besides the family in the photograph.

She looked at the picture and read Josh's letter until they were nearly worn out. She knew every sentence by heart, and she could have picked Josh's handwriting out of hundreds of others.

At the end of three days she knew what she had to do. Just as she had originally planned, she was going to marry Mr. Joshua Greene. Josh seemed to think he needed a woman who knew about milking cows and whatever else one did on a farm, but Carrie was convinced that what he actually needed was her.

When Carrie told her friends what she was going to do, they were outraged. Even Helen, who was still smoldering with resentment over Carrie's highhandedly taking Josh away from her, was upset.

"You are out of your mind," Euphonia said. "You could have any man you wanted. With your looks and your money—"

At that, there was a gasp from the others, because it had always been prohibited to speak of Carrie's money.

"*Someone* has to speak the truth," Euphonia said with a sniff. "And this man wants a farm wife. Carrie, you can't even sew, much less plant corn." She narrowed her eyes. "You do know that corn silk isn't really silk, don't you?"

Carrie knew no such thing, but that was hardly the issue. "I have considered the possibility that if I were to write Mr. Greene, he might not think me suitable as a wife. Since he seems to believe that he needs a hired hand instead of a wife, I have therefore decided to marry him before I go to this town of his in Colorado, this Eternity."

This announcement set the women to talking at once as they tried to reason with Carrie, but it was like talking to a wall. They pointed out that she would have to lie to Mr. Greene, and one of their policies had always been that they weren't to lie to the men who requested brides. They didn't tell a man who wanted a sweet-tempered wife that they were sending him a dear woman and then send him a virago. Mr. Greene had asked for a farm wife, and he should have what he asked for.

"He won't be disappointed in me," Carrie said with a little smile of confidence.

At this the women sat back in their chairs and looked at Carrie. She was so pretty that everywhere the women went men fell over themselves to get Carrie's attention. Carrie had a way about her that every woman who saw her would have sold her soul to possess. Men liked Carrie. Men *adored* Carrie. Maybe being raised with seven older brothers and a father had taught her all there was to know about men. But whatever the reason, the fact was that Carrie could have any man she wanted. All she had to do was choose.

After two days of trying to "reason" with Carrie, the women gave up. They were tired of talking, and Carrie hadn't budged an inch. Carrie said that if they were really her friends, they'd help her try to figure out how to get herself married to Mr. Greene so that he couldn't back out of the marriage when he found out she knew nothing about farming. "He might be a bit, well . . . upset when he first finds out that I've embellished the truth of my abilities. He might be tempted to, maybe, tell me to return home. You can never tell about men. When they think they've been wronged, they don't act rationally so I want to force him to give me a chance to prove to him that I am the perfect wife for him."

The women had their opinions of what Mr. Greene would do when he found out that Carrie had lied, connived, plotted, and schemed, all in order to trap him into a marriage that he didn't want. But Carrie was so determined that after a while they began to try to help her in her plan to deceive Joshua Greene. After all, it was all divinely romantic.

The first thing they did was try to find out about farming. All of the women had grown up around the sea, and all of them had lived comfortable lives with servants to care for them. Food came from the kitchen, and they had absolutely no idea how it got into the kitchen. Sarah said that a man brought it to the back door of the house.

With a goal in mind, the women set about researching farming just as they would have done a school project. Within a few days they realized that the subject of farming was very boring, so they asked a woman who came to them looking for a husband to write a sample letter. Carrie copied the letter in her own handwriting and sent a messenger off, at her father's expense, to take it all the way from Maine to the tiny town of Eternity in Colorado.

Carrie and her friends had come up with an elaborate story to tell the unsuspecting Mr. Greene about how the woman who was perfect for him had to be married by proxy before she could come to Eternity. If Mr. Greene agreed, all he had to do was sign the enclosed papers, and the marriage would take place in War-brooke. If he agreed, then when Carrie arrived to meet him she would already be married to him.

"Your father will never sign the papers," Euphonia said.

Carrie knew that she was right. Her father would never allow his youngest daughter to marry a man she'd never met, a man he had not met. He would laugh at her statement that she had fallen in love with a photograph of a man and his two children.

"I'll find a way," Carrie said with more confidence than she felt.

After she sent the letter to Josh, she had to wait for months for his reply, for even with a messenger on the trip to Colorado, it took a long time for mail to get there and back. She had made a copy of her long letter to him, and as the days went by, she criticized every sentence of it. Maybe she shouldn't have written this; maybe this sentence should have been left out; maybe she should have included this.

During the long months of waiting, she may have had her

doubts about the letter, but she never once wavered in her conviction that what she was doing was right. Each night she kissed her fingertips and gave kisses to her future family, and every day she thought of them. She purchased fabric to make dresses for the little girl who was going to become her daughter, and she bought a sailboat for the boy. She purchased books, whistles, and boxes of hard rock candy for the children and eight shirts for Josh.

After six months of waiting, one morning Carrie walked into the old house, and her six friends were standing and waiting for her. With such looks of anticipation on their faces, Carrie didn't have to be told that Josh's letter had arrived. Silently, Carrie held out her hand for the letter.

With trembling hands, Carrie opened it, quickly scanned his letter, then hurriedly looked at the legal papers. As though the air had left her, she sat down hard on a chair. "He signed them," she said, half in wonder, half in disbelief.

At first the women didn't know whether to rejoice or cry.

Carrie grinned. "Congratulate me. I'm almost a married woman."

They congratulated her, but they also let her know that they thought she was crazy, and they couldn't resist telling her for the thousandth time that Mr. Greene was going to be quite angry when he found out how he'd been tricked.

Carrie ignored them, for she was delirious with happiness. Now all she had to do was get her father to sign her papers because she was so young, then she had to find a minister to perform the proxy service.

Carrie handled it all in the same way that she had handled Joshua Greene: She lied.

She went to the offices of Warbrooke Shipping, which her family owned, and nonchalantly volunteered to deliver a sheaf of papers to her father to be signed. Slipping the proxy papers in with the business papers, her father signed them without reading what he was signing. Money found a minister who would perform the service.

So, on a late summer morning, one year after the War Between the States had ended, Carrie Montgomery legally became Mrs. Joshua Greene, with Euphonia acting as the stand-in for Josh.

At the end of the service, Carrie threw her arms around each of her friends in turn and told them that she was going to miss them, but that she was going to be very, very happy in her new life. The women bawled copiously, wetting the front of Carrie's new dress with their tears.

"What if he beats you?"

"What if he drinks?"

"What if he's a bank robber or a gambler or he's been in jail? What if he is a murderer?"

"You didn't worry about the hundreds of other women we've sent out, why should you worry about me?" Carrie asked, annoyed with the women for not being happy for her.

Her friends just cried harder into their handkerchiefs.

To Carrie, all that she'd done so far was easy compared to what she still had to do: tell her parents. When she did tell them, her mother wasn't nearly as stunned as her father. Her mother gave her husband a look of disgust and said, "I told you that all of you spoiled her, and *this* is the consequence."

Carrie thought her father might start crying. He adored his last child, and it had never crossed his mind that she might grow up, much less marry someone and go hundreds of miles away to live.

Carrie's mother suggested that the marriage was illegal and that they could have it annulled. With utter simplicity and absolute conviction, Carrie said, "I will run away."

Studying her daughter's humorless face, her mother nodded. The Montgomery stubbornness was infamous, and she knew that if her daughter had made up her mind to stay married to a man she'd never met, then she would stay married.

"I wish 'Ring were here," her father said, speaking of his oldest son.

Carrie shuddered. Had her oldest brother been there, she would have waited until he left before presenting the fact of her marriage to her soft-hearted parents. Her oldest brother was not soft-hearted nor particularly indulgent of his sister's schemes. In fact, Carrie would not have told her parents while *any* of her brothers were home.

"I don't see that there's anything we can do," her father said sadly. "When will you leave?" His voice was heavy with tears.

"As soon as I can pack," Carrie answered.

Her mother squinted at her youngest child. "And what do you plan to take to this wilderness?"

"Everything," Carrie said in answer to what she thought was an odd question. "I plan to take everything that I own."

At that, her parents' long faces changed from sadness to mirth. They looked at each other and began to laugh, but laugh in a way that made Carrie feel defensive.

Straightening her back, Carrie stood up. One could almost take offense at the tone of their laughter. "If you'll excuse me, I must go to my room and start packing for the journey to meet my husband." Stiffly, she walked from the room.

Chapter Three

Mrs. Joshua Greene fanned herself with an ivory-handled, feather-tipped fan, stroked the little dog beside her, and tried to still the beating of her heart. In another few minutes she and the other stagecoach passengers would be in Eternity. Since they were a full four days later than scheduled, she wondered if her husband would be there to meet her.

Every time she thought the word *husband* she smiled to herself. She thought of the pleasure she was going to see on Josh's face when he realized that his new wife was not a woman with a back meant to pull a plow, but was instead a young lady of some . . . well, appeal.

Thinking of their first night together, Carrie began to fan herself harder. Even though her brothers thought they had been successful in keeping their little sister's mind pure and uncluttered with any knowledge of the world, Carrie had learned a great deal about men and women from sitting quietly and listening to her brothers' remarks about bachelor life. She was certainly sure that she knew more than most young women. And if she was sure of anything at all, she was sure that she wasn't afraid of what happened between a man and a woman. According to the laughs and comments of her brothers, what a man and woman did together was the most exciting, pleasurable, worthwhile event on earth. All in all, Carrie was very much looking forward to the experience.

When at last the coach pulled into Eternity and stopped before the depot, she saw him long before the vehicle halted.

"Is he there?" the woman across from her asked.

Carrie smiled shyly and nodded. She and this woman had traveled together for the last seven hundred miles, and Carrie had told her that she was going to meet her new husband. She had not told all the details, preferring to leave out that her letter to Josh had contained some untruths, but she'd told her all the most romantic parts of the approaching love affair. Carrie had told of the adventure of being a mail-order bride and being married by proxy because they had fallen in love through letters and that now she was going to meet her husband for the first time.

The woman, who lived with her husband and four children in California, leaned over and patted Carrie's hand. "He'll be even more in love with you the moment he sees you. He's a very lucky man."

Looking down at her hands, Carrie blushed.

When the stage finally stopped, Carrie found herself suddenly frightened, and every word that her friends and parents had said to her came back to her. Quite suddenly, she thought, What in the world have I done?

Two men got out of the coach, but Carrie hung back, drawing the coach's leather curtain aside and looking out at the man standing on the porch gazing at the coach with unreadable eyes.

She would have known him anywhere. This was Josh, this was the man who was her husband. In secret, behind the cover of the leather shade, she examined him. He was shorter than her brothers, standing about five foot nine or ten, but he was as strongly built as they were, just as broad shouldered and slim hipped, and he was just as handsome. He had piercing dark eyes that stared at the coach intently, and he was leaning against the wall of the stage depot, looking for all the world as though he didn't have a care in the world. He was wearing a black suit of excellent cut and quality, and Carrie's expert eye knew that when it was new it had been very expensive, but the suit was a bit worn now, frayed here and there.

Wiping her hands on her traveling skirt, Carrie listened to the stage driver unloading the bags from the top of the coach, but still she sat where she was, holding Choo-choo on her lap and looking out at Josh. She wanted to see him to make sure that what she had felt from the photo was true when she saw him in person. What kind of man was he?

He didn't move from his place against the wall even when there seemed to be no more passengers disembarking. Standing very still, he watched and waited.

He knows that I'm inside, Carrie thought. He knows it and he's waiting for me. At that thought she relaxed and smiled, and the woman across from her smiled also.

Putting the loop of Choo-choo's leash over her wrist, Carrie got up from her seat and went to the coach door.

The moment Josh saw a skirt in the doorway, he stepped away from the wall and came forward, and when he saw Carrie, he paused.

In the instant Carrie met his eyes, she knew without one doubt in the world that she had made no mistake. Mr. Joshua Greene was hers and would be for the rest of her life.

She smiled at him. It was a tremulous smile, for her heart was beating in her throat so hard that she seemed to have trouble thinking.

Without smiling, Josh came forward quickly. By the expression on his handsome face a person might not have known he was anxious, but he nearly knocked the stage driver to the ground in his rush to get to Carrie. Putting his strong hands up toward her waist, he waited to help her down.

As Josh's hands touched Carrie's waist, the moment they connected, the two of them froze in place. He held her waist, looking up at her as she stood in the doorway, and there was a charge of such excitement between the two of them that Carrie was sure her pounding heart was going to burst her bodice.

For minutes the two of them stood there, Josh's hands about her waist, Carrie's feet barely grazing the stage step, neither of them moving as they stared at each other. To an outsider they might have been statues except for the fact that every visible blood vessel was engorged and throbbing.

"You two lovebirds mind gettin' out of my way?" the stage driver said as he tried to push Josh aside. But Josh was as firmly rooted where he was as though he'd been planted and grown roots a hundred feet deep.

It was Carrie who broke the spell when she smiled at her husband.

When Josh returned her smile, Carrie thought she might melt. He had the most beautiful smile in the world, with perfect, even, white teeth and lips that were finely shaped.

Slowly, ignoring the stage driver who stood looking at them in disgust, Josh lowered Carrie to the ground. As he lowered her, his hands—strong hands—moved from her waist all the way up to her armpits. When his palms went past her breasts, Carrie was sure she was going to faint.

When Carrie's feet were on the ground (literally speaking), Josh stepped away and tipped his hat. "Ma'am," he said softly.

If Carrie hadn't been in love with him before, she was sure she would have been after she heard his voice. Odd, but in all her imaginings she hadn't thought about what his voice would be like. It was deep and . . . and, well, beautiful, almost like a singer's voice.

She knew she should introduce herself, but suddenly the words stuck in her throat. What could she say? "Hello, I'm your wife?" Or "Did you really, actually, truly want a farm girl?" Or should she say what first came to her mind, which was, "Kiss me"?

After discarding all those alternatives, she didn't say anything, but stepped away from the coach, Choo-choo panting and following her, and walked to the shade of the porch of the stage depot. Standing there, she took the fan from her wrist and used it as she watched Josh turn back toward the stage.

As Carrie watched, the woman who had traveled with her stepped from the coach, and Josh politely put his hands up to help her down. The woman was at least fifty pounds overweight, as well as being several years older than Josh.

"Are you Miss Montgomery?" she heard him ask. "I mean, Mrs. Greene?"

The woman smiled at Josh. "You can get that worried look off your face, young man, I'm not your bride."

Instantly, Josh removed his hat and bowed before her. (What lovely hair, Carrie thought.) "Had I been so honored, my lady, I would feel myself the most fortunate of men," he said.

The woman, nearly old enough to be Josh's mother, blushed and giggled at his gallantry.

Behind them, Carrie smiled. If she'd had any doubts left about what she'd done having been right, they would have left her when she saw Josh's chivalric courtesy. Now it was up to her when she told Josh that the two of them belonged together—and she wanted to do that in privacy.

She watched as Josh looked into the empty stage; then he went to the driver and questioned him, where he was told that there were no other passengers on board.

Sitting down on a dusty bench on the porch of the stage station, Choo-choo at her feet, Carrie watched Josh as he removed her letter from his coat pocket and reread it. She looked at the way his hands moved. They were expressive hands, and she remembered his touching her.

When the stage driver called for the continuing passengers to reboard, one by one, they did. When the coach was loaded and the driver seated on top, Josh turned to Carrie and looked at her in question. Carrie was well aware that he hadn't forgotten her presence for even a split second. He had been as aware of her as she was of him.

"May I help you onto the stage?" he asked softly, and just his eyes on her made Carrie's heart beat faster.

She managed to shake her head no, but couldn't seem to speak.

The driver yelled to the horses, and in a cloud of dust, the coach pulled away. After the depot manager went inside the building, Carrie and Josh were left alone outside.

Standing in the sun, his back to Carrie, Josh watched the departing stage coach. When it was out of sight, he slowly turned back to her, moving so he was standing in the shade, but still a few feet from her. "Are you waiting for someone?" he asked.

"My husband," she said, then smiled a bit at his crestfallen face. "And you? Are you waiting for someone?"

"My—" Breaking off, he cleared his throat. "My wife."

"Mmmmm," she said. "What's her name?"

He was staring at Carrie so intently that for a moment he couldn't seem to think. "Whose name?"

"Your wife. What is the name of your wife?"

Reaching inside his coat, he withdrew the letter, then with obvious reluctance, he drew his eyes from Carrie's and looked down at the letter. "Carrie. She's named Miss Carrie Montgomery."

"You don't seem to know much about her," Carrie said teasingly.

"Oh, but I do." There was a heaviness in Josh's voice that almost made Carrie giggle. "She can plow ten acres of farmland in a single day. She can raise hogs, slaughter them, and cook them, and she can doctor mules, chickens, and children. She can shear sheep, weave the cloth, and make clothes, and, in a pinch, she can build her own house."

"My goodness," Carrie said. "What a competent woman she sounds. Is she pretty?"

"I rather think not." As he said this he looked Carrie up and down, and there was such hunger in his dark eyes that Carrie felt a little river of sweat run down the back of her neck.

"Then you haven't met her?"

"Not yet." As he answered, he took a step closer to her.

At that moment Choo-choo decided to chase a rabbit that was running across the mountain grass, and when Carrie lost hold of his leash, he went flying across the countryside. Instantly she was on her feet and running after the dog that had become so precious to her. He was the only live thing that she had been able to bring from home with her.

But Josh was running before she was. Taking off after the dog as though its recapture meant his life, he ran across the field after the animal.

For several minutes the two of them were both running after the dog, Carrie in her hoop skirt, which gave her legs great freedom, and Josh in his black suit. It was Josh who caught the little dog before it went scurrying down a rabbit hole, and in gratitude, Choo-choo bit Josh's hand.

"Bad dog!" Carrie said, even as she scooped Choo-choo into her arms and turned to Josh. "Thank you so very much for saving him. He could have been hurt."

Holding his bleeding hand extended in front of him, Josh smiled. "There are rattlers around here. You'd better hold onto that leash."

She nodded, put the dog to the ground, hooked the loop of the leash over her arm then took out her handkerchief. "Let me see your hand."

After a token protest, Josh held out his hand to her, and she took it in both of hers.

Carrie wasn't prepared for the shock that went through her as her flesh touched his. They were standing under the shade of an old cottonwood tree, the high mountain air was fragrant, and it was silent and empty around them. For all they were aware of it, the rest of the world might not have existed.

Trying not to tremble, but not succeeding, Carrie dabbed at the blood on Josh's hand. "I . . . I don't think the wound is too deep."

Josh was looking at Carrie's hair. "He doesn't have enough teeth to go very deep."

She looked up at him and smiled, and for a moment she was sure that he was going to kiss her. With every morsel of her being, she tried to send thoughts to him that would make him take her into his arms and kiss her until she couldn't think any more.

Abruptly, Josh stepped away. "I have to go. I have to see what's happened to my . . . to my . . ."

"Wife," Carrie supplied.

He nodded in agreement, but he didn't say the word. "I have to go." At that he turned on his heel and started back toward the stage depot.

"I'm Carrie Montgomery," she said.

Josh stopped in his tracks, his back to her.

"I'm Carrie Montgomery," she repeated a bit louder.

When Josh started to turn, she smiled in anticipation of his happy surprise.

When he looked at her, his face was an unreadable mask. "What do you mean?" he asked softly.

"*I* am Carrie Montgomery. I am the woman you're waiting for. I am—" Her voice and eyes lowered. "I am your wife," she whispered. She felt rather than heard him take a few steps toward her, and when he was so close that she could almost feel his breath on her face, she looked up at him. He was not smiling. In fact, had he been one of her brothers, she would have thought that the expression he wore was rage.

"You've never pulled a plow in your life," he said.

Carrie smiled at that. "True."

With shaking hands, Josh pulled the letter from inside his coat. "She wrote to me about what she could do. She said that she'd run a farm since she was little more than a child."

"Perhaps I embellished the truth a bit," Carrie answered modestly.

Josh took a step closer to her. "You lied. You bloody well lied to me!"

"I think that's a curse word. I'd rather you didn't—"

He took another step toward her, but Carrie was already in that space so she had to back up. "I wrote that I wanted a woman who knew about farming, not some . . . some socialite carrying a long-haired rat she calls a dog."

As though he heard himself mentioned, Choo-choo began to bark at Josh. "Now see here," Carrie began.

But Josh didn't allow her to speak. "Was this your idea of a joke?" Putting his hand to his forehead as though he were in great agony, Josh stepped away from her. "What in the world am I going to do now? I was suspicious when I received that proxy marriage paper, but I thought it was because the woman was mud-ugly. I was prepared for that." Turning back to Carrie, he looked her up and down with great contempt. "But you! I wasn't prepared for *you*."

Shushing Choo-choo, Carrie looked down at herself, wondering if she'd suddenly turned into a frog, for she'd certainly never before had a complaint about how she looked. "What's wrong with me?"

"What *isn't* wrong with you?" he said. "Have you ever milked a cow? Do you know how to chop the head off a chicken and pluck it? Can you cook? Who made your dress? A French modiste?"

Carrie's dressmaker at home was French, but that was of no consequence. "I can't see that any of those things matter. If you'd just let me explain, I can clear up everything."

At that Josh went to the tree, leaned back against it, and folded his arms across his chest. "I'm listening."

After taking a deep, calming breath, she told her story. She started by telling him how she and her friends had organized the mail-order bride office, hoping that it would show him that she was good at a great many things. He didn't speak, nor could she read his thoughts, but she continued by telling him how she had seen the photo he'd sent and known from the first moment that she loved him. "I felt that you and your children needed me. I could see it in your eyes."

He didn't so much as move a muscle.

She told him in great detail of her indecision, of how she had given the matter great consideration. (She didn't want him thinking that she was a featherbrain who did things without thinking them through first.) Then she told about all the complicated arrangements she'd made in order to marry him, and when she told of leaving her family and friends and home to come to him, there were tears in her eyes.

"Is that all?" Josh asked, his jaw rigid.

"I guess so," Carrie answered. "You can see that I didn't do this to be mean. I felt that you needed me. I felt that—"

"*You* felt," he said, moving away from the tree toward her. "*You* decided. You and you alone decided the fate of everyone around you. You gave no consideration to anyone else. You put your friends and your family through hell all because of some romantic notion you had that a man you never met—" He glared at her. "*Needed* you." He said the word with a great deal of derision.

Stepping toward her, he leaned over her so that she bent backward. "For your information, you spoiled, overindulged, little rich girl, what I *need* is a wife who can run a farm. If I *needed* some empty-headed, worthless bit of fluff like you, I could pick her up anywhere in the world. I could have had a half-dozen women like you right here in Eternity. I don't need a feisty bed partner. I need a woman who can *work!*" With that last declaration, he turned away and angrily started walking back to the stage depot.

Blinking in bewilderment, Carrie stood where she was. No one had ever talked to her as this man had just done—and no one was going to. Pulling her bodice down as though to emphasize her resolve, she went after him. Since he was walking very quickly, he wasn't easy to catch, but she managed. She stepped in front of him.

"I don't know how you decided that you know all about me, but you don't. I—"

"Appearances," he said. "I have judged you on appearances. Isn't that how you judged me? You took one look at my photograph and decided to alter the course of my life. You never so much as considered that I might not want my life altered."

"I didn't decide to alter your life. I decided—"

"Yes?" he asked, his eyes blazing. "What *did* you decide if not to change my life? And the life of my kids." He gave a snort of laughter. "I told them that I would bring someone home tonight who could cook dinner for them, and I swore that they'd never have to eat my cooking again." Roughly grabbing her hands, Josh looked at them as though her hands were his enemy. Carrie's hands were creamed and soft, the nails trimmed and filed. "I have a feeling that I've cooked more meals than you have." Tossing her hands down in disgust, he started walking again.

Determinedly, Carrie moved in front of him again. "But you

liked me. I know that you did. I didn't tell you who I was immediately because I wanted to see if you liked me or not."

At that Josh's face changed from anger to almost amusement. "Is that what you thought, that when you met me I'd be so bowled over with your beauty that I wouldn't notice that your only use is to sit in some rich man's parlor and play minuets on the spinet? Did you think that I would be so blinded by your beauty and my raging desire to get you into bed at night that I'd not be able to hear the hungry cries of my two children?"

"No," Carrie said softly, but he had hit nearer to the truth than she liked to think. "I didn't think that. I thought—"

The rage came back to his face. "You didn't think at all. It never seems to have occurred to you that I could have taken a wife here. Did you think that no woman would *want* to marry me? Do you think I'm too ugly to attract a woman?"

"Why no, I think you're—"

He didn't allow her to finish her sentence. "Yes, of course you do. A lot of women do. I can get a woman if I want her, but I have neither the time nor the inclination for courting, and *all* women want courting, no matter how ugly they are. I sent to that lunatic company of yours so I could get a helpmate, not a girl with a head filled with romance, so I could feed my children and myself." With what was close to being a sneer, he gave her one more look up and down. "Now, Miss Montgomery," he said, tugging on the brim of his hat, "I bid you good day, and good-bye. I hope in the future that you think before you act."

He walked away from her, leaving her standing there, her little dog at her feet.

Carrie wasn't sure what she was to do now because what had just happened was not something that she had considered. Trying to give herself time to think, she wondered when the next stage ran. She dreaded going back to Warbrooke, but she guessed she'd have to. Looking up, she glared at the back of Josh as he walked toward the depot.

"Mrs. Greene," she said softly to his back, then called out louder, "My name happens to be Greene. Mrs. *Joshua* Greene." By the time she said the last, she was fairly shouting.

Stopping where he was, Josh turned and looked at her.

Carrie crossed her arms over her bosom and glared at him defiantly.

With anger in his every step, he started back toward her. There was so much anger on his face and emanating from his body that Carrie stepped away from him.

"If you touch me, I'll—"

"Half an hour ago you were practically begging me to touch you. If I'd started undressing you, you wouldn't have protested."

"That's a lie!" Carrie said, but her face turned red.

"You should know about lying if anyone does." Reaching out, he clamped his hand on her upper arm and began pulling her along behind him as he started toward the stage station.

"Release me this instant. I demand—"

Halting, he put his nose almost to hers. "As you reminded me, you did such a thorough job of hornswoggling me that I find I am now *married* to you. You are going home with me until next week when the stage runs through here again and I can send you back to your father where you belong."

"You can't—"

"I can and I'm going to," he said, dragging her along behind him as he walked. When he reached the depot, he stopped. "Where are your bags?"

Carrie stopped trying to push his hand off her arm and looked about her. While they had been under the tree, her baggage wagon had arrived, and, when she looked at it, she saw that the driver's seat was empty so the man must be inside the depot. "There," Carrie said, nodding toward the wagon. "I can take care of myself. I can—" She broke off at the look on Josh's face, for he looked as though he had just seen a swamp monster. He was horrified, shocked, immobile with disbelief. Following the direction of his eyes, she saw nothing unusual, only her baggage wagon.

But what Josh saw was a mountain of trunks, all of them tied down with heavy rope onto a big wagon drawn by a four-horse team. He doubted if the sum total of all the belongings of the people of Eternity was enough to fill that many trunks. "Heaven help me," he whispered, then looked back at her. "What in the world have you done to me?"

Chapter Four

By the time Carrie was seated atop Josh's old buckboard, she was beginning to wish that she had never seen his photograph. He was so angry at her that he wouldn't look at her or speak to her. He yelled at the horses and snapped the reins as though the horses were the cause of his problems, and they rode off into the setting sun, Carrie's baggage wagon following them.

"I really didn't mean—" Carrie began, but Josh cut her off.

"Don't say a word to me. Not one word. I need to think what to do about this."

"You could let me prove myself," she said under her breath.

When Josh heard what she'd said, he gave her a sideways look of such contempt that Carrie tightened her lips, refusing to say another word to him.

After a long ride over a dusty, rutted road, they turned down a weed-infested road that was hardly more than a path and slowly made their way into the tall trees. After some minutes the trees cleared away, and Carrie could see the house.

Never in her life had she seen such a forlorn, unhappy-looking place as that dilapidated little house. She had seen poverty in Warbrooke; some of her Taggert cousins were poor, but their houses didn't have the miserable, sad, forlorn look about them that this place did.

All the ground in front of the house and surrounding the little shed behind the house was bare of grass and plants, and the cheerless house itself had no glass in the windows, just oiled paper. There was light coming from inside the house, but not much, and there was no smoke coming from the ragged-topped chimney.

The house itself was nothing but a box, with a door and a window on each side. Another perfectly square, perfectly boring box was attached to the back of the house, and she wondered if it was a bedroom.

Turning, she looked at Josh in the moonlight, her face showing her disbelief at what she was seeing. For the life of her she could not picture this man living in a place like this.

With a set-jawed straight-ahead stare, he refused to meet her glance, but she knew he was aware that she was staring at him. "You see now why I wanted someone who knew how to work. Could you, Miss Rich Princess, live in that?"

Carrie thought it was odd that he could see how appalling the place was yet he hadn't done anything about it. Her Taggert cousins lived in semisqualor, but they all seemed to love the mess. When they visited her house, they were uncomfortable and couldn't wait to leave.

Angrily, as though the house and everything about it was somehow her fault, he halted the wagon in front of the house and got down. When she was closer to the place, Carrie could see that the house was even worse than it had looked from a distance. The missing roof shingles made her wonder if the house leaked. The front door was hanging by one hinge, giving the place a drunken appearance. Since there was no porch on the house, there was what looked to be a permanent mud puddle in front of the door.

With what seemed to be a permanent mood on his part, Josh angrily came to her side of the wagon and lifted her down. But there was no lingering of his hands on her waist this time. In fact, he didn't so much as look at her as he left her standing while he went to the baggage wagon.

After one more look at the house, she turned to the baggage wagon and asked the driver to hand her the two small carpet bags that were loaded on the front of the wagon. One was full of her night things and the other contained her gifts for the children.

"Are the children inside?" she asked Josh.

"Inside waiting in the cold and the dark, and I'm sure they're hungry." The anger and bitterness in his voice made it sound as though the condition of the place was Carrie's fault.

She didn't say any more to him, but turned and went toward

the house. It wasn't easy trying to balance the two bags and Choo-choo at the same time, but Josh made no effort to help her. He was giving orders to the baggage wagon driver about where to unload Carrie's trunks, and he let everyone within hearing distance know what he thought of all her baggage. The broken hinge of the front door made it nearly impossible to open, and when she did get the thing open, the frame nearly hit her in the face. It was a struggle, but she managed to get it open enough to go inside the little house.

If she thought the house was bad outside, she wasn't prepared for the inside. Grim, she thought. A bleak, unhappy, colorless place that was guaranteed to make its inhabitants wretched. The walls were of bare planks darkened with soot from many fires. In the middle of the room was a dirty, round table with four mismatched chairs, one of which was leaning to one side from a leg that was too short.

In the corner of the single room was a cabinet that seemed to be the kitchen of the house, for the top of the cabinet was piled high with chipped dishes that hadn't been washed in so long that they were dusty as well as encrusted with dried food.

As Carrie stood with her back to the broken door and looked about the dreadful place, at first she didn't see the children. They were standing in the shadows of the doorway to what Carrie assumed was the bedroom, standing quietly, watching, waiting to see what was going to happen.

They were beautiful children, even more beautiful than their photograph showed. The boy looked as though he might grow to be more handsome than his father, and it was obvious that the girl would someday blossom into splendor.

In spite of their good looks, the children looked as unhappy as the house did. Neither of them had combed their hair in days, maybe months, and, although they were fairly clean, their clothes were dirty and torn and had that faded look that only hundreds of washings could give to cloth.

As Carrie stood looking at them, she knew that she had been right: This family needed her.

"Hello," Carrie said as cheerfully as she could manage. "I'm your new mother."

The children looked at each other then back at Carrie, their eyes wide in wonder.

Carrie went to the table and set her bags on it, noting that the table was greasy and needed a good cleaning. Sniffing around her legs, Choo-choo pulled to be free, and when she unsnapped his leash, he went immediately to the children, both of whom looked down at the animal in astonishment. Neither of them made any move to touch the little dog.

Opening the first case, Carrie withdrew a porcelain-headed doll, an exquisite creature, made in France and dressed by hand all in silk. "This is for you," she said to the girl, then waited for a seemingly endless moment until the child came forward to take the gift. She looked as though she were afraid to touch the elegant doll.

Carrie took the sailboat from the bag. "And this is for you." Holding out the boat to the boy, she saw by his eyes that he very much wanted to take the present, and he even took a step forward, but then he stepped back and shook his head no.

"I brought it just for you," Carrie said coaxingly. "My brothers sail ships from Maine to all over the world, and this is very much like one of their ships. I'd like for you to have it."

The boy looked as though he were fighting some inner demon, fighting the part of him that so much wanted the toy, and fighting the other part of himself that for some reason wanted to refuse the boat.

At last the boy tightened his lips—and in doing so looked exactly like his father—and said belligerently, "Where's Papa?"

"I believe he's helping a man with my baggage."

The boy gave a firm nod then ran out the door, obviously used to the broken hinge as he seemed to work it without nearly killing himself.

"Well," Carrie said and sat down on one of the unbroken chairs. "I think he's angry at me. Do you know why?"

"Papa said that you were going to be ugly and we weren't to mention it. He said that lots of things were ugly, but they couldn't help it," the girl said, then cocked her head to one side as she studied Carrie. "But you're not ugly at all."

Carrie smiled at the little girl. For all that she couldn't be more than five, she was certainly articulate. "It seems to me to be a little unfair to be angry just because someone isn't ugly."

"My mother is beautiful."

"Oh, I see," Carrie said, and she did see. If her own beautiful mother died and her father had married another beautiful woman, Carrie wouldn't have been too happy about it either. If her father had remarried, she would have much preferred him to marry an ugly woman, a very, very ugly woman.

"You don't mind that I'm not ugly, do you? I can be ugly if you want." At that Carrie began to make faces, pulling her eyes down with her fingers, and pushing her nose up with her thumb.

The little girl giggled.

"Think Temmie would like me better if I looked like this?"

Giggling again, the child nodded.

"Why don't you come here and let me brush your hair and you can tell me what you're going to name your doll."

When the child hesitated, as though trying to decide if this would be something her father would want her to do, Carrie withdrew her silver-backed hairbrush from her case. After a little gasp of awe at the sight of the pretty brush, the child went to Carrie and took her place between Carrie's knees and allowed her to gently brush her hair.

"And your name is Dallas?" Carrie asked, stroking the child's fine, soft hair. "Isn't that a rather unusual name?"

"Mother said it was where I was made."

"Like in a factory?" Carrie said before she thought, then cleared her throat, glad the girl couldn't see her red face. "Oh, I see. What are you called? Dallie?"

The child seemed to consider that for a moment. "You can call me Dallie if you want."

Behind her, Carrie smiled. "I should be honored to be allowed to call you a name that no one else calls you."

"What's his name?" Dallie pointed to Choo-choo.

Carrie told her. "It's because the day my brother gave him to me, he sneezed many times. Do you know that since that day I don't think he's sneezed once?"

When Dallas didn't laugh but nodded solemnly, Carrie felt a tug at her heart. It wasn't right that a child as young as she was should be so serious. "There now," Carrie said. "Your hair is very tidy and what lovely hair it is, too. Would you like to look?" When she held out a silver-backed mirror, the child took it and looked at herself as though she were studying herself.

"You are very pretty," Carrie reassured her.

Dallie nodded. "But not beautiful. Not like my mother." She handed the mirror back to Carrie.

What an odd thing for a little girl to say, Carrie thought as she looked about the cold, dreary little room. "Shall we see about dinner? What is there in the house to eat?"

"Papa said that you would make dinner. He said that you knew how to cook anything in the world and that you would never let us go hungry."

Carrie smiled. "Then that's what I'll have to do." Standing up, she went to the single cupboard and opened the doors. Her heart sank when she saw how little there was inside. The sight of half a loaf of stale bread, three cans of peas, and nothing else made a surge of anger at Josh shoot through her. Even if she were the greatest cook in the world, she wouldn't be able to prepare a meal with these few ingredients.

She searched the cupboard, and way in the back, she found a jar of homemade strawberry preserves. Withdrawing the jar, she smiled. "For dinner tonight we shall feast on bread and jam. I have a fat packet of China tea in my case so we shall be able to have a very elegant tea party."

"We can't eat that," Dallas said, motioning toward the jar of jam. "Papa says that we must save them for something special. Aunt Alice made them. They were a present."

Carrie smiled. "Every day is special. There is never a day when you can't find *something* to celebrate, and today, especially, there are lots of things to celebrate. I have arrived and you have a new doll and Temmie has a new toy and—"

"He won't like for you to call him Temmie. He's Tem and that's all."

"Oh, I see. He's too old to be Temmie, is that it?"

Dallas nodded solemnly.

Carrie smiled. "I'll try to remember that he's too old to be a Temmie. Now, let's get the table set for dinner."

It was obvious that the child had no idea what Carrie meant by "setting the table," so Carrie set her bags on the floor and withdrew a lovely, enormous Paisley shawl. The reds and pinks of the shawl seemed to sparkle in the dull little room that was lit by a single candle set on the mantelpiece. Dallas's eyes widened as she watched Carrie spread newspapers from a short stack by the fireplace on the table, then spread the shawl over the papers. Next

Carrie began looking for clean dishes but could find none. She gave a glance at the stack of dishes in the sink but didn't think much about them. At home, Carrie knew that dishes went out of the dining room dirty and came back clean, but she wasn't sure what happened in between.

Since there were no clean dishes, Carrie looked in her bag and withdrew four linen handkerchiefs. "We shall have a picnic," she said as she spread them on top of the shawl then withdrew four small silver tumblers from the bag. She always carried them when traveling, because her mother said that she was never to use the communal cups that the other passengers used.

Standing to one side, Dallas watched all of this in fascination, and after Carrie brought the silver cups from the bag, the child went to peer into the bag as though it were something from a fairy tale and contained everything in the world.

Removing her cut-crystal hairpin holder from the bag, Carrie wiped it out with a clean handkerchief and filled it full of strawberry preserves. Dallas didn't remember ever having seen anything but jars put on the table, so this concept of putting food into pretty dishes was new to her. Carrie sliced the bread and placed it on another handkerchief in the middle of the table, then stepped back to look at the results.

"Rather pretty, don't you think?"

Dallas could only nod. Candlelight played on the silver tumblers and the crystal of the hairpin jar, and the colors of the shawl glowed. It was the most beautiful table Dallas had ever seen. Next to this woman who said she was her new mother and the doll that Dallas was clinging to and that little dog, the table was the most beautiful thing Dallas had ever seen in her whole life.

When Dallas looked up and smiled at Carrie, Carrie smiled back.

It was at that moment that Josh and his son came back into the house, and Carrie saw that having to unload twenty-some trunks full of women's clothes had not put Josh into a better mood.

"All of them are stacked in the shed," Josh said, his mouth rigid, his jaws clamped together. "Of course, there's no room for the horse's feed and the tools had to be set outside, so if it rains tonight we're sunk, but those trunks of yours are inside, all safe and warm and protected." He looked at the table, which his son was staring at in open-mouthed astonishment. "What's this?"

"Dinner," Carrie said proudly, waiting for him to admit that he had been wrong about her. He had promised his children their new mother would feed them dinner tonight, and that's just what she was doing. "The children are hungry."

Without relinquishing his frown, Josh picked up the crystal jar full of jam and looked at the bread so neatly sliced and laid out on the monogrammed handkerchief. "Bread and jam," he said contemptuously. "That's not a very good dinner for children, is it?"

Carrie glared at him, thinking that he was incapable of admitting when he was wrong. "I used what there was. No one, not even the paragon of work that you were expecting, could cook a meal from the little food that you have in this house."

"There are canned goods," Josh said, not giving an inch. "You can at least heat something from a can, can't you? And why has the fire been allowed to die down? Why didn't you build it up? It's cold in here."

The children looked from Carrie to their father in consternation. He had talked to them at length about how they were to be nice to this woman who was coming to take care of them, yet he wasn't being very nice to her at all.

Carrie just looked at Josh, refusing to reply to his accusations.

At last Josh shook his head in disbelief. "I see. You have no idea how to open a can, do you? And it's my guess that you've never so much as thrown a log on a fire."

He was right, but Carrie wasn't going to tell him so. Instead, she just stood where she was and looked at him.

Looking from one to the other, Dallas felt like bursting into tears. "Papa, I *like* bread and jam. Would you like to see my doll? You can name her if you want, but if you like the name Elsbeth, so do I."

As Carrie watched him, Josh's face changed when he looked at his daughter. So far, she had seen two expressions on his face: She had seen him when he didn't know who she was and desired her, and she had seen rage on his face since he'd found out who she was. But now she was seeing love on that dark, handsome face—a face she already felt she knew so well. She watched as he smiled at his daughter, then sat down and asked to see her doll. Carrie listened as Dallas told her father all about the doll, which was surprising because Carrie hadn't been aware that the child had even looked at the toy. Dallas showed her father the doll's pretty underclothes and its legs made of stuffed kid leather.

"I think Elsbeth is the best name for her," Josh said softly, stroking Dallas's hair, noticing that it was brushed and neat, and for one brief flash, he looked at Carrie in gratitude.

"I brought Tem a gift too," Carrie said as she picked up the boat from where she'd put it on the mantelpiece.

Tem gave a longing look at the toy, but turned to his father for permission to take it. Carrie could see by Josh's face that he didn't want his children to take anything from her, but she also saw that his children's happiness meant more to him than any feud in the world. With a smile, Josh nodded to his son.

Hesitantly, Tem stepped forward and took the boat, then went back to stand near his father, the boat behind his back, as though he didn't dare look at it. Even though Tem didn't look at the boat, Carrie saw that he was stroking it with his hands.

"Papa," Dallas said, "I'm hungry."

With a sigh, Josh looked at the table, then nodded for his children to take their seats.

"If you have a teapot, I could make tea," Carrie said softly, for she was ready to make amends. This man who looked at his children with such love was the man she'd seen in the photo, the man she'd fallen in love with and had lied her way into a marriage with.

But when Josh looked up at Carrie, the love left his face. "You can make tea in a pot?" he practically sneered. "But then I guess that's a ladylike occupation, isn't it?" Angrily, he got up, tended to the fire, put an iron kettle of water on to boil, then rummaged under the stack of dirty dishes until he found a chipped teapot, which he set on the table.

They sat in silence while the water heated, all of them morose, looking down at the handkerchiefs that served as plates and saying nothing.

How ridiculous, Carrie thought, looking at the three of them. How utterly absurd to be alive and healthy and to be so sad. Poverty and living in a house like this didn't make it necessary for people to be gloomy.

"I have seven older brothers," she said brightly into the silence. "And every one of them is as handsome as a prince in a fairy tale, and all of them travel all over the world on ships. Some months

ago, not long before your father and I were married—" she ignored Josh's startled look at this statement—"my brother Jamie
brought Choo-choo to me. Would you like to hear some of the
stories he told me about the places he visited? He went to China."

"Yes, oh please, yes," Dallas said, her voice and face showing
that she was practically begging for some relief from the never-
ending sadness.

Carrie looked at Tem, and although he tried to act as though he
couldn't care less what Carrie did, his eyes were eager. He nodded his consent.

Carrie looked at Josh and waited, forcing him to be part of the
family.

"Whatever pleases the children," he said gloomily.

With enthusiasm, Carrie began to tell what Jamie had told her
about China and especially about the palace her brother had visited, describing in lurid detail the silks and ornaments. Maybe she
embellished a bit, but then maybe Jamie hadn't told her all there
was to tell. Leaning forward, in a voice reserved for ghost stories,
she told the children about the custom of binding the feet of Chinese women.

During this, the water came to a boil, she got up, brought the
kettle to the table, filled the teapot with water and her delicious
tea, then began heaping strawberry jam on thick slices of bread,
and handed them round to the children and Josh. Since Carrie
was by this time telling about foot binding, Josh was as absorbed
in her story as the children were, and he didn't remember to tell
her that he could serve himself.

Carrie talked all through the meal, at one point telling a Chinese fairy tale about true love that had ended abruptly and the
woman had become a ghost. When all of the bread and jam was
gone, she went to her case and withdrew a box of chocolates and
served two pieces to each person while she finished telling her
ghost story.

When all the food and all the tea were gone, Carrie stopped
talking, and for a moment there was silence at the table.

"Golly," Dallas said into the silence, her eyes wide.

"Is any of that true?" Tem asked, trying to sound like a skeptical
grownup.

"All of it. My brothers have been all over the world, and they've
told me the most extraordinary tales. You should hear about In-

dia. And then there're the desert countries and Egypt, and two of my brothers have fought pirates."

"Pirates!" Tem gasped, then caught himself.

"And one of my brothers was in the U.S. Army and fought Indians, but he says he liked the Indians better than he did most of the soldiers. I brought some things my brothers have given me, things they bought or stole or traded for on their trips."

"Your brothers *stole* things?" Dallas asked, aghast. "Uncle Hiram says that stealing is a sin."

"It is and it isn't," Carrie assured her. "One of my brothers stole a pretty young woman from a slave trader, but that's another story that I'll have to save for another night. Right now I think it's time you two were in bed."

Again there was silence, but then Josh spoke. "Yes, of course. It's time for bed. Past time. Now scoot."

Carrie watched as the children hugged their father, kissed his cheek, and told him good night, then both of them turned to Carrie and didn't seem to know what to do.

She smiled. "Go on, go to bed," she said, still smiling and relieving them of their dilemma.

As she watched, they scurried up a ladder leaning against the wall in the shadow of the fireplace. Overhead, she could hear them in what must be a tiny attic as they settled down for bed.

Still smiling, Carrie looked back at Josh, but he wasn't smiling. All humor, all happiness had left his handsome face, and his dour expression made the smile disappear from her face.

"I'll clean this up," Carrie said.

"Unless you plan to leave it for the maid."

Her teeth gritted, she stopped with her hands on the handkerchiefs. "What is it that angers you the most about me? Is it that I have so far succeeded where you predicted failure?"

Sitting down on the chair, her hands clutched in front of her, she looked at him. "I can see now that what I did wasn't fair to you or your children, but I think you should give me a chance. I think you've misjudged me."

For a moment she saw that look of desire in his eyes, and the hairs on the back of her neck stood up, but then it was gone again and he looked at her coldly. "Let me explain something to you, Miss Montgomery, I—" He put his hand up when she started to speak. "All right, then, Mrs. Greene. My children mean more to me than anything else in the world. They mean *everything* to me, and I want to give them the best that I can, and by the best I mean a life that has a great deal of stability to it. I want them to have a father and a mother as well. I want them to have what I didn't have, and I want them to grow up in the country in the fresh air; I want them to have food—home-cooked food. In order to obtain those things for my children, I am willing to do anything I have to. If I have to marry a woman who is part horse in order to give them what they need, then I'll do so. Do you understand me?"

"What about love?" Carrie asked softly. "Doesn't love matter to you?"

When he answered, he didn't meet her eyes. "I love them enough for a dozen people. What they *need* is good food and a clean house and clean clothes."

"I see. And you have decided that I can't give them any of those things. You've known me for only a few hours, yet you've decided exactly what I'm like."

He smiled at her in a patronizing way. "Look at you. How much did that dress cost you, and are those real pearls you're wearing? You don't have to answer me. I unloaded your trunks, remember? Do you think I'm so stupid as to think that someone like you is going to be happy living in this . . ." He waved his hand. "This hovel?" He leaned toward her, the table width between them. "You know what I think, Miss Montgomery? And yes it is and will always be Miss *Montgomery*, because I don't mean to actually make you into Mrs. Greene, if you know what I mean."

Carrie couldn't help herself, but she glanced toward the bedroom, which she hadn't yet seen.

"Exactly," Josh said. "What I think is that this is a great adventure to you. You probably grew up spoiled and pampered by these too-magnificent-to-be-believed brothers of yours and you think you can do anything you want. Right now you want to spread your cheery little self around the house of some poor man and his children. But what happens to us after you get tired of us? Do you come into our lives, make us laugh with your stories, make the children and—" He sighed. "Make the children come to love you, and for that matter, maybe make me come to adore you, too, then when you're tired of us, you go back to Daddy and your fascinating brothers? Is that what's going to happen?"

"No," she said and started to defend herself, but he wouldn't let her speak.

"How old are you, Miss Montgomery? Eighteen? Nineteen? Twenty, at most, is my guess."

Carrie didn't answer him, for he seemed to have everything figured out, so why bother trying to dissuade him?

"You haven't had time to see anything of the world or to experience anything. Quite romantically, you fell in love with a photograph, and you thought you'd give marriage a try. How exciting to travel all the way out West with hundreds of dresses and—"

Abruptly, he broke off and stood up. "What the hell's the use trying to explain? You'd never understand in a million years." He gave a sigh of resignation. "All right, Miss Montgomery, here's the way it's going to be. You may stay here for one week—until the stage travels through again—then I'm sending you back to your father as intact as you were when you arrived. You were so clever at arranging this marriage all by yourself, so you can arrange the annulment all by yourself."

Carrie stood up also. "Are you through? Have you finished insulting both me and my family? Maybe I should tell you about the town where I grew up so you can insult that too. It's true that I grew up with money, but as far as I know you don't have to be poor in order to want to give and receive love. And whether you believe me or not, love is why I came to this place. I—" She stopped because if she didn't, she was going to start crying. When she thought of all her expectations and the reality of meeting the man she thought she was going to love, she could do little else except cry.

With all the dignity she could muster, she picked up her night case, tucked her dog under her arm, and walked toward the bedroom. "I shall stay here one week, Mr. Greene, not because of you, but because those children of yours need a little happiness in their lives, and if I can give them one week of happiness, that's better than nothing. At the end of the week I shall return to my father just as you wish." She took a step into the bedroom, her hand on the door. "As for your not touching me during that week, that is *your* loss." With that she slammed the door.

She managed to maintain her anger for about three minutes, then she flung herself on the none-too-clean bed and began to cry. Choo-choo licked her face and seemed as sad as she was.

Chapter Five

The next morning, Carrie was out of bed before dawn—or at least it seemed so to her. Usually, she awoke early, but she had a talent for turning over and going back to sleep, but this morning it took her a moment to remember where she was. Her eyes were puffy from crying herself to sleep, and she had a bit of a headache.

Reluctantly, she got out of the warm bed, opened the bedroom door, and went into the parlor—if it could be called that—and smiled when she saw that it was empty. Good, she thought, she was up before they were. But then she saw that there was a note on the table. They couldn't have come and gone already, could they? It was barely dawn.

Ignoring the note, she turned back to the bedroom, trying not to look at the dreariness of the little room. A bureau that didn't look as though it would make good firewood was against one wall and on top of it was a pocket watch that she assumed was Josh's. Squinting against the early morning light, she looked at the watch. Eight o'clock. Good heavens, she had never been out of bed this early in her life. Even when she was going to school, her tutor had started her classes at eleven.

Yawning, she went back into the big room and picked up the paper from the table. Recognizing Josh's handwriting, she was instantly transported back to the time in Maine when she had read and reread his letter asking for a wife, and later she had memorized his letter saying he agreed to her terms of a proxy marriage.

Sitting down, Choo-choo on her lap, she read Josh's letter.

Dear Miss Montgomery:

I didn't sleep much last night as I was thinking about our few conversations—if you can call them that. Whatever has happened, I believe you meant well. I now believe that your intentions were good and maybe there's some truth in my children needing more than just clean clothes and hot food. But whatever your intentions, my children do need those things.

Twice you have asked me to give you a chance to prove yourself, to allow you to show me that you are not what you appear to be, so I have decided to give you that chance. You have proven yourself to be capable of caring for my children in a maternal way—at breakfast they could hardly keep their eyes off the bedroom door. In fairness to you, you seem to genuinely like my children, but I wonder if you can do the chores necessary to be a farmer's wife.

I am enclosing a list of chores that I will expect you to complete within the week that you are to be with us. If you can do these things, then I am willing to discuss what possible future there is for you as the mother of my children.

> *Sincerely yours,*
> *Joshua T. Greene*

After reading the letter, Carrie picked up the list of chores, her mouth dropping open when she saw that the list was at least a foot long. Five women in six weeks couldn't complete all the things that Josh had given her to do.

She sat back in the chair, her eyes narrowed at the list in one hand and the letter in the other. "You will allow me to be the mother of your children, will you?" she said to the air. "Not your wife, but somebody's mother." Tossing the papers aside, she scratched Choo-choo's head. "Rumpelstiltskin. That's what this is like. King Joshua gives me a list of chores just as the king in the fairy tale gave the young woman a roomful of straw to spin into gold. If she performed that impossible task, then she got to marry the king. In this case I get to mother the king's children."

She looked about the room. Impossible to believe, but it looked even more barren and hopeless in the daylight than it had the previous evening. "I wonder what they had for breakfast? Peas?" Carrie gave a delicate shudder, then stood and put Choo-choo to the floor. "Shall we go find our own Rumpelstiltskin?" she said to the dog. "Someone to help us perform the tasks the king has set before us?"

An hour later when Mrs. Carrie Greene née Montgomery rode into the town of Eternity on Josh Greene's old swayback work-horse wearing the finest riding habit that had ever been seen west of the Mississippi, the town came to a virtual standstill. Every person in sight stopped what he or she was doing and looked at this vision of loveliness. Her habit was dark red, trimmed in black velvet, and she wore the sauciest little veiled hat perched over one eye that anyone had ever seen.

"Good morning," Carrie said to each person she passed. "Good morning."

People stared and nodded at this fashion plate vision of loveli-ness, too dumbfounded to move or reply.

Carrie stopped the horse—if the poor thing could be called that —in front of the mercantile store, where the owner had paused in sweeping the front porch to gape at her. Nodding to him, she said, "Good morning," then went inside the cool, dark store.

When the store owner had recovered himself, he leaned his broom against the wall, smoothed his apron front, and went into the store.

Carrie had seated herself on a chair near the empty wood stove and was removing her riding gloves.

"What can I do for you, Miss, ah . . ."

"Mrs. Greene," she said confidently. "Mrs. Joshua Greene."

"I didn't know Josh got married. Hiram didn't tell me anything about it."

That was the second time Carrie had heard mention of Hiram, and she had no idea who he was, but she wasn't going to let this man know that. "It was rather sudden," she said demurely, trying to make it seem as though she and Josh hadn't been able to help themselves, that their marriage had been a love match.

"I understand," the store owner said. "Now, what may I do for you?"

By this time a quarter of the townspeople had decided that they had to buy something at the mercantile store and so had slipped through the door as quietly as possible. They were lining up against the wall opposite Carrie, standing quietly, looking at her as they would have a circus performer.

"I should like to make a few purchases," Carrie said.

Carrie knew that Josh thought she had no talents because she didn't know how to wash dishes or open cans, but there was a talent that Carrie had in abundance and that was: She knew how to buy things. That statement might cause laughter in some people, but the ability to use money properly is an underestimated talent. Some people with great wealth squander their money on bad investments; they hire incompetent people; if they buy art, they buy fakes.

But Carrie knew how to handle money. She knew how to get ten cents out of every nickel. There was a joke in her hometown that it was better to work for any Montgomery other than Carrie, for she'd get twice as much work out of you for half as much money. Carrie had a way of looking at people with her big blue eyes that made them fall over themselves to do what she wanted.

"I wonder if someone in this lovely town could help me," she said innocently. "My husband has asked me to do a few things for him, and I really don't know how to get started."

When she held up the list of tasks Josh had written out for her, the store owner looked at it, then gave a long, low whistle and passed the list to the man behind him, who passed it to the person beside him.

"Why, you poor thing," one woman said upon reading the list. "What in the world was Josh thinkin' of?"

Carrie sighed. "I am a brand-new wife and have no idea how to do anything. I don't even know how to open a can."

"*I'd* like to show her how to open a can," one man mumbled, but his wife poked him in the ribs.

"I may not be able to actually *do* the things my husband wants, but I thought perhaps I could get someone to help me."

They were willing to give lots of sympathy, but no one rushed forward to volunteer to repair the roof on that shack of Josh's. Compassion was one thing but sweat was another.

Carrie removed the fat purse from her wrist. "My father gave me a bit of money before I left home so I wondered if I could hire some people to help me." She opened the drawstring and poured several coins into her pretty little palm. "Does it matter that the only coins I have are gold?"

After the initial intake of breath, all hell broke loose as people began shoving, kicking, and shouting as they offered Carrie their services to do anything that she wanted them to do. They were her slaves—or perhaps highly paid employees would be more accurate.

Standing up, Carrie went to work. She was a sweet-voiced drill sergeant, but a drill sergeant nonetheless. First, she hired half a dozen women to clean that pigsty Josh called a house, then she bargained with two other women to take Josh's chipped and cracked dirty dishes away in trade for three rose bushes that grew in front of their own houses. Planting was part of the trade.

She bought home-canned goods from nearly every woman in town (all of whom were in the store by now), and she purchased produce from gardens. For the future, she arranged with a woman named Mrs. Emmerling to cook meals and deliver them to Josh's house every other day, paying for a month in advance.

When she was finished with the women, she started on the men. She arranged for the roof to be repaired and the shed to be mended, then hired a carpenter to repair the front door. When she asked if anyone had a porch on his or her house, a porch that they'd like to take down and put up on the front of Josh's house, there was a bidding war on the porch. Carrie went with the man who had the porch with the white posts. She arranged for the house to be painted.

"How soon do you want this done?" one man asked.

Carrie smiled sweetly. "For every job that's done by sundown tonight, I will pay twelve percent more than the agreed-upon price."

About twenty people tried to get out the door at the same time.

"Now," Carrie said, turning back to the store owner. "I'd like to make a few purchases."

She bought one can of everything he had in his store. She bought bacon and ham and flour, as well as anything the store owner's wife told her she'd "need" as a wife. Smiling as though she knew what she was doing, Carrie purchased a can opener, a strange-looking contraption that made no sense to her. She purchased a cookstove that the store owner said anyone could cook on.

She bought lace curtains and panes of glass, then hired people to install them.

By this time people were running into the store and offering Carrie things to buy, for Eternity was a poor town, and people used any opportunity to earn money. Carrie bought rag rugs, more rose bushes, a solid oak kitchen cabinet, four matching chairs (she traded Josh's chairs for these), quilts, blankets, pillows, and sheets. She bought dishes and silverware (plate, unfortunately, not sterling) from a widower, and she hired women to come once a week and do the laundry.

When a wagon full of furniture came rolling by, owned by a family moving out of Eternity, she bought several pieces, including a big tin bathtub.

By two o'clock she rode out of what was nearly a deserted town, for most of the townspeople were already at Josh's house working, but two big, strong boys came running up and asked what they could do. Carrie hired them to go into the mountains, dig up four sapling trees, and plant them in Josh's front yard.

By three she was back at Josh's house. A circus would have seemed calmer than the chaos around his house, as women tried to plant roses right where men wanted to stand while they painted. Women stole ladders from men fixing the roof, then the painters stole the ladders back. Tempers were short, and there was a great deal of shouting while everyone tried to get his or her job done before the sundown deadline.

Carrie sat on the sidelines, eating bread and butter, feeding tidbits of this and that to Choo-choo, and paying men and women as they finished their jobs. She didn't have to worry about quality of work, for the people were glad enough to report any task that was only half done.

It was summer, so, thankfully, sundown was late in coming, and by the time there was a reddish glow on the horizon, the house was unrecognizable. Smoke poured from the repaired chimney, and over the stench of fresh paint, she could smell roast beef and possibly carrots simmering.

It was almost dark and, thankfully, there was still no sign of Josh or the kids yet when the last tired woman left the house, her money clasped in her hand. Carrie left her place under the shade tree and went back to the house, knowing that what she most wanted was a long, hot bath. She certainly deserved one after the day of work she had done. Having anticipated this need, she had arranged for several buckets of hot water to be waiting by the tub set up in the bedroom, so all she had to do was undress herself—a task in itself, considering all the buttons on her habit—and step into the water.

Sighing and smiling, pleased with herself and anticipating Josh's forthcoming apology, she went back to the house.

Chapter Six

When Josh and the children rode up the path toward the house, all of them on the same horse, they halted and stared in disbelief. At first Josh thought he'd made a wrong turn, so he reined the horse away and started back down the path. But there was that big clump of aspens that he knew was at the corner of the woods and there was the old fence post so he knew he was in the right area. Turning the horse, he started back toward the house and halted in front of it.

Moonlight shone down on the little building, but the wreck of a house he'd left this morning was gone. In its place was a house with a porch on the front of it. *This* house was whitewashed instead of being covered with dingy gray boards, and roses grew in front of it; there was sparkling clean glass in the windows.

"Did the Good Fairy come?" Dallas asked, rubbing her eyes, thinking she was asleep and dreaming.

"Something of that nature," Josh said through clenched teeth. "A good fairy with lots of money. Her *father's* money."

Josh urged the horse forward, helped the children down, and opened the front door of the house—a door that now moved easily on oiled hinges.

Inside the house, light reflected from several candles and lanterns set about the room, and against one wall set a new cookstove, enameled in bright blue and looking very cheerful. The walls, no longer bare but covered in pretty, rose-printed wallpaper, gleamed. There were rugs on the floors, furniture in the room, the table laid with a cloth and pretty porcelain dishes.

"It's a fairy castle," Dallas said and Josh winced. The child was too young to remember a time when she'd lived in anything but a hovel, and she didn't remember anything but poorly cooked food and bare floors and an unhappy father. She didn't remember a time when it was her father rather than an outsider who gave her what she needed.

When Josh looked at his son, he saw that Tem, too, was impressed by his new surroundings, and Josh felt angry because he had not been the one to give his children simple, basic things such as good food and a pretty house. Instead, some rich, empty-headed do-gooder from the East Coast had come into their lives and decided to bestow her charity on the poor little family in the mountains. It must have given her great satisfaction to act the Good Fairy, as Dallas called her, Josh thought. When Carrie left, she could tell herself that she had done well, that for a whole week she had given happiness to the dreary little family. She would be able to leave with her conscience clean and free of guilt knowing that she had done so much for the poor dears. But it was going to be Josh who'd have to hold the children when they cried.

Looking at the closed bedroom door, his mouth set, he went to it and turned the handle. But when he opened the door, he almost forgot his anger, because Little Miss Charity was sitting up to her neck in a bathtub full of suds. Her face was pink from the hot water, her hair was loosely piled on top of her head in a jumble of fat curls, and her breasts were just breaking the surface of the water. Josh stood gaping in dumbfounded stupefaction.

"Good evening," Carrie said, smiling, brushing a lock of damp hair off her brow. That look of desire was on his face again, and it felt so very good to have wiped that smug, patronizing look off his face. "Did all of you have a good day?" she asked as if they were in a drawing room, but as she spoke, she noted Josh's torn and dirty work clothes and thought that they suited him much less well than his suit had. Some men look good in canvas pants and cotton shirt, but Josh looked out of place, as though he were pretending to be someone he wasn't.

As Josh struggled to get himself under control, he realized that his life was very different from what it used to be. No longer did women often greet him in their bathtubs, and no longer was he free to do what he wished with them. Now he was a sensible, serious, responsible person—a father—and he had to think of serious matters. And serious matters did not include what he most wanted to do in the world right now, which was to close the door to the bedroom and climb in the tub with this delicious, delectable, luscious young woman.

He straightened. "I'd like to speak to you," he said as sternly as he could manage, but then a curl fell over her eye, and she tried to brush it away with a soapy hand. She was going to get soap in her eye, he thought, and someone ought to help her.

Dallas pushed in front of her father and stood for a moment staring in wonder at the bedroom. There was wallpaper on the walls in this room too and a new brass bed and fluffy covers on the feather mattress. "It's beautiful," Dallas said.

Carrie smiled. "I'm so glad you like it, but I don't think your father does."

Dallas looked up at her father in disbelief. "But it's beautiful." The child sounded as though she were going to cry. "Can we keep it?"

Picking up his daughter, Josh hugged her. "Of course we can keep it. There isn't any way to return wallpaper." He looked over Dallas's shoulder to frown at Carrie, but she just smiled at him.

Carrie looked at Dallas, in her father's arms, and at Tem, peering from behind his father and said, "If you children would excuse us, I think your father would like to talk to me in private."

Josh did have some things he wanted to say to Carrie, actually rather a great many things, but he wasn't going to be alone with her while she was sitting in a bathtub. From what little he knew of her, he wouldn't put it past her to stand up in the tub and ask him to hand her a towel. If she were to stand up, he knew he'd be lost. "What I have to say can wait," Josh said as gruffly as he could manage and put Dallas down.

Moving to the tub, Dallas picked up a handful of suds, looking at them in question.

"They are foaming bath salts," Carrie said, "and they're from—"

"Let me guess," Josh said sarcastically. "France. One of your dear brothers brought them back to you."

"As a matter of fact he did, along with six new dresses," she said sweetly. She was not going to defend her brothers to this man.

"How charming for you to have been born wealthy. The rest of us slaves of the world have to work for our bread and . . ." He looked about the room. "We have to work for the rugs and the wallpaper and the dresses."

Carrie smiled at him. "Then it seems that it's the duty of the rich people to share their wealth, doesn't it?"

"Perhaps, but charity doesn't sit well with all of us."

Carrie refused to allow him to make her angry. She wanted to remind him that they were now married and that what was hers was his, too, and that she had purchased these items for her own family. As for his pride, which seemed to be hurt, she had not bought a house in town, even though there was a rather nice one for sale, but had merely decorated *his* house.

Carrie bit down on her feelings of injustice and, instead, offered to share her tub with Dallas. The little girl looked at her father for permission, then hurriedly undressed herself, and her father lifted her into the tub. As the child settled into the tub, Carrie was very pleased to see Josh frowning fiercely before he turned away and left the room.

Once he was out of the bedroom, Josh felt that he could breathe again, but that didn't last for long, for now the parlor was so very, very different from the way it had been. The whole room seemed to reek of Carrie. Everywhere he looked he could see her touch, and when he glanced at Tem and saw that the boy was looking into the big pot that set bubbling on the stove, he knew that his son felt it too. Tem jumped guiltily when his father glanced at him, as though he knew he shouldn't be enjoying what Carrie had done for them.

Turning away, Josh went to the fireplace. Since the fire was no longer sending clouds of smoke billowing into the room, he was sure that Carrie had had the chimney cleaned. In spite of himself, Josh took a seat in one of the two rocking chairs set in front of the fire, leaned back against the pretty cushions tied to the back and seat of the chair, and enjoyed the sights and sounds around him. When his father was seated, tentatively, Tem sat on the chair across from him.

Leaning back, Josh closed his eyes, and for a moment he could imagine that life was how he had imagined it would be. He could hear his wife and daughter splashing in the bedroom, and the sound of their laughter seemed to fill the room—and him—with warmth. He could smell food cooking and hear the stew simmering, and he could hear the fire crackling. When he opened his eyes and looked at his son, who was so comfortable in the chair, Josh knew that all of it was almost exactly as he'd hoped it would be. This was how he'd imagined his life would be when he'd sent for a bride who knew how to cook and clean and run a farm. He had wanted the best for his children and had been willing to sacrifice his own happiness for that of his children.

But Josh was too well aware that all of this was an illusion, that it wasn't real, and that it wasn't going to last. Looking at Tem, Josh saw that he was about to fall asleep in the chair. It was going to be Josh who had to hold the children and dry their tears after Carrie got bored with her life as a farm wife and left them. And Josh was going to have to try to explain to the children about adults and about selfishness, and he was sure that he was going to be as good at it the next time he had to do it as he had been when the children's mother had left them.

Looking up when the bedroom door opened, he saw Carrie had dressed Dallas in a white cotton nightgown that Josh was sure was fresh from the shelves of the mercantile store, and Josh felt a fresh surge of anger. It had been a long time since he had been able to buy his children gifts.

But Josh forgot his anger as he looked at Carrie, for her hair was wet and hanging in a tangle down her back, flowing over a gown of dark pink silk covered by a red cashmere robe. When he looked at her, Josh had to swallow, and his hands gripped the arms of the chair until his knuckles were white. More than anything in life he wanted to slip that robe off her shoulders and kiss her clean, white neck.

"And now," Carrie said, holding up two tortoiseshell combs, "the men may comb our hair." She looked from Josh to his son, then back to Josh, and she smiled at the expression on his face.

Tem protested. "I can't do that. That's girl's work."

Immediately, Josh told his son to be quiet. "There's no reason why you can't comb your sister's hair."

Smiling, Dallas went to stand between her brother's knees, and, in spite of his protest, Tem began to gently untangle Dallas's wet hair.

Carrie stood in the doorway, smiling confidently at Josh, the comb held out to him in invitation.

"I don't think—" Josh began, but then Tem stopped combing and looked at his father in question. His expression said that if his father couldn't comb a girl's hair, then he wouldn't either. With a groan that sounded a bit like a trapped animal, Josh held out his hand for the comb.

Smiling even broader, Carrie went to Josh, handed him the comb, then sat on the floor between his knees. From the first instant he touched her—being careful to touch only her hair and not her skin—Carrie knew two things. One was that the very air between them was charged and, two, that he had combed other women's wet hair. From the deft, experienced way he gently pulled the comb through her hair, she was afraid that he may have done it several times in the past.

Turning her head a bit to look at Tem, she saw that he was watching his father and learning. But then Josh's hand touched Carrie's forehead, and she forgot all about anyone else. Leaning her head back toward her husband, her eyes closed as she felt his touch through her hair and throughout her body.

Josh pulled her hair back from her face and in doing so, his fingertips touched her cheek. At the contact, both of them stopped moving, his fingers pausing as Carrie moved her head just a bit so that one fingertip touched the corner of her mouth. Without moving, sitting utterly still, her body seemed to vibrate with feeling. Turning until his finger was on her lips, she kissed his finger.

Josh moved his hand so that his two fingers covered her mouth, then his fingers began tracing the outline of her lips. When Carrie parted her lips, he ran his fingertips on the inside of her lip, just touching her teeth.

"Josh," Carrie said in the slightest whisper, then very gently, one by one, she bit his fingertips. He moved his hand over her mouth, and she kissed/bit his palm, then slowly moved to his wrist.

Bending down to her face until his lips were on her ear, his soft, warm breath on her ear was the most exciting thing Carrie had ever felt in her life.

"Golly," Dallas said, her eyes wide as she stared at the adults.

With a jolt, both Carrie and Josh became aware of their surroundings. Josh started to jump away from Carrie, but she wouldn't allow him to—not that it required much strength to hold him to her, but she leaned against his knee, and Josh rapidly started combing again.

Carrie looked at Tem and Dallas staring at them in big-eyed wonder and tried to put on a good-mother face. "Sometimes husbands and wives—" Carrie began.

"Shut up," Josh said sharply. "Is there anything to eat tonight? There, I think your hair's done." He looked at Tem. "What about your sister's?"

Tem was still staring, blinking at the two of them. He knew he had just seen some important adult-thing, but he didn't know what it meant.

"Have you finished combing your sister's hair?" Josh asked in a loud, piercing voice, snapping Tem out of his trance.

"Oh. Yeah," Tem answered, looking from Carrie to his father then back again.

"Good, then we can eat." With businesslike efficiency, Josh gave Carrie's hair one more stroke, then handed her the comb. "Could we eat now?"

"Of course," Carrie said sweetly, then, as though she'd done it all her life, she began to serve dinner to her family. Just as she had the night before, Carrie was the one who had to sustain the conversation throughout dinner. But tonight it was easier because the children asked her questions, and instead of hiding their interest in what she told them about her brothers' travels, they allowed their eagerness to show.

After dinner, when she bid the children good night, after Dallas had kissed her father, she didn't hesitate as she flung her arms around Carrie and kissed her too. Tem stood to one side, his hands in the pockets of his dirty work pants and looked as though he didn't know what to do.

"Go on," Josh said gruffly, motioning his head toward Carrie, giving his son permission to kiss her.

Shyly, Tem bent to Carrie and quickly kissed her cheek. He was a bit red in the face when he did it, but he gave a self-conscious smile as though he were proud of himself, then hurried up the ladder to his bed.

When the children were out of the room, Josh didn't say a word, but left the table to stand by the fireplace and stare at the flames. Silently, Carrie cleared the table, putting the dirty dishes in the sink. She had no idea what to do to clean them, and she certainly had no desire to learn. She liked beauty, and dirty dishes had nothing to do with beauty.

Carrie turned to Josh. "Would you like to go outside?" she asked.

"Why?" Josh asked suspiciously. His arms were folded across his chest, as though he were determined that none of himself was going to escape.

"So you can shout at me, of course. I got the distinct impression that that was your number one desire when you came home today. You haven't forgotten already, have you? Or maybe you've changed your mind. Or maybe you want to yell at me in the house so our children can hear."

"My children."

"So, you *do* want them to hear?"

At that, Josh grabbed Carrie's upper arm and pulled her out of the house into the cool, starlit night.

She walked toward the privacy of the trees, but he didn't follow her, so she turned back to him and sighed. "All right, I'm ready."

"What you did was wrong," he began. "You've made a laughingstock of me in front of the entire town."

"Actually, I rather think the townspeople think you're the luckiest man on earth, but then they don't have the deep knowledge of my character that you believe you do."

"Character has nothing to do with this. You may as well have told everyone that I can't take care of my own family."

"You love your children as much as any person I've ever seen. You just don't seem to have any money. Personally, I'd rather have love than money."

Josh didn't know whether to wring her neck or shout at her. No matter what he said to her, she didn't seem to hear him, didn't listen, didn't understand. When he spoke again, his voice was quieter. "A man likes to think he can support his own family, that his wife—I mean, his—"

"Yes, go on. What am I to you if not your wife?"

He didn't answer her, but stood there in silence.

Carrie sighed. "All right, King Joshua, I have fulfilled task number one, not by the rules, according to you, so what is task number two? I hope there are only three tasks involved."

At that inanity, Josh looked confused.

Carrie explained. "In all the fairy tales the princess is set three tasks. This morning you gave me a list that one human could never have completed, but I managed to do it—with the help of

Rumpelstiltskin, of course. Rumpelstiltskin being the entire town of Eternity. So now, sire, what is task number two?"

As understanding began to dawn on Josh, he grimaced. "It's as I thought: You think that all of this is a source for humor, something that you can tell your rich friends when you return home to Maine."

"And *you* think that everything in life is a reason for gloom. What is it that I have to do to prove myself to you?" She stopped. "No, wait a minute. You know something that I never did understand in the tale of Rumpelstiltskin? I couldn't understand why the young woman *wanted* the king. The king said that if she didn't spin the straw into gold, he'd cut her head off. How was I to believe that she lived happily ever after if she had to *marry* a creep like that?"

"There is no happily ever after, that's what I've been trying to tell you," Josh said heavily.

"Maybe you don't believe there is, but I do," Carrie practically shouted. "And it's what I mean to have. I apologize profusely, Mr. Greene, for having played such a dreadful trick on you as lying to you and marrying you. Since your major concern in life seems to be money, then perhaps what I spent on your house will partially make up for what I did to you. Now, if you'll excuse me, I have to pack."

As she started toward the house, Josh caught her arm. "It's the middle of the night. You can't go anywhere."

"Yes I can. If you can spare your second-best horse, I mean to go into town. Surely, after the amount of money I spent in that town today, someone will give me a bed for the night. And think, sir, of the satisfaction you will have in telling your children that I have gone. You can give them a much-needed lesson in the perfidy of women."

"Carrie," Josh said, reaching out his hand to touch her.

"Oh, so you know my name. I had no idea I was so honored. I thought that Miss Montgomery was all that you knew of me, but then, for you, my name is all you've needed to know—that and my looks, of course."

When Carrie marched onto the porch of the house and flung open the door, she was greeted by two white-faced, scared-looking children who had obviously heard everything that had been said outside.

"You aren't going to leave, are you?" Dallas said in a tear-filled voice, her little face white.

With a quick glance at Josh, Carrie saw that his face had an I-told-you-so smirk on it that she wished she could knock away with a baling pin. It was at that moment that Carrie decided to tell the children the truth. She'd often thought that adults terrified children by telling them there were things they were too young to understand and that it was ignorance that frightened people, not knowledge.

"I want both of you to sit down and I want to tell you everything," she said.

Just as she thought he would, Josh began to protest, but she turned on him in fury. "Whether you like it or not, I am legally part of this family."

The children sat at the table solemn and quiet while Carrie told them everything about how and why she came to be at their house.

"You loved us from the picture?" Dallas asked.

"Yes," Carrie answered. "I did. But now I have to leave, because your father is afraid that if I stay here longer, when I do leave, I will hurt you very much, and he doesn't want that to happen."

"*Will* you leave us?" Tem asked in a very adult voice, but there was a child's fear underlying the voice.

"If your father and I don't love each other, then I guess I'll have to. I'm afraid that I played a rather nasty trick on your father, and he's very angry about it."

Tears welled in Dallas's eyes. "Don't be angry, Papa."

Taking the child onto her lap, Carrie held her in her arms. "Don't blame your father. He's probably right. I might get bored living here in this little town. You see, where I live I'm used to parties and dancing and laughter." She was lying, but she knew it was for a good cause. She couldn't bear to leave and make the children think her departure was their father's fault. It was better that they dislike her than their father.

As Dallas clung to Carrie, Josh looked away. A five-year-old little girl was still a baby, for all that Dallas sometimes acted very grown-up.

"You can stay with us for the week, and we won't cry when you leave," Tem said, for once not looking at his father for approval.

Everyone turned to the boy.

"I don't think—" Josh began.

"She can stay!" Tem shouted, and it was easy to see that he was on the verge of tears, all his self-control about to break.

It was Carrie who at last spoke. "Temmie," she said, gently. "I am genuinely flattered that you've come to like me so much, but I know what you're thinking, that maybe I'll stay. I can assure that I will not. The only way I'd stay would be if I fell in love with your father, and I can promise you that will not happen. I rather stupidly thought that I knew what your father was like from looking at his photograph, but I didn't. Your father is a judgmental, pigheaded, know-it-all who has no sense of humor whatsoever, and I could never possibly love anyone like him."

Josh was looking at Carrie in horror as she delivered this pronouncement of him, while the children were staring at their father as though considering her opinion.

"Papa used to laugh," Tem said seriously. "But since Mother—"

"That's enough," Josh said sharply, cutting his son off.

"Stay," Dallas said, begging. "Please stay. It's so nice when you're here."

As Carrie held the child, she had to blink back her own tears. Perhaps it was the children she had come to love from the photo, for they were just as she'd hoped they'd be. She knew that if she'd come to love them this much in two days, it would be unbearable if she stayed a whole week and then had to leave them. "I think it's better that I leave now," Carrie said softly.

"We will vote," Tem said, but looking at his father for permission.

Josh took a moment, but he nodded his consent. Carrie was sure that the vote was going to be a tie, two for her leaving, two for her staying, but when Tem asked who was for Carrie staying as long as she could, both children put up their hands, then, slowly, so did Josh.

Carrie looked at him. "I want my children to be happy," Josh said softly in explanation, "even if it is only for a matter of days."

Carrie sighed, for she felt that she was making a mistake. She already loved these children, and she was going to love them more in the next few days. She didn't know how she was going to be able to leave them in just a few days' time.

"Sometimes the stage is late," Tem said, hope in his voice.

Smiling, Carrie reached across the table and took his hand in hers. Yes, she thought, who knew what could happen in a week? "All right," she said at last. "I will stay for as long as I can."

Chapter Seven

"**H**ow do people fall in love?" Dallas asked her brother.

It was early morning in the loft, and since Carrie had arrived, Josh had tried each night to fit himself into Dallas's narrow bed, but he complained that Dallas wiggled too much. This morning he had risen early and gone down to chop wood for the new stove so Carrie could cook breakfast. Dallas had heard her father mumble that the idea of Carrie cooking was a joke, but she hadn't heard her father laughing.

"I don't know," Tem said, but he'd given the idea some thought. "I think the man gives the woman flowers and they hold hands, then they get married. I don't know what else."

"Could we ask someone? Aunt Alice maybe."

"I don't think Uncle Hiram knows about love," Tem said, and Dallas nodded in agreement. One couldn't very well put love and Uncle Hiram in the same thought.

Silently, Tem got out of bed, put his dirty work clothes back on, then helped Dallas into her plain, worn brown dress before they went down the ladder together.

Both of the children stood out of the way as Carrie and their father went about preparing breakfast. Tem knew that Dallas was much too young to understand what was going on, besides, she was too busy spending her time running her fingers over the roses on the wall to pay attention to much else, but Tem was all too aware of everything that went on between his father and Carrie.

Carrie and his father sniped and spat at each other like a dog and cat. Josh said that Carrie couldn't cook, that for all that she could buy a stove with her father's money, she didn't know what to do with it. Then Carrie said that if Josh had any decency, he'd teach her how to cook.

Tem nearly groaned at that, for as far as he could tell, his father was the *worst* cook on the face of the earth. Before Carrie came, if it hadn't been for the women in town and Aunt Alice taking pity on the children, who kept growing thinner by the day, they might have starved. Their father once set eggs on to boil, then went out to feed the horses. When he came back, he discovered that he'd cracked the eggs when dropping them into the pot and the insides of the egg had come out. They'd had white goo for breakfast.

Now Carrie was asking Josh to give her cooking lessons. Tem expected his father to tell the truth, that he knew as much about cooking as Carrie did, but Josh didn't tell the truth. Instead, he told Carrie that he didn't ask her how to farm and she shouldn't ask him how to do her job. Josh said that according to the letter she sent she knew all there was to know about cooking. In fact, Josh was thinking about bringing home a live goat and Carrie was to slaughter it and do all the rest to it. Tem knew that his father had no idea what else was done to a goat to make it ready to be put on the table, but it didn't sound that way. It sounded as though his father knew all there was to know about goats and everything else on the farm. Carrie got very angry and told Josh he was an idiot and she would be glad to see the last of him. Josh said that he was also thinking about buying rabbits so his wife could cook them, too.

In the end they had oatmeal and bacon and eggs for breakfast. The oatmeal was only half-cooked, some of it still dry flakes. The bacon was half-burned, half-raw, and the eggs were cooked so solid in the center that Tem knew he could have used the yolks for ice hockey pucks.

Both the children sat at the table, dabbing at their food, while Josh told Carrie in detail everything that was wrong with the meal. He said that the children couldn't even eat it. At that Tem kicked Dallas, and the two of them started eating as though they were dying of hunger and the food was delicious. When Dallas started to complain that her oatmeal tasted bad, Tem put three tablespoons of sugar on top of it and that stopped her complaints.

After breakfast—the longest meal of Tem's life—Josh put on his hat and said that the children had to get ready to go with him to the fields. Dallas made a long face and said that she wanted to stay with Carrie, that Carrie was going to leave and she wanted to see her. Tem could see that this hurt his father, so Tem said loudly that he wanted to stay with his father, that he was looking forward to hoeing turnips and pulling bugs off the corn.

With an angry look, Josh said that Tem was to stay with Carrie too. Tem protested, but Josh said that he didn't want or need his son with him, then he slammed out of the house.

"What a jolly, cheerful fellow," Carrie said. "What a joy he is to have around."

Dallas said, "When Mother—"

Tem kicked her so she'd shut her mouth. Their father had talked a great deal about not telling anyone anything about the past, but it was sometimes hard for a baby like Dallas to remember. Tem knew that his father hadn't always been as he was now, that there had been a time when their father had been very happy. Tem remembered when he used to run to his father's outstretched arms, and he remembered his father laughing and taking his children to fairs and the circus and to see plays. He remembered the way his father used to talk to their mother. In fact, Tem remembered the way his father had seemed to talk to *all* women. Their mother used to say that Josh was a real ladies' man, that he charmed them all—but Tem didn't think Carrie found their father "charming."

Josh didn't talk to Carrie in the way he usually talked to women. He talked to her as though he hated her. But, for some reason, Tem wasn't sure that his father did actually hate Carrie. First of all, how could he? Tem was sure that, next to his mother, Carrie was the prettiest woman on earth. And second, she was funny and she was exciting and she made people smile. How could anyone hate Carrie?

And, also, there was the way his father acted when he got too close to Carrie. Three times this morning Tem was sure he'd seen his father's face turn red when she leaned over him or walked close to him. And every time Josh's face turned red, he said something mean to Carrie. He even said bad things about her little dog.

And there was the way his father watched Carrie. Whenever she had her back to him, Josh was watching her. He couldn't seem to take his eyes off her. And this morning Josh had gone into the bedroom to get a clean shirt from out of the bureau Carrie had bought, and Tem had seen his father look inside one of the drawers and just stand there staring. Then Josh had put his hand in the drawer to touch whatever was in there. He had the very strangest look on his face, like that time he'd hurt his foot and he'd said that it didn't hurt but it actually did. After his father had left the room, Tem had sneaked in and looked in the drawer. Carrie's nightgown was in there, the one she'd worn the night before when Josh had combed her hair and she'd kissed his hand.

All and all, it was very confusing to Tem. His father seemed to hate Carrie, but then he didn't seem to hate her. He seemed to like to look at her and to listen to her stories at night, and he seemed to like to stand real close to her, so Tem couldn't understand why his father said such mean things to Carrie.

As for Carrie, Tem didn't understand her either. She said things to Josh that were just as bad as he said to her, but then he saw her pick up his father's shirt and sort of hug it to her. Tem thought maybe he saw tears in Carrie's eyes while she was holding it, but he wasn't sure about that.

"What shall we do today?" Carrie asked. "Would you like to go fishing?"

Tem looked about the kitchen. There was a three-foot-tall stack of dirty dishes on the cabinet and the floor had mud on it and there were dirty clothes and the animals needed to be fed. He wasn't sure, but he thought that Carrie was supposed to clean things during the day. Aunt Alice was somebody's wife, and she always seemed to be cleaning things and she talked a great deal about a woman having pride in her house.

Tem cleared his throat. "I can show you how to wash dishes," he said.

Carrie smiled. "I'm sure that I could figure it out if I needed to, but I really have no desire to learn how to do dishes. Don't look so worried, Tem. They'll get cleaned. I have a woman coming from town to do them."

Tem tried again. "But aren't *you* supposed to wash the dishes?"

"I'm sure your father thinks so. But then I'm also sure that I could spend the entire week scrubbing, and he'd still find something wrong with me. If a person's determined to dislike you, he will. Besides, if I have only a few days with the two of you, I'd rather go fishing." Carrie watched as Tem contemplated this. "Tem, it's up to you. If you want to stay here and scrub, that's what we'll do. But if you'd rather fish, then we'll do that."

"Tem," Dallas said in a whine, begging her brother to let them have a day of fun.

Tem knew that he should choose scrubbing, since it's what his father seemed to want in a wife, what he seemed to think was the most important thing a wife could do, but then he asked himself if Carrie was right. Would Josh be happy if he came back to a clean house? Last night he had come back to a house that was filled with light and walls with roses on them, yet all Josh had done was grumble, so Tem thought that maybe a clean floor wouldn't make him smile. "Fishing," Tem said at last, and Dallas started jumping up and down in happiness, Choo-choo jumping with her.

Tem tried to forget the problems between his father and Carrie, but as the day wore on, he seemed to think of them more. Maybe Carrie couldn't cook, but she sure could do other things. She took the children into the barn—that's what Papa called the shed, and calling it that had made Uncle Hiram laugh—and showed them her trunks.

When she started opening them, it was like Aladdin's treasure trove, and it took her over an hour to find the fishing poles— handmade in England she told the children. They didn't have to ask to know that her brothers had given her the poles.

Carrie shut the trunks, and they started off toward the stream. Tem was impressed at how well Carrie could fish. She seemed to sense where the trout were hiding, and she wasn't the least bit afraid of baiting her hook with worms. As they fished, she told the children stories of fishing in the sea and about catching lobsters and other strange creatures.

"Mother fed us lobster," Dallas said, then yelled at Tem when he hit her arm.

"Are you not supposed to talk about your mother?" Carrie asked.

Dallas shook her head, while Tem glared at her in warning.

"Does the mention of your mother make your father sad?" Carrie asked.

"Not sad," Dallas began, but said no more after catching a look at Tem.

Tem covered for his big-mouth sister. "Very sad. Maybe that's why he says such mean things to you."

Carrie nodded at that. Maybe it was true that Josh didn't think anyone could replace his children's mother.

"Look at the time," Carrie said. "It's past time for lunch."

"Papa didn't take any food," Dallas said. "He'll be hungry."

"Then we shall see what Mrs. Emmerling has made for us to eat, and you can take something to your father."

When they got back to the house, they found it was as dirty as they'd left it. The woman Carrie had hired from town hadn't come yet, and Tem wondered if she would come. If their father came home to all the dirt, he'd be angry, and he'd be hungry and there'd be no supper either.

"Tem," Carrie said, smiling, "don't look so sad. It's not a tragedy. I can make luncheon for your father. I'll make him a fried egg sandwich."

Tem had to put his hand over his sister's mouth to keep her from groaning out loud. "He'll like that," Tem said, and when Carrie turned back around, both children were smiling angelically at her.

While Carrie fried the eggs, Tem put cans of things in a bag and a jar of pickles in the bag too, then the three of them and Choochoo set off to the fields where Josh spent all day every day. On the walk there, Dallas chattered nonstop, asking Carrie a million questions about the sea and China and her brothers, so Tem had time to think. Time to dream, actually.

He imagined Carrie handing his father his sandwich and then his father saying that the sandwich was so good that he'd love Carrie forever, then he'd ask her to stay with them for always. Carrie would say yes, and then they'd become a family. And Carrie would make his father laugh as he once did, and everyone would be happy. The only problem that Tem could see was what to do about the dirty dishes that Carrie didn't want to do, and then, too, there was her cooking that could stand a great deal of improvement. Tem had no idea what to do about those things. In fact, the thought of Carrie's cooking made the dream a little less rosy.

The dream lost all its rosiness when Carrie saw the three fields that Josh worked on all day. Tem had seen his Uncle Hiram's fields and knew that they looked like something out of a storybook, but Tem was proud of his father no matter what he did and had given no thought to the fact that his father's fields were full of bugs and weeds and that some of the corn was tall and some short.

After one look at the fields, Carrie started laughing. Tem was already used to the idea that Carrie seemed to find humor in everything, but Josh didn't seem to understand that. Tem saw his father get very angry when Carrie laughed, and he got angrier when Carrie said that Josh was as bad a farmer as she was a housewife. Considering the way Carrie had left the house and the sight of his father's cornfield, Tem thought she was telling the truth.

But his father didn't seem to see any truth or humor in what Carrie was saying. In fact, the more Carrie laughed, the angrier his father became. He only laughed when he bit into Carrie's sandwich and crunched down on a big wad of eggshell. He seemed to think that was *very* funny.

Carrie turned around and walked away, Choo-choo barking furiously at Josh, as though he knew that Josh had made his mistress angry, and now Carrie was as angry as his father had been.

The children stood still for a moment, not knowing whether to stay with their father or go with Carrie, but Josh told the children to go with Carrie. "You seem to like her better than me now, so go with her." He stomped back into the fields.

Dallas burst into tears, so Tem picked her up and carried her back to the house.

Thank heaven that when they got to the house Mrs. Emmerling was there cleaning and cooking. Carrie went to the bedroom and slammed the door, and the children were sure they could hear her crying.

Tem sat down on the rocking chair in front of the fireplace while Dallas took her new doll and Choo-choo and went outside to play. Mrs. Emmerling bustled about the kitchen, then swept and dusted while Tem sat on the chair and thought. After a while Mrs. Emmerling sat on the opposite rocker and began to sew up some of the holes in Josh's shirts.

"You look as though you have a very serious problem," Mrs. Emmerling said. "Anything I can help you with?"

Tem didn't know this woman, but he liked her. She was nice and fat, and her face and hands were red. He shook his head no.

"Are you sure? I have eight kids of my own so I'm used to listening to problems."

"What makes people love each other?" Tem blurted out.

Mrs. Emmerling sewed for a moment. "Why would you want to know that?"

Tem blinked rapidly. He didn't want to cry. He *wasn't* going to cry. "Carrie won't stay unless Papa loves her, and Papa won't love her because Carrie can't cook. Could you teach her how to cook?"

Mrs. Emmerling smiled. "Cooking doesn't have to do with love. Being a good cook helps make a marriage a more pleasant place, but I doubt if a man ever gave a thought to cooking before he asked a woman to marry him. And if he did, he's not the type of man a woman would want. She'd want a man who wanted *her,* not her apple pies."

This helped Tem none at all, and his face showed his continued confusion.

"If your father isn't in love with a lovely lass like Carrie, then there's something else wrong. Why don't you tell me what's been going on?"

Tem told her as best he could, but he didn't really understand it himself. He said that his father had wanted to marry someone who could do farm things, but Carrie had come instead and it had made him angry.

"Your father wanted someone to help him take care of you kids," Mrs. Emmerling said softly.

"Yes," Tem said brightly. "And Carrie *does* take care of us. She tells us stories and makes us laugh, and she can fish real good. But—" Tem looked down at his shoe toe.

"But what?"

"But she laughed at Papa's farm fields."

Mrs. Emmerling had to hide a smile. So did everyone else in town laugh at Josh's fields, but they didn't let him hear their laughter. No one in Eternity had ever seen anyone try harder at farming than Josh with so little success. He so much wanted to make a good home for his children.

Mrs. Emmerling looked about the house that a day ago had been a disgrace and now was downright pretty. No doubt Josh's pride had been severely hurt by Carrie. She had come into town and done in a day what Josh had been struggling for months to do—and he had failed at it miserably.

Personally, Mrs. Emmerling didn't see any hope for Josh and Carrie's staying together. It was her experience that men didn't like women who bested them in anything. She gave Tem a sad look. Everyone in Eternity felt sorry for these poor, motherless children, and every unmarried woman had at one time or another tried to get her hooks into the handsome Josh, but all of them had failed. It was as though he'd developed an aversion to women—or at least to women who wanted to marry him.

So now, Josh was married to the lively, laughing Miss Carrie, and she was laughing at his fields.

"You see, Tem," Mrs. Emmerling began, "when two people marry, they have to think that each other's the greatest person on earth. They may be very ordinary people in reality, but they have to *think* that the other one can . . . well, can move mountains, can make the sun rise and set, that sort of thing."

Tem looked at her as though she were daft, not understanding a word she was saying.

"Your father wants Carrie to think that he's wonderful, that he's the best and bravest and finest man on earth. He wants her—"

"But he *is!* My father *is* the best."

Mrs. Emmerling smiled. "Yes, he is, but Carrie doesn't see that. All she sees is that, well, your father isn't as good a farmer as, say, your Uncle Hiram."

"Nobody can farm as good as he can," Tem muttered. If Uncle Hiram was an example of what a man should be, then he was glad his father was so bad at farming.

"Exactly. I'm afraid Carrie sees that your father's not a very good farmer, and your father sees that she sees."

"You think Carrie will fall in love with Uncle Hiram?"

"I doubt that," Mrs. Emmerling said, chuckling.

Tem still didn't understand. "But Carrie didn't like Papa before she saw his fields. I think Carrie liked Papa at first, but Papa didn't like her. He said she couldn't feed us or wash clothes."

"But that's the same thing, isn't it? Your father doesn't think that Carrie is the greatest person on earth, just as she doesn't think that about him. If they don't start thinking that about each other, they'll never love each other."

Tem was silent for a moment. "What about the dirty dishes?"

Mrs. Emmerling laughed. "If your father falls in love with Carrie, I think that your father may start washing the dishes himself. And he'll honestly think that whatever she cooks is delicious."

"Even her eggs?" There was absolute disbelief in Tem's voice.

"Especially her eggs." Mrs. Emmerling watched the boy for a while longer, then got up to finish cleaning. For herself, she was glad Carrie didn't know how to clean, since she and her family needed the money Carrie paid her.

After a while Tem got up, left the house, and went outside. Dallas was sitting under the shade of a tree at the edge of the woods and jabbering away to her doll. When Choo-choo saw Tem, he left Dallas's side and ran to him. As Tem sat down on the edge of the porch, stroking the little dog, he thought about what Mrs. Emmerling had told him.

If Carrie left, he was sure that his father would let the roses she'd had planted die. And both he and Dallas would have to spend all day in the fields with their father. Josh didn't too often make Dallas do things in the fields, but she had to stay within his sight, and she got awfully bored sometimes.

If Carrie left, everything would go back to the way it was, and right now that looked like a hideous prospect to Tem.

"What can I do?" Tem whispered to Choo-choo. "How can I make Papa and Carrie think that each other is great?"

Tem tried. He knew that if he never did anything else in his life, at least he'd tried to show Carrie and his father how great the other one was. But by the time he went to bed, he was past unhappiness.

Throughout dinner he had pointed out every good quality he could think of about each of them. He told his father how pretty Carrie was. He talked about her trunks full of wonderful things and how, if Carrie stayed, she could bring them into the house for Josh to see. This had made his father say some unpleasant things about Carrie's brothers who he said spoiled her, which made Carrie say that her brothers were a great deal nicer than Josh was.

Tem told Carrie about his father's taking care of them. Tem very much wanted to tell Carrie about the past, but he couldn't because talking about the past was forbidden. His father had said, "That part of my life is done, and there's no use speaking of it ever again."

Dallas seemed to sense her brother's frustration, so she said,

"Papa gives speeches. He gives good speeches, and the ladies like him."

Josh gave his daughter a look that silenced her.

Carrie, however, showed great interest in what Dallas had said and asked several questions, but Josh wouldn't answer her or allow the children to answer her.

Tem sighed and tried again, trying to think of things for the two of them to do together. He suggested they go fishing together, but Josh snorted at that, saying he had to work for a living. Tem suggested that Carrie help his father debug the corn plants.

"Sorry, but she only does things that Daddy's money can buy."

At that, Dallas had started crying at the tone of voice her father was using. When Josh pulled his daughter into his arms, he said that Carrie had made Dallas cry.

"Your rudeness, not to mention your intractability, has made her cry."

Tem didn't know that word, but his father seemed to.

Josh got very angry and opened his mouth to say something to Carrie, but she jumped up from the table and went to the bedroom. "You can clear the table yourself, since it seems to mean so much to you," she said before slamming the bedroom door.

Tem and his sister kissed their father goodnight, but he didn't seem to notice them as he stood in front of the fireplace and stared into it.

When he came up the ladder to try to sleep in Dallas's bed, Tem was still awake. He had been thinking a great deal.

"Papa?"

"You should be asleep."

"Do you think that Carrie is wonderful?"

"I think that Carrie has never been anything but adored in her life. She's never had to work; she's never been denied anything in her life." Josh turned and knelt by his son's bed. "I know that you like her. I know that she's cheerful, and, Lord knows, you children deserve some laughter in your life after what you've been through in the last couple of years, but you're going to have to trust me on this. Carrie is not the mother for you children."

Tem sat up on his elbows. "Is she the wife for you? If you didn't have us, would you marry her?"

Josh smiled. "I might just be fool enough to do so. But you children have made me wise, much too wise to stay with a butterfly like Carrie. Now, go to sleep. A month after she's gone, you won't even remember her." He kissed his son's forehead and began to undress.

But Tem didn't go to sleep as he lay back on the bed and looked at the attic ceiling. It was his fault that his father and Carrie didn't love each other. His and Dallas's fault.

Chapter Eight

The next day, Carrie and Josh didn't find out that Tem was missing until Josh came home from the fields. Since Josh was still smarting under the hurt of Carrie's laughing at his fields and the desertion of his children, he didn't return to the house until nearly nine o'clock at night.

The scene that greeted him upon opening the door should have made him happy, but instead, it made him even more angry than he already was. Dallas was standing on a stool, and Carrie was pinning up the hem of a new dress for her—a dress that Josh could not afford to buy for his daughter. The little house was cheerful and redolent of good smells, and Carrie, his wife who was not his wife, looked lovely. More than anything in the world Josh wanted to shout that he was home and have his wife and child run to his open arms.

As it was, he walked in quietly and hung his hat on the peg by the door.

"Papa!" Dallas cried and started to leap down from the stool, but Carrie helped her.

His warm, clean daughter flew into his arms and snuggled into his neck. This was what made the fields bearable, he thought, this was what made his unhappiness worth something.

"We have roast beef for dinner and Mrs. Emmerling made cookies and I think my doll's hair is growing."

As Josh stroked his daughter's hair, he thought that it was good to see her clean again. In the months that he had been running the farm, he hadn't had time to see to the cleanliness of his children. He had too much to do in trying to feed and clothe them.

"Her hair's growing, is it?" Josh asked, smiling. He hadn't even been able to give his daughter a doll.

Standing behind them, Carrie was smiling, and Josh knew he'd never seen a prettier female in his life, with her trim little waist and her blonde hair—and her body that wasn't his.

"Good evening," Josh said stiffly. "I take it the woman you hired has prepared dinner."

Carrie turned away, the smile gone. "Yes, she did." She looked back at Josh. "Where's Tem?"

"He's with you," Josh said quickly as though she were too dumb to know that she'd had Tem all day.

Carrie stood there blinking for a moment, then began to turn a bit pale. She went into the bedroom and returned with a note from Tem saying that he was going to spend the day with his father.

Without a word, Josh reached inside his shirt pocket and withdrew another note from Tem. This one said that Tem was going to spend the day with Carrie.

"Maybe he wanted to go fishing," Carrie said, but she didn't believe that. Without a doubt, she knew that wherever Tem was and whatever he was doing had something to do with her and Josh.

Josh was across the room in seconds as he grabbed Carrie's shoulders. "Where is he? Where is my son?" he shouted into her face.

"I don't know," Carrie answered. "I thought he was with you all day."

Josh gave her a shake. "Where is he?" he yelled, as though the very loudness of his voice would make her remember something she didn't know.

"Don't hurt Carrie," Dallas cried, clutching her father's legs. "Tem will be back. He said he would."

Both Carrie and Josh turned to look at her, then Josh dropped to one knee. "Where is your brother?" he asked softly.

Dallas backed into the safety of Carrie's skirt. "He made me swear not to tell. He said something bad would happen to me if I told."

"Something bad will—" Josh began, but Carrie picked Dallas up and set her on the table.

"What time was Tem supposed to be back?"

Dallas looked as though she was going to cry. "He said he'd be home before Papa."

Carrie looked over the head of the child to Josh, then back at Dallas. "He's very late, isn't he?"

Josh stepped between the two of them. "Dallas, you have to tell me where Tem went. You have to—" He broke off when Dallas began to cry.

Pushing Josh aside, Carrie bent down to Dallas. "But you can't tell, can you? And not just because Tem said you couldn't tell. You can't tell because it's a point of honor, isn't it? You know what honor is, don't you, Dallas?"

"No," the child sniffed.

"Honor is when someone tells you a secret and you'll die before you tell that secret."

"For God's sake!" Josh said. "That was thunder. I think there may be a storm coming."

Carrie put her face close to Dallas's. "But sometimes honor and helping someone fight each other. Like right now. If you tell, you won't be honorable, but if you don't tell, Tem might be in trouble."

Dallas nodded and glanced nervously at her father.

"So," Carrie said, "let's see if we can't find out about Tem and keep your honor too. Suppose you tell me a story, like I tell you a story every night?"

"For the love of—" Josh said, but was cut off by a flash of lightning followed by a loud clap of thunder.

Dallas squealed, and Choo-choo hid under the table.

"Once upon a time there was a young prince who was very unhappy," Carrie began. "Let's say that the king and queen were having problems, and the prince wanted to do something about those problems. What do you think the prince would do?"

"Look for a rattlesnake," Dallas said firmly.

Carrie straightened. "What would he do with the rattlesnake?" she asked in barely more than a whisper.

"He'd put it in your—I mean the queen's—bed, then when she was afraid, the king could save her and she'd know he was great. Then they'd love each other forever."

Slowly, Carrie turned to look at Josh, wondering if she was as pale as he was. Already, she could feel herself beginning to shake.

Josh knelt before his daughter. "Where would the prince get the rattlesnake?"

"On Starbuck's Mountain," the child said. "Tem—I mean the prince—saw some up there. He saw a whole bunch of rattlesnakes on the mountain."

Another streak of lightning and clap of thunder made Dallas leap into her father's arms.

"Get her some warm clothes," Josh said as he carried Dallas to the bedroom. "I want her wrapped up against the storm."

Carrie caught his arm. "What are you going to do?"

It was obvious that he hadn't much interest in Carrie at the moment. "I'm going to take Dallas to my brother's house and I'm going to get my horse, then I'm going to find my son." He started walking again.

Carrie put herself in front of him. "I want to go with you."

Another flash of lightning that lit the house allowed Carrie to see the look of contempt on Josh's face.

Carrie put her hands on both his arms, her fingers digging into his muscles. "It's my fault that he's alone on the mountain. If I hadn't come here—"

"It's too late to think of that now." Pushing past her into the bedroom, he stood Dallas on the bed.

Carrie moved to his side. "I may be helpless in the kitchen, but I'm not helpless in the rest of my life. You may think you know all there is to know about me, but you really don't know anything. I come from a family of sailors and I know about survival, and I can ride anything on four legs." She handed him a woolen shirt, and he wrapped Dallas in it.

Picking Dallas up again, he started for the front door, but Carrie placed herself in front of the door. "Whether you 'allow' me to go or not, I'm going to search for Tem. Whether I go with you or by myself, I'm going."

Josh looked at her for a second. He didn't have time to argue with her, nor did he have time to spend with a frightened woman. Now his only concern was his son. "Go or stay, I don't care. But if you can't keep up with me, don't expect me to bring you back."

"You won't have to bring me back. Can you get me a proper horse? Something other than those nags of yours?"

He nodded once, then he was out the door. When he was gone, Carrie grabbed bread and bacon and put them into an oiled sack, then she began gathering equipment for a rescue mission. Having lived all her life by the sea, she knew a great deal about rescue. She went to the shed, rummaged in her trunks until she found her large knife, then took a long, heavy rope from the wall. When she went back to the house, she had to fight the rising wind. She put matches in the bag, then tore up a petticoat for bandages and stuffed heavy waxed canvas in a bag.

When her equipment was ready, she took off her skirt, petticoats, and hoops and put on a pair of Josh's heavy canvas pants, tying them at the waist with a wide leather belt.

She had just finished when Josh returned. He looked her up and down, but didn't say anything as he took the bags, looked inside them, seemed to be satisfied with what she'd put in them, then took the rope from her.

"My brother has sent to town for help. In a few hours the mountain will be full of searchers. You should stay—"

She handed him a thick slice of buttered bread. "Shut up and eat it on the way. Come on, we're wasting time."

Taking the bread, he gave her a curt nod, and after that he stopped treating her like a woman who should have been left behind. Standing outside were two of the finest horses Carrie had ever seen; one was an enormous black stallion with a white blaze on his nose and the other, a dark brown mare that looked proud and fast.

"Get on her," Josh shouted, for the wind was now quite loud. "And stay with me. If you can't keep up, come back here and wait for me. Understand?"

Nodding, Carrie easily vaulted into the saddle, then reined the animal away behind Josh's big stallion.

He can ride, Carrie thought. He can ride as well as anyone I've ever seen, she thought, as she watched him take off at breakneck speed down the rutted path that led from the house, Carrie right behind him. When he reached the foot of the mountain, he didn't so much as hesitate, but began moving straight up. After taking a deep breath for courage, Carrie followed him. He must have eyes like a cat's, she thought, for she couldn't see anything. Thank heaven there was a white spot on the stallion's back hoof, for at times that was all she could see.

Twice the mare she was riding wanted to give up and go back down the mountain, but Carrie wouldn't let her stop. Up and up they went, over hard rock surfaces that made the horses' feet slide, then through scrub oak groves that scratched at Carrie's face and tore at her clothes.

Carrie realized that Josh was going up no path, but was taking the fastest, most direct route to the top of the mountain. He didn't seem to be aware of her, his only thought being that he was going after his son and there was nothing or no one else on his mind. Once Carrie and the mare came to a hard, rocky surface, and the animal's foot slipped. The mare screamed, and Carrie had to use every muscle in her body to keep the big animal from turning and going back down the mountain. Applying her crop to the animal's rump, she pulled hard on the reins, knowing that if she lost control of the animal now, she'd never regain it. To help relieve the fear that was inside her, she began to curse as only a sailor knows how to curse. The words she knew were in at least six languages, all from places her brothers had been. Her brothers thought she wouldn't know they were cursing if they used a foreign language, but Carrie had heard and remembered the words, and right now she used them all on the mare.

When she thought her wrist was going to break, the mare stopped fighting and started back up the mountain. As Carrie began to move, there was a flash of lightning, and she looked up to see Josh on his horse, standing on a ridge and watching her. For all his avowals that he wouldn't wait for her, he was doing just that. She wasn't sure, but she thought he gave her a nod of approval before moving on.

The rain started as they reached the top of the mountain, coming down in a fury, as cold as only rain at a high altitude can be. Carrie was wet through within minutes. At the top of the mountain, Josh was waiting for her—or actually, he was looking about him, as though trying to decide which way to go.

"Where are the rattlesnakes?" Carrie shouted. "Did you see them with Tem?" It was a question she should have asked before.

He glanced at her long enough to nod once, then he flicked the reins and took off to the west. Carrie followed him closely, the mare giving her no trouble now. Within minutes, Josh halted and dismounted, looking at what appeared to be an enormous hill of rock in front of them. Down the center of the rock was a crack that widened at the bottom. Josh was walking toward the rock, and she knew that this must be where he and Tem had seen the snakes.

With the rain lashing in their faces, Josh came to Carrie, and when her horse skittered, he put his hand on her leg. "If anything happens to me, find Tem," he shouted.

Carrie nodded to him as the rain dripped down her face, then, silently, she watched as he moved toward the crack in the rock. Just as he touched the rock, he lit a match, shielding the flame from the rain and wind with his hat, then leaned into the crack.

Even over the rain, Carrie could hear the hiss of the snakes. She could see in the flame of the match the writhing bodies of the snakes inside the rock, and she held her breath as Josh took a step forward, closer to the snakes, only releasing it when he stepped back to safety.

"He's not in there," Josh shouted up at her. "I'm going to search the area. Stay here."

Carrie wasn't about to remain where she was. She wasn't going to be a useless woman sitting on top of a horse and waiting. Josh's beautiful stallion was standing untied where he was in spite of the lightning and the nearby snakes, but Carrie knew that her mare wouldn't stay put. Riding back the way they had come for a bit until the sound of the snakes was too distant to hear, she tied the horse firmly to a big pine tree.

Fighting the wind, her eyes shielded by her hand from the rain, she went back to Josh.

He grabbed her shoulders. "I told you—"

"NO!" seemed to be the most appropriate answer to what he was saying, and she shouted it into his face.

He didn't spend precious time arguing with her. "There," he shouted back. "Search those trees."

Carrie moved away from him and into the trees, starting to walk in an ever-widening circle as she searched and with every step knowing how futile their search was. Tem could be lying on the ground not ten feet from them, and with this rain and wind they'd never see or hear him. And how could two people search the entire mountain? Even when the people of Eternity showed up, they wouldn't be able to search every rock and tree. And it would be hours before the townspeople arrived, for she didn't think they would come up the way she and Josh had. No one in their right minds would come up that way.

She screamed when Josh put his hand on her shoulder. When she turned, she saw in a flash of lightning that he was thinking exactly what she had been thinking, that it was no use, that the only way they'd find Tem was by accident.

"I'm going above," he yelled, pointing to above the boulder that contained the snakes.

Carrie nodded at him, then returned to her search, but a moment later came a piercing whistle that she knew was from Josh. She went running toward it, scrambling up rocks, scraping her hands, her feet slipping.

Josh was standing on the side of a ledge, and when she reached him, he held out his hand. In it was a piece of blue cloth, and she knew it was from Tem's shirt.

Turning away, he started climbing again, Carrie right behind him.

At the top of the rock was a ridge, a ridge that was on the side of nothing. For many, many feet down they could see nothing but darkness.

"The river," Josh shouted, pointing down into the black nothingness.

For the first time Carrie felt cold. The piece of cloth proved that Tem had come this way, but if he'd fallen, he would have fallen down into that ravine.

Josh was moving ahead, leaving Carrie standing and looking down into the blackness. When a flash of lightning came, she turned, then screamed at what she saw.

Josh was beside her in seconds. "What is it?" he shouted.

Carrie pointed into the darkness.

Lightning came again, and then Josh saw her too. For a moment Carrie had thought the child she'd seen was a figment of her imagination, for she was just a bit of a thing, no more than six or seven years old, but she looked more like some unusual breed of animal than a child. In spite of the hard, driving rain, her hair was standing out from her head in a wild, tangled mass, and she wore torn, primitive leather clothing, her feet bare.

Stepping in front of Carrie, Josh began to walk toward the child, but when the lightning came again, she was gone. "Where is he?" Josh shouted into the darkness, the rain lashing him in the face. "Where is he?"

Moving toward Josh, Carrie put her hands on his shoulders and her head against his back.

When more lightning came, the child was there again. This time Josh practically ran after her, but she was too elusive to catch.

"She knows where Tem is," Josh shouted. "I know she does."

At the next lightning streak, the child showed herself again, this time standing on the very edge of the ridge, so close that Carrie held her breath in fear. As the light highlighted the girl, she pointed—and she was pointing straight down the side of the ridge.

"Is it Tem?" Josh shouted, and the girl nodded once before the dark again hid her.

"I'm going down," Josh said as he turned to Carrie. "Stay here and wait for me. I'll get the rope. Don't leave this place."

Seconds later Josh was half-running, half-sliding down the rocky slope to the horses and equipment below.

Carrie stayed in exactly the same spot, afraid to move even a step for fear of losing the place where the girl had pointed. Every time there was a flash of lightning, she looked for the girl, but she didn't see her. Yet, she knew as well as she'd ever known anything that the child was nearby and watching them.

Josh came back up the rock with the rope coiled about his arm, but when he went to a tree to tie it, Carrie yelled at him, "No!"

"I'm going!" Josh shouted back at her.

It took Carrie a moment to make him understand that she wasn't protesting his going, that her objection was to the knot he was using to tie the rope around the tree. Taking the thick rope from him, she expertly and quickly tied it to the tree in one knot, then looped the rope and tied another. It was so difficult talking that she didn't try but made motions to tell Josh that she would help pull on the rope when he came back up, when he returned carrying Tem, that is.

When Josh realized what she was doing, he looked at her in a way that he'd never looked at her before: with admiration and thanks.

Holding on to the rope, Josh walked to the edge of the ridge and began to lower himself. He did it as though he'd done it many times before and knew exactly what he was doing.

Carrie stood at the top, her eyes straining to see him, listening should he whistle.

Within minutes Josh came back up the rope, climbing hand over hand with the agility of the very best deckhands, and Carrie wondered if he'd ever spent time on a ship.

There was joy on his face, such joy as Carrie had never seen before, and she knew then that Tem was all right. Tears mixed with the rain on her face.

"He's there and he's alive, but he's unconscious. I have to get him up," Josh said, shouting into her face. "I need to make a sling of sorts."

Carrie knew instantly that he was asking her advice, that he was asking for her help. Frantically, she began searching her mind for what they had brought. Please, they couldn't have to go back down the mountain to get something to make a sling to carry an unconscious child in. The canvas bags they had brought weren't strong enough to hold a sturdy little boy, and they didn't have enough rope.

Suddenly, Josh reached out and put his hand on Carrie's waist, his fingers moving around her stomach as though feeling for something.

It took her moments to understand, and when she did, she smiled. Yes, her corset. Immediately, with Josh's nimble-fingered help, she unbuttoned her shirt and pulled it out of the trousers she wore, and Josh deftly helped her with the corset strings. When Josh had it in his hands, he opened the corset, frowning at its small size, not sure if it was going to be big enough to go around him and the child.

Unbuckling her trousers, Carrie gave Josh the belt, then slipped out of the trousers and held them up to him, demonstrating that he could tie the legs around Tem's inert body.

Josh nodded at her, then, with most of her clothing tied about him, he took the rope and walked to the edge of the ridge, Carrie right beside him. "When I have him, I'll whistle and you pull. Understand?"

"Yes," Carrie shouted back.

When he was on the brink of the ridge, he paused. Carrie knew what was in his mind, knew what he felt, because she felt the same way.

As though they had been friends and lovers forever, she leaned forward and kissed him. "Good luck," she whispered against his lips.

"Break a leg," he said, then he was over the ridge.

Carrie couldn't see a thing, and she was sure that the time that Josh spent down below was the longest of her life. Hanging over the side, she strained to see or hear anything. She lay down on the sodden ground, oblivious to the fact that now she wore only her boots, knee-length drawers, and chemise. The thin cotton was no protection against the cold and the wet, but she didn't feel the storm, for she was too intent on what was going on below to worry about herself.

At long, long last, a whistle came and she gave a little prayer of thanks as she ran to the tree and grabbed the rope. She was young and she was strong and she was determined. At another time, she might not have had the strength to pull on the rope as she did now, but knowing that Tem and Josh were at the end of it gave her a great deal of strength.

At one point she thought there was someone helping her pull, but when she looked back, she saw no one. Then, lightning flashed, and she nearly screamed at the sight of an old man, a man who wore patched leather clothes and was dirty even in the rain, standing behind her and pulling on the rope. Swallowing the scream that came to her throat, she nodded thanks to him, then kept on pulling.

At long last she saw Josh's head appear. She held her breath. Then, as he came over the ridge, she saw Tem harnessed to the front of him by the means of a corset, a pair of men's trousers, and Josh's shirt sleeves.

Dropping the rope, she ran to them, grabbing at Tem frantically. From what she could see of him, he didn't look to be alive.

Turning into the darkness, where she could see no one, but knew that the old man and the little girl were there, she shouted, "Where can we go? Help us, please."

They had to wait for the next flash of lightning, then they saw the little girl again and she was pointing east. Neither Josh nor Carrie hesitated, but began scrambling down the rock face toward the horses, Josh holding his son to him as though he were fragile and precious—as he was.

When they reached the horses, Josh handed Tem to Carrie. She struggled under the weight of the child who was almost as tall as she was while Josh mounted and reached down for his son, easily taking him onto the saddle in front of him. Carrie ran to her mare, pulled on the reins and freed the knot, then mounted.

The little girl appeared to them twice more before they found the cave. When Josh had dismounted with Tem in his arms, Carrie pulled both of the horses into the mouth of the cave.

The cave had a sandy bottom, and there was dry firewood stacked along one wall. In the back she could see a stack of what looked like blankets. There was also an ancient coffeepot and half a dozen mugs. For all that it was a cave, it looked as though it were used as a guest house.

"Get him out of his wet clothes and wrap him up while I build a fire," Josh said.

Carrie lost no time in obeying. She had Tem out of his sodden clothes in seconds, but before she wrapped him in a dry blanket, she inspected him to see how badly he was injured. No bones were broken. There were bruises all over him, and there was a cut on the side of his head, but for the most part he just seemed to be cold.

Wrapping him in two blankets, covering his head, she pulled him to her and rubbed his back and sides.

Josh came to her and carried Tem to the fire, where he had put the coffeepot filled with rainwater and a handful of Carrie's tea. "Get out of those wet clothes," he ordered.

It was then that Carrie realized that she was nearly as cold as Tem. Moving to the back of the cave, she took off her clothes and wrapped herself in a blanket, then went back to Josh and Tem.

Josh was holding his son to him as though he meant to put life back into him, and as Carrie watched, Tem's eyes fluttered.

"Tem," Josh said. "I want you to talk to me."

Lazily, Tem opened his eyes and smiled at his father. "I fell. I saw the wild girl and I fell."

Josh looked up at Carrie. The poor child must have felt guilty at scaring Tem. "It's all right," Josh said, stroking his son's damp hair. "You're safe now and your wild girl told us where to find you."

"I didn't get a rattlesnake."

"I'm glad that you didn't."

Turning his head, Tem looked at Carrie, then back at his father. "You brought her."

"She wouldn't let me leave her behind." He smiled at his son. "Wait until you see the knots she can tie. Beautiful."

Tem closed his eyes. "Do you think Carrie is the best person in the world? The greatest?"

"Right this moment I do."

Tem smiled, and within moments he was asleep.

Moving close to them, Carrie stroked Tem's forehead. "He's still cool to the touch." She looked up at Josh. There was blood running down the side of his head, and Carrie reached out to touch the place, but pulled her hand back.

"You'd better get into something dry," she said. "There are more blankets over there." When Josh hesitated, Carrie said, "I'll take care of him. You don't have to worry about him."

For a moment she wasn't sure that Josh was going to turn the precious burden of his son over to her, but then she sat down by the fire, and he placed Tem in her arms. Carrie thought that it was perhaps the most precious gift anyone had ever given her and surely the most trust that had ever been shown her.

While she held Tem, Josh stood behind her undressing and wrapping himself in a blanket. When he was done, he went to the horses and unsaddled them, but the blanket kept slipping so Josh, with a curse of frustration, wrapped the blanket about his waist.

Carrie smiled at the sight of his strong, muscular bare back. No matter how bad his farming was, it had put muscle on him. He dropped the saddles by the fire, then brought the bags of food and pulled out a big chunk of bacon.

"I should have brought a skillet," Carrie said guiltily. "I wasn't thinking too well when I packed."

Taking a knife from his saddle bag, Josh sliced the bacon. "I can cook it on a stick," he said, then looked up at her in a teasing way. "Or you can cook it with your cursing."

Feeling herself blushing, Carrie looked down at Tem. "I didn't know you heard me."

"They probably heard you in Eternity."

She laughed. "That mare wanted to go down the mountain when I wanted to go up."

"She's a bit lazy and frightens easily." He was holding a piece of bacon on a stick and watching it fry in the fire. "Truthfully, I didn't think you'd get her up here."

"Is that why you gave her to me? You wanted her to carry me back down the mountain?"

"The thought did cross my mind."

Carrie didn't say anything; she didn't have to. He had not wanted her with him, had thought she'd be a hindrance, so he'd given her a horse that he didn't think she could control. But she had controlled the horse, and she'd been a help to him when he'd found Tem.

"I couldn't have brought him up without you," Josh said softly. "If you hadn't been here, I don't know what I would have done."

"You'd have managed," she said, but she was pleased by his praise. She watched him for a few moments as he fried bacon. "You were certainly skilled at getting me out of my corset," she said in a voice of mock indignation. "Have you had much practice with corset strings?"

Josh didn't look at her, but concentrated on the bacon. "I'm better with corsets than with corn."

Carrie smiled because he had come very close to making a joke about himself. "Where did you learn so much . . . about corsets, I mean."

"Not the same place I learned about corn."

Carrie frowned, because he had told her nothing.

After putting three slices of bacon on a chunk of bread, Josh filled a mug with boiling hot tea. "Wake him up. I want to get this down him."

Carrie pulled Tem to a sitting position, although it wasn't easy since her arms had gone to sleep while holding him. Tem was tired and sleepy and he had no desire to wake up, but neither Carrie nor Josh would allow him to continue sleeping.

When he had drunk three cups of hot tea and had eaten a large bacon sandwich, he snuggled down by Carrie and went back to sleep. Sitting by him, she stroked his forehead, smiling down at him.

"Nothing makes you realize how insignificant everything else is until you come close to losing a child," Carrie said, and when she looked up at Josh, she saw that he was staring at her from across the fire. He was cooking more bacon for the two of them. With the rain closing off the outside of the cave and everything being darkness at the edges of the fire, it felt very intimate to be together. The firelight glistened off Josh's bare chest. "Who do you think the little girl is? And did you see the old man? He helped me pull the rope up."

"I didn't see him," Josh said, "but it's my guess that he's Starbuck. No one that I've ever talked to has actually seen him. He's a hermit."

"And the child?"

"I don't know. I've never heard of her, but then I haven't been in Eternity long."

She watched him put bacon on bread. "Maybe your brother knows."

"Maybe," Josh said in a way that let her know that was the end of that conversation. He handed her a sandwich and a cup of very strong tea.

"Where were you before you came to Eternity?" She watched his face and was sure that she saw a flicker of pain go across it. What had he done that caused such a look? What had he done that made him keep his past a secret? Carrie was well aware that his children had been instructed to never tell anything about where they had come from or where they had been. Poor Dallas was so confused about what she could and could not tell that sometimes she thought she wasn't supposed to mention Carrie's brothers to Carrie.

"I've been many places," Josh said, and Carrie knew he wasn't going to say any more.

The intimacy was broken, for he was reminding her that she was an outsider. If she sometimes looked at the children and couldn't imagine a life without them, she knew that Josh didn't feel that way about her. To him she was someone who was going to leave in a few days, and he wasn't about to share any secrets with her.

In silence, Carrie ate her sandwich and stared at the fire, no longer attempting to make conversation. She chastised herself, for what had she expected, that she'd help him when he needed it and he'd say that he had misjudged her? Was he going to tell her that she wasn't an empty-headed piece of fluff after all? If she hadn't come to Eternity, if she hadn't played a trick on Josh in the first place, Tem wouldn't have decided to go after rattlesnakes, and Josh wouldn't have needed to climb down a ravine and—

"No stories about your brothers tonight?" Josh asked.

She knew he was trying to lighten the silence between them, but it didn't help. "Why don't you tell me about *your* brother?" She said it with more venom than she'd meant.

Josh looked at the fire for a moment. "He's the best farmer in the world. Perfect corn; perfect beets. Everything in straight, even rows. I don't think a bug would dare attack his plants."

"Why does he have your horse?" Carrie didn't have to be told that the black stallion was Josh's horse. A man and a horse don't work as well as Josh and the stallion did unless they had spent a great deal of time together and had learned to trust each other.

"I sold it to him," Josh said softly. "Or rather, gave it to him as partial payment for the farm."

Carrie tried to hide her frown at that. It didn't sit well with her that one brother would take another brother's horse, no matter what the reason. Carrie wanted to ask more questions, but she didn't because she knew she'd be rebuffed once again.

After more long minutes of silence, Josh got up and came to her side of the fire. "It will be daylight soon, so we'd better get some sleep."

Carrie yawned. "I could sleep for a week." When she saw Josh looking at her oddly as she stretched, she realized that her blanket was slipping. She started to draw it more fully over her breasts, but then she stopped, for she didn't really care. He was the one who had decided to reject her and was continuing to reject her, not the other way around.

Stretching out on the sandy floor beside Tem, she put her arms around him and closed her eyes, opening them when Josh lay down on the other side of his son. Carrie looked into the dark eyes of her husband and forgot her anger. Reaching out her hand, she started to touch the bloody place on the side of his head.

"Don't," Josh whispered, sounding as though he were in pain.

Carrie left her hand where it was, hovering over his temple.

Josh looked at her a moment longer, so close yet so far away, then he turned on his other side, facing away from her, and unbidden, sharp tears came to Carrie's eyes at his rejection of her. "Good night," she said with as little emotion in her voice as she could manage. Josh didn't reply.

Chapter Nine

Carrie awoke with a smile. She was warm and dry, and she knew that Tem was safe beside her, and, too, there was a warm hand on her cheek. With her eyes still closed, she turned toward the hand.

"Carrie," Josh whispered, and she slowly opened her eyes. He was dressed and kneeling beside her, touching her. It was cold in the cave, and although the rain had stopped, it was still dark outside. When she smiled at him, he moved back from her abruptly.

"I don't bite," she said dreamily, then raised her bare arm out of the blanket. "Is everything all right?"

"I have to find the searchers and tell them Tem is safe."

Carrie's eyes opened wide at that. "I forgot all about them. Do you think they've been looking all night?"

"If I know my brother, he didn't go into town until it stopped raining. He wouldn't get himself wet merely because a child was lost."

Carrie gaped at him in disbelief, but Josh's face showed that he wasn't going to answer the questions that ran through her mind. She'd already found out that he didn't answer questions about his brother.

"I want you to stay here with Tem, and I'll come back for you after I've found the searchers." He hesitated. "Will you do that?"

She laughed. "I obey when the orders are worth obeying."

He gave her a little smile. "When your brothers are captaining their ships and the sailors disobey because they don't think the orders are worth obeying, what do your brothers do?"

She gave him a look of mock innocence. "You don't expect me

to know what goes on on a man's ship, do you? I think I might be shocked to the very depths of my soul if I were to be told something like that."

When Josh grinned at her, a lovely, warm grin that showed his fine white teeth, Carrie thought she might swoon at the sight of him. She was sure that there was no better-looking man on earth than Mr. Joshua Greene. She lifted herself onto her elbows. "Josh," she began, "do you think—"

He put his fingertips to her lips to silence her, then drew back as though he'd been burned. "Wait here and keep Tem warm."

She nodded at him, and he was gone.

When Carrie got up to dress, she saw that before he'd left, while she and Tem were still asleep, Josh had raked the fire and put more wood on it. He had filled the coffeepot with water and tea and set it to boil. As Carrie poured herself a mug of tea, she smiled. He may not be a great farmer, but he knew how to take care of people and he knew how to climb up and down ropes in the middle of a storm and he knew how to ride—and he knew how to love.

"I could stand a little of that love," she said out loud, as she stood up and went to the mouth of the cave to look out at the dawning of the day.

By the time Josh, Carrie, and both children, as well as Choo-choo, were once again assembled in their pretty little house, it was almost noon. Mrs. Emmerling had come and gone, the house was clean, and there were ham sandwiches made, as well as a pot of bean soup simmering on the stove and two fat apple pies in the oven.

"I'm hungry," Tem said.

All the way down the mountain, Josh had held his son tightly in front of him, as though he couldn't believe the boy was well and safe, but now Josh turned a stern face to his son. "You and I are going to have a little talk," Josh said, and Tem looked at his father in disbelief.

Carrie took Dallas outside while Tem and his father "discussed" what Tem had done.

While Carrie and Dallas sat under a tree with Choo-choo, the child's doll, and a stack of buttered bread and mugs of fresh milk,

Carrie kept glancing back at the house. "You don't think that your father will . . . you know, do you?" she asked Dallas.

"Beat the stuffin' out of Tem?" Dallas asked without much concern in her voice.

"Where did you hear such an expression?"

"Uncle Hiram says that's what's wrong with us. He says that Papa should beat us now and then, and it would do us a world of good."

"Does he?" There was a tone of challenge in Carrie's voice. "And what does your father say to that?"

"Papa doesn't talk to Uncle Hiram much. He just sits and listens." Dallas's voice lowered. "I think Papa hates Uncle Hiram."

Carrie opened her mouth to tell Dallas that she was sure that Josh didn't hate his own brother, but she couldn't make herself say the platitude. From what she'd heard about Josh's brother, she already hated him. "*Will* your father strike Tem?"

Dallas gave Carrie a smile that was as sly as any adult's. "Naw. Papa couldn't hit us. He'll just talk a lot."

Carrie laughed. Her own father would have died before he hit one of his children. Of course most of the townspeople were in agreement with Hiram and thought that she and her brothers and sister would have benefited by a good, sound beating, but it never happened.

When, at long last, Josh came out of the house, Tem behind him, Tem looked fine, but Josh looked miserable. Carrie knew that Josh fully realized how close Tem had come to death, but Tem was already beginning to look on last night as an adventure.

Slipping her arm through Josh's and holding tight when he tried to pull away from her, Carrie said, "I declare today a holiday. No corn bugs today and no anything that we must do."

Josh gave her a look of irony. "You look on *every* day as a holiday."

"Thank you," Carrie said. "I think that may be the nicest compliment I have ever received."

The snide look melted from Josh's face and he smiled. "All right, you win. No bugs today. No weeds." When he looked down at Carrie, his eyes were teasing. "And for you, no dishes to wash, no floors to scrub, no laundry to scour. For once you can do just as you please. You can be as lazy as you want."

She didn't like the implication that she led a life of constant frivolity. "I don't think I'm lazy," she said in a hurt voice, then saw that he was teasing her. When she raised her hand to strike him on the chest, he agilely danced away from her, so Carrie ran toward him and tried to hit him, but she couldn't catch him. A minute later, the two of them were chasing each other like children, while Tem was standing by and smiling and Dallas was laughing and clapping her hands, with Choo-choo barking excitedly.

Carrie couldn't catch Josh, but when she struck at him once and he sidestepped her, he caught her in his arms, her back to his front, and wrestled her arms to her side.

"I am *not* lazy," Carrie said, trying to wiggle away from his grasp.

"You're the laziest person I ever saw," Josh said, then, without thinking what he was doing, he bit her earlobe, and before he realized what he was doing, he was kissing her neck.

Carrie stopped struggling and leaned back against him, her eyes closed in ecstasy.

It was at that point that the worried Choo-choo, who didn't understand what was being done to his mistress, bit Josh on the leg.

One minute Carrie was being kissed and the next Josh's shout sounded in her ear. Squealing in pain as Josh released her, Carrie saw him go after Choo-choo with his hands made into claws.

"Run, Choo-choo," Dallas called.

When Josh caught the little dog and said he was going to wring its scrawny neck, both children leaped on their father, trying to knock him down. Josh dropped the dog, held both of his children in his arms, and twirled them about. Choo-choo, who seemed to think Josh was hurting the children, snipped at him again, so Josh, still holding the kids, went after the dog.

This time, Carrie leaped on Josh, and the four of them went tumbling to the ground, while Josh yelled that they were too heavy for him and they were going to crush him. Dallas started giggling, then Tem got the giggles and Carrie joined in. Josh rolled over and over, the three of them in his arms, all the while protecting them from the rough ground.

When they had rolled far enough to reach the edge of the woods, Josh flopped on his back, his arms flung outward, and declared that they had worn him out, that he was dying.

Carrie, with both children, was half on top of Josh, half on the ground, and she saw right away that this was a game the children had played many times before.

"What will make you live again?" the children said in unison, their voices ecstatic with happiness to once again see their father laughing.

"Kisses," Josh said quickly, and both children began kissing their father's freshly shaved cheeks with damp enthusiasm.

"You too, Carrie," Dallas said.

Josh opened his eyes. "I don't think—"

He didn't say any more because Carrie moved her body full on top of him and pressed her lips to his. She had to displace a couple of kids to command all of his body to herself, but she did it without a thought.

She hadn't had much experience at kissing, but Josh seemed to have had some. Putting his hand behind her head, he turned her head, then, with a few delicious movements of instruction, showed her how to open her mouth.

Carrie had never felt anything so divine in her life as kissing Josh, and her enthusiasm made up for her lack of experience. She tried to put her arms around Josh, but she couldn't lift him so he rolled over until she was beneath him, never once breaking the contact of their lips.

Putting her arms around his chest, she pulled him to her as tightly as she could, and when the tip of his tongue touched hers, she moaned and tried to pull him closer.

When Josh pulled away from her, she made a sound of protest, then opened her eyes to look at him. He had turned his head to look at his children.

His children had placed themselves flat on their stomachs, one on each side of Carrie and Josh, their heads propped on their hands as they unabashedly, interestedly, watched their elders kissing.

Carrie could feel her face turning red.

"I think you like Carrie's kisses best, Papa," Dallas said solemnly, as though making a scientific discovery.

Josh didn't miss a beat. "She had some jam on her mouth. I was trying to get it off."

"On her *tongue*?" Tem asked in disgust.

At that, Carrie and Josh, still wrapped together, began to laugh.

"I don't know how anyone ever has *two* children," Josh said as he got off Carrie then reached down a hand to help her stand. "After the first one, a man has no privacy."

"The husband and wife sleep together," Carrie said, batting her eyelashes up at him. "In the same room with the door closed."

Josh grinned. "You win. All of you win. Now, did I hear someone say that Carrie is great at fishing? A *girl* who can fish? Ha!"

After that, challenges were issued and accepted, with the boys against the girls. Carrie went to get the fishing poles, but Josh declined her fancy English pole and said that he had his own. Tem groaned when his father unearthed two of the rattiest-looking old bamboo poles that had ever been seen.

"We can't beat her with those," Tem wailed.

"Then we'll cheat," Josh whispered.

Tem perked up at that proclamation.

The four of them packed a lunch, then went to the stream and put their poles in the water. Carrie and Dallas caught fish almost instantly. An hour later they had four, and the boys hadn't caught one. Then an hour went by, and no fish were caught by the females.

It was Dallas who saw what her father was doing. Every time a fish nibbled at Carrie's or Dallas's pole, Josh pointed out something in the woods to Carrie, and while she was looking away, Tem threw a stone at the fish.

Showing unusual cleverness for a child so young, Dallas didn't yell about what she was seeing. Instead, the next time a fish nibbled at Carrie's pole, she screamed that a bee had stung her, and while her father was tending to his daughter, Carrie reeled the fish in. It took Dallas three attacks of bees, wasps, and a killer bird before her father realized what she was doing. Tem was complaining nonstop about having girls along on a manly fishing trip, but when Josh realized that he had been beaten at his own game by a five-year-old, he picked his daughter up, twirled her around, and laughed gleefully. Carrie and Tem watched the two of them in consternation. "Crazy," Tem finally declared, looking back at his pole.

By the afternoon, the girls were two fishes ahead and declared themselves the winners. Josh and Tem outdid themselves in coming up with excuses as to why they hadn't caught as many fish as the females, talking about their poles, their bait, about how Tem was tired from his ordeal of the night before, how Josh was tired from working all the time, and how it wasn't the right time to fish. On and on they went.

Dallas, imitating Carrie, put her hands on her hips and listened to the excuses.

When the two males finally began to wind down, Carrie said, "Dallie, honey, aren't men the worst losers in the world?"

Dallas gave a very solemn nod, took Carrie's hand, and walked toward the lunch basket, the males trailing behind, all the while sputtering that they weren't bad losers, that they just . . . well, you know.

Carrie allowed the losers to serve lunch to the winners, and she and Dallas had a lovely time asking the men to hand them things that they couldn't reach. Of course, sometimes they had to lean backward to keep from reaching the items, but their thank yous dripped with sugar.

After they'd eaten, Carrie brought out a newly published book that she'd bought in Maine before leaving. It was Lewis Carroll's *Alice's Adventures in Wonderland*. She asked the children if they'd like for her to read to them, and both kids and Josh, stretched out drowsily on the quilt they'd brought, nodded.

But Carrie hadn't read more than two pages before the children grew restless. When she asked them if they wanted to do something else, they both declared that more than anything they wanted to hear the story, so Carrie started to read again. This time Dallas and Tem began to give each other looks, rolling their eyes skyward.

Carrie put the book down. "What is wrong with you two?" she asked. "And I want the *truth*. No lies."

She could see that Tem didn't want to say, so she looked at Dallas.

"Papa reads much better," Dallas said simply.

Carrie was surprised and maybe a little hurt by the comment, for she had often read books to shut-ins and to children, and quite often she'd been told that she was the best reader they'd ever heard.

Without a great deal of grace, she held the book out to Josh. "Please," she said, her voice dripping with sarcasm. "I do hope you can read as well as you can fish."

Giving her a smile that was more smirk than smile, he took the book from her. From the moment he began reading, Carrie knew that there was no contest. Josh could indeed read. No, he didn't just read, he created the story. He made the listener see and hear Alice. When Josh read, you could see, feel, almost touch the White Rabbit.

Carrie couldn't see how he did it. Some people when reading aloud exaggerate every scene, doing the voices of all the characters with such enthusiasm that after a while the listener is tired just from hearing them. But Josh's rendition of the story was subtle, molding his voice around the words in a way that made them live, never stumbling once, never stammering, never pausing over a story that was too new for him to have possibly read before.

Lying back on the quilt, her eyes closed, Carrie fell into the story, imagining everything she heard about Alice and all the people she met in her strange adventure.

When Josh stopped reading, she wanted to beg him to go on. As she opened her eyes, she was surprised that she wasn't still in the Red Queen's garden. She was also surprised to discover that it was nearly sundown and Josh had been reading all afternoon, yet his voice wasn't hoarse nor did his throat seem to be dry.

"That was wonderful," Carrie breathed when she managed to bring herself back to the present. Rolling over, she looked at him, her eyes shining. "I've never heard a reading like that. Josh, you are . . ."

"The best?" Tem asked eagerly, as though her answer was of life and death importance to him. "Is Papa the greatest person on earth?"

Carrie laughed. It was what he'd asked his father about her last night. "Close," she said. "He's certainly the best reader in the world."

"Papa used to—"

"Dallas!" Josh snapped.

Carrie grimaced, for the spell was broken. Josh had once again reminded her that she was an outsider.

Getting up, Carrie began putting things in the basket.

Josh seemed to understand what was wrong with her as he put his hand on her wrist. "Carrie," he began, "there are reasons—"

She cut him off. "You don't have to explain anything to me." Her voice was angry. "I'm not part of your family or your life, remember? I'm going back to my father in two days." She almost choked on the words. In a mere three days she'd leave her new family and go back to Maine.

When he started to say something else, she pulled away.

They walked back to the house together, the children talking about the fishing, but it wasn't the same as it had been since the adults were now silent.

At the house, Carrie set the table and served Mrs. Emmerling's bean soup with freshly baked bread.

"Can we go fishing again tomorrow?" Tem asked.

"Tomorrow is Sunday," Josh said in a heavy voice.

At those few innocent words, Tem looked back at his bowl and Dallas burst into tears.

This burst of grief made Carrie feel a little like Alice in Wonderland. "What is so dreadful about Sunday? You children couldn't hate church that much, could you?"

"We don't go to church," Josh said gloomily, pulling Dallas onto his lap and drying her tears.

Suddenly it was all too much for Carrie. She slammed her fist onto the table. "I've had it! I've had all the secrets I can take. I demand that someone tell me what is so awful about Sunday."

Looking as though he were going to cry too, Tem said, "Uncle Hiram comes to our house for dinner on Sunday and he makes everyone sad."

"A dinner guest doesn't sound like such a tragedy. And I doubt if he can make us sad if we don't allow him to."

"You don't understand," Josh said softly. "There are things that you don't know about. Our . . . welfare, our being together as a family depends on Hiram's good nature." Josh nearly choked on the last words.

"I see," Carrie said tightly. "And of course you don't plan to tell me any more than that, do you?" She waited, but Josh said nothing more. "All right, then I won't ask. Does your brother like food?"

Dallas giggled.

"Does that mean he *does* like food?"

At that Tem got up from the table, blew out his cheeks to make them look fat, held his hands out in front of him as though he had an enormous stomach, and began to walk like a very fat man. "What is this, little brother?" Tem said in a deep voice. "Something else you cooked? Maybe some worms from that field of yours? Ha! Ha! Ha! What's the matter with you? Can't you do *anything* right? Look at me. Use me as an example of how a man should be. I know right from wrong. I *decided* right from wrong."

Dallas was laughing and Josh was smiling, but Carrie was staring at Tem in wonder, because she was sure that his parody of a man she'd never met was perfect. From Tem's impersonation, she could see this man as clearly as though Tem had grown two feet taller and gained a couple of hundred pounds.

She turned to Josh. "He's quite good, isn't he?"

He set Dallas on the floor and raised one eyebrow as though to say, If you think that's something, watch this. "Be a duck," he said.

Carrie watched, at first in wonder, then in uncontrolled mirth as Dallas imitated a duck. Imitated it perfectly. Dallas put her head back to preen her feathers, pointed her feet outward, even twitched her tail when her duck rose from the water.

Not to be outdone by his little sister, Tem became a cow. Then Dallas did a chicken. Tem couldn't bear his sister getting so much attention so he began circling her, and within minutes they had become two dogs at first meeting.

Abruptly, Tem stood upright, his shoulders back, and gave Dallas a stern look. "I will *not* laugh, Miss Moneybags," he said in a deep voice. "We are a *serious* family."

Right away Carrie knew that Tem was mimicking his father—he even had Josh's posture down, that proud walk of his, that jaw that could be so inflexible.

Dallas stepped in front of her brother, and when she looked up at him, her lashes fluttered. She had gone from being a little girl to being a sexy, flirtatious woman. "Dishes," she said, falsetto. "I do declare they are dirty. We shall leave them and when we return the Good Fairy will have cleaned them."

Carrie was a little afraid that Dallas was imitating her, but she was sure when she heard Josh laugh out loud. Giving him a look over her shoulder that said, Laugh too hard and you will regret it, she turned back to the children.

Carrie was amazed at them, truly amazed as she watched them enact a hilarious parody of her and Josh. They argued over the most insignificant things, making Carrie and Josh laugh in a nervous sort of way. But it was when the children started imitating how Carrie and Josh reacted when they touched each other that the adults began to clear their throats.

"You have touched my arm!" Tem said. "I cannot bear it. I must hold you, kiss you." Putting the back of his hand to his forehead, all the while pulling Dallas toward him, he looked like a man in great agony. "But no, I mustn't. I cannot touch you."

"Oh, please touch me, my big handsome man. Please," Dallas said, looking up at Tem with adoring eyes.

Carrie turned to Josh. "Your children are brats."

"I thought they were *our* children."

"Not at this moment, they're not."

With a grin at her, he clapped his hands once. "Bed, you hams. Bed, this minute."

They ran up the ladder, but not before taking bows and waiting for the long, loud applause they so very much deserved.

"What extraordinary children," Carrie said when she and Josh were alone.

Rolling up his sleeves, Josh turned toward the sink full of dirty dishes. "I'm going to teach you about dishes."

Carrie didn't shudder, but she came close. "Sorry, but I can't tonight. I have to run an errand."

"You can't go out now," Josh protested, then stopped, knowing from experience that it was useless to tell Carrie what she could and could not do. "Where are you going?"

"I am going into Eternity to arrange the most heavenly meal your brother has ever eaten," she said. "And don't you say a word about what I can and cannot do. You can't give orders to someone who isn't part of your family, someone you don't share your secrets with."

With that she flung on her short, wool cape and left the house.

After staring at the door for a moment, Josh smiled. She was a handful, he thought, as he turned back to the dishes. "And I'm the one who'd like to have my hands full of her," he said aloud. Still smiling, he thought of Tem and Dallas's performance tonight, knowing he hadn't seen them that happy, that animated, since their mother—

He cut himself off and poured water into the dish pan. He was *not* going to think about their mother.

Chapter Ten

By the time Josh's brother and his wife arrived for Sunday dinner the next day, Carrie was so nervous she was shaking. She'd had only four hours of sleep the night before, because she'd spent hours in Eternity arranging the dinner. Josh had waited up for her and he'd made it clear that he thought asking other people to do the cooking was the easy way out. He seemed to think that a "real" wife spent the day hanging over a hot stove.

Without bothering to answer him, she went to bed and slept until the next morning when the first woman arrived with a covered dish. To wake her, Josh opened the bedroom door and allowed the children to jump into bed with Carrie.

After that ruckus, she got up and dressed, then, with the children's help, began rummaging in her trunks. By noon she had set the dining table with an Irish linen cloth and napkins and porcelain dishes from France, and the centerpiece was Georgian silver. The serving dishes, filled with delicious food that had been cooked by nearly every woman in Eternity, were either silver or French porcelain.

"Golly," Dallas said, for she didn't remember having seen anything like the table.

At exactly one o'clock, Hiram and his wife Alice pulled up in what Carrie knew was a very expensive carriage. Hiram was a large man, with a belly that stuck out like a shelf in front of him. Looking down at Tem in conspiracy, she smiled, for Hiram looked just as Tem had portrayed him.

While Josh and his children stood in the doorway looking glum, Carrie, after a look of disgust tossed their way, went forward to greet Hiram and his wife. As Carrie crossed the yard, she got a closer look at Alice. Alice was a thin little woman, who probably wasn't as old as she looked, but she looked to be the tiredest person in the world, so tired in fact that Carrie wanted to take her in the house and give her a chair to sit on.

Smiling at them both, Carrie continued across the yard, her hand extended in welcome. For all that Josh had warned her that his brother was a formidable person, Carrie wasn't afraid of anyone, for in all of her short life she had never been treated with anything but respect and love. Her family was the richest in her hometown, in fact, there were very few people in the town who didn't work for her family. On top of that, she was pretty and generous and she was fun to be with. Until she'd met Josh, no man, woman, or child she'd ever met had failed to like her.

"Good afternoon," she said cheerfully to Hiram. "May I help you?" She said the last to Hiram's wife.

Looking at Carrie with startled eyes, as though she were surprised that anyone saw her, Alice's tired expression changed to one of pleasure.

Hiram leaned back and looked at Carrie, looked her up and down in an insolent way. Had Carrie been at home and some visiting sailor had looked at her as this man was doing, one of her brothers or one of her family's employees would have knocked the man down.

Ignoring Carrie's extended hand, Hiram looked away to Josh standing not too far behind her. "So this is the little wife you sent away for," he said, smirking. "I heard her cooking was as good as your farming. It's just like you to marry a useless woman."

With that Hiram swept past all of them, ignoring the children as he went into the house.

"Why that—" Carrie began and started after him. No one was going to say something like that to her!

Josh caught her arm. "Don't," he said, his eyes pleading. "He leaves in precisely two hours and twenty minutes, and I find that one can bear him for that length of time."

"I don't believe I can," Carrie said.

"Someone with your money doesn't have to," Josh said meanly. "You'll never believe what we poor people have to put up with in order to survive."

Now she had been insulted by *both* of the men. Looking down her nose at her husband, she went into the house.

"Your rich wife give you all of this?" she heard Hiram saying as she entered the house. He was looking over his fat belly toward the table that she had worked so hard on. "Be sure she doesn't take it with her when she leaves you," he said to Josh and began to laugh nastily at his own joke.

When Carrie started to open her mouth, Josh looked at her, his eyes begging her to keep quiet. "When he kicks us off the farm, are you going to buy us another one?" Josh said softly, with such derision in his voice that Carrie clamped her mouth shut. At that moment she wasn't sure which of the men she disliked the most.

Carrie was determined to endure this odious man for the full two hours and twenty minutes. After all, Josh was making her leave tomorrow and maybe she'd never see this family again, so it wasn't as though she had any right to care what happened to them. If they wanted to sit still and endure this man's insults, that was their business.

And insult them he did. He talked about the children's lack of education, wanting Dallas to quote "The Rime of the Ancient Mariner." When the five-year-old said that she had never heard of the poem, Hiram gave his brother a look of disgust. Keeping his head down, Josh didn't answer his brother.

When Hiram looked at Tem's small hands, he declared them unfit for work, saying that when he was Tem's age he was practically running a farm by himself. He also berated Tem for getting lost and causing problems that made the Greene name a laughingstock in town.

When he'd finished with the children, he started on Josh, laughing at Josh's cornfield and announcing that he had always known that Josh could never make it as a farmer.

It was only when Hiram began to talk of Josh's past that Carrie's ears perked up. From what she could gather from Hiram's cryptic tirade, Josh had done something atrocious in his past and that was why he'd lost what money he'd had. Hiram spoke of Josh being "on the run," and when Carrie looked at Josh, she saw the way he was staring down at his plate, not saying a word.

What could Josh have done that was so bad? she wondered. According to Hiram, Josh had once been quite wealthy, for Hiram mentioned that Josh must be very used to the silver and the pretty dishes, but that Josh had had everything taken away from him.

Taken away by whom? Carrie wondered. By the law? Had Josh gained his wealth in some nefarious way and been caught at it?

Hiram finally ran out of words about Josh, then turned to his wife, telling everyone at the table everything that Alice had done "wrong" that week. He told of clothing stains that she had not been able to remove and food undercooked and overcooked. He told of cobwebs hanging from the ceiling.

Carrie looked at the watch pinned to her breast. Only one hour gone. It was amazing that one person could pontificate for so long.

When Hiram was at last finished with his wife, he paused—not that talking nonstop had caused him to miss so much as a bite—and looked at Carrie.

Carrie was well aware of the other people at the table, all of them sitting solemnly, all of them saying nothing in their own defense at what this man was saying about them. When Hiram turned to her, she didn't look down at her plate, but met his eyes. Money, she thought. That's what gave this man his power. He owned his own farm and Josh's, and because he had the power to evict them, in essence to take the roof from over their heads and food from their mouths, he thought he had the right to denigrate them.

But Carrie knew about money. Many, many times she had felt the power of her family's money, but, thank heaven, there had always been someone from her family nearby to tell her that money did not give a person special privileges. Just because she had money didn't mean that she got a free ride in the world. She had to give something back to the earth besides money.

Hiram looked at Carrie long and hard, then turned away with a little smirk and looked back at Josh. "I can see why you got her," he said in the most leering tone that Carrie had ever heard.

Hiram looked back at Carrie, as though trying to ascertain what she was going to say to him.

When Carrie smiled at him sweetly, Hiram turned away with a smirk of self-satisfaction.

It was his look that broke Carrie. Not his words. She could handle them, but she couldn't handle that smile, for he seemed to assume that here was yet another person to browbeat and humiliate.

"More corn, Brother Hiram?" Carrie asked sweetly.

With that smirk still on his ugly face, he said, "Don't mind if I do. Of course it isn't corn that my little brother has grown, is it? Too many worms for me."

Picking up the heavy silver dish, she offered it to him, but when he put his hand on the bowl, he leered at her and said, "You may be useless as a wife, but I bet you have some uses as a *woman*."

Carrie looked him in the eyes, smiled, then poured the bowl of corn in his lap. In the ensuing silence of horror that came from everyone at the table, Carrie managed to pour creamed spinach on Hiram's head, coleslaw in his face, and hit him with a greasy ham in the chest. She had her hand on the carving knife when Josh grabbed her wrist.

"He has no right to—" Carrie began.

Josh's hand tightened on her wrist. "You don't know anything," he said.

"And no one has bothered to tell me, either," she said, then, with one more look at the children, she ran out of the house. It wasn't her business. Just because she was married to Josh, just because she loved the children with all her heart and soul, that didn't seem to count.

She ran until she reached the road, and then she kept on running—wanting to run all the way back to Maine. She kept going until her lungs were bursting and her legs were weak.

When she could go no further, she turned to the nearby river and slipped into the trees to sit on the bank by the rushing water. She hadn't caught her breath before she started crying.

She cried for a long time, her knees pulled up to her chin, hiding her face in the folds of her dress. She had tried so hard and had failed so completely.

"Here," said a voice beside her, and a handkerchief was held out to her.

Looking up through her tears, she saw Josh sitting beside her. "Go away. I hate you. I hate all of you. I wish I could leave today instead of tomorrow, and I'll be glad to never see any of you again."

Without any comment on her little speech, his eyes on the wa-

ter, he handed her a bottle of whisky. "It's good single malt
Scotch, the best there is. My last bottle."

Taking it from him, Carrie swallowed a healthy-sized amount of
the smoky liquid, then took another drink and another, until Josh
pulled the bottle out of her hands.

"About my brother . . ." he began.

Carrie waited. The whisky was making her feel better, hazy,
relaxed. Leaning back on her arms, she looked at the water.
When Josh didn't say anything more, she gave a nasty little laugh.
"I knew you wouldn't tell me anything. I knew you couldn't part
with a secret." She turned to look at him. "I must say that your
brother doesn't look much like you."

"We're not blood relatives. My mother married his father when
I was ten and Hiram was already an adult by then."

"Was his father like him?"

"No." Josh took a long drink of the whisky. "I think my stepfather was a bit horrified by Hiram."

Carrie giggled. "I can understand that. Has he always been like
that?" She gestured in the general direction of the house, which
was over a mile away.

Taking another drink, Josh handed the bottle back to her.
"Men like Hiram are born, not created. He was born thinking he
knew the right way and that it was his duty to instruct the rest of
us."

"Why do you live here on land that he owns?"

Josh was silent at that.

Carrie took a deep drink of the whisky. "I beg your pardon.
That's a question I shouldn't have asked. I forget from one mo-
ment to the next that I'm not good enough to be part of the
Greene family, that I'm merely an empty-headed little rich girl
who has no right to be here." She got up. "Excuse me, but I think
I'll go back to the house."

Josh grabbed her skirt. "Carrie, I'd tell you, but—"

She looked down at him. "But what?" she yelled at him.

"It would make you hate me."

This was not the answer she had expected.

Releasing her skirt, he looked back at the river. "I've made a
mess of my life and I've done some things that I'm not very proud
of. The children are the only thing I've ever done that was any
good."

Carrie remembered Hiram's insinuations. *Had* Josh been a criminal? Maybe they had allowed him out of prison only if he agreed to put himself under his brother's care and run the farm and take care of the children.

Sitting back down beside him, much closer than she had been, she took another drink from the bottle, then returned it to him. "Let me stay," she said softly.

"More than anything in the world I'd like for you to stay, but it can't be. This isn't the life for you. This isn't the life for anyone, and I can't keep living off your money."

She nodded, not in understanding, but in acceptance. "Josh," she whispered, then turned to look at him, her eyes full of tears. "This is the last day."

When he looked at her, he told himself that his life would be better after Carrie left, that she had upset him and that wasn't good. He knew that the kids would be unhappy for a while after she left, but they'd recover, and soon the little family would be back to normal. And what was normal? His cooking? His farming? His misery, which the children reflected?

"Oh, Carrie," Josh said, then pulled her into his arms.

The minute their lips touched, they ignited, for they had hungered for each other since they had first seen the other. Their desire for each other had started the first time Josh had put his hands on Carrie's waist to help her out of the stage, and daily contact had increased it until the two of them were tightly strung.

Day after day they had watched each other, had looked at each other's bodies, had broken into cold sweats at the sight of so much as an inch of bare skin. For all that they pretended to dislike each other, each of them had felt vibrations whenever the other entered a room.

The children had been well aware of the adults' reaction to each other, the way their eyes never left the other, the way they were obsessed with each other.

Now they were alone, with nothing about them but trees and rushing water, and there was nothing to stop them from doing what they'd wanted to do since that first day: They tore at each other's clothes.

Josh was much more experienced at removing a woman's clothes than Carrie was at taking off a man's, but Josh had never in his life been this eager. When he pulled on Carrie's sleeve, it ripped away, but care for her clothing was the last thing in his mind as he stroked the bare flesh of her upper arm and put his mouth to it.

Josh tried to undo the buttons at the back of her dress, but it was easier to tear them away. When he could reach her shoulders with his mouth and he heard Carrie's moan, he no longer thought of clothes. He thought of nothing but his own desire.

Within moments there was a flurry of garments flying through the air. There was a torn silk dress, petticoats made of yards of soft cotton, and hoops that entangled Josh, but he dispatched them quickly.

Carrie had seen her brothers in various states of undress and had a good idea of how to get Josh's clothing off of him. She found that she was very good at pulling off shirts and even socks.

By the time they were nude, there was no caressing, there was only lust, pure and simple lust. Frantic lust. A lust both of them had waited a lifetime to relieve.

With his mouth fastened on Carrie's breast, with his hands on her hips, Josh entered her, making Carrie cry out in alarm at the pain, but the pain didn't last for long. She had wanted Josh for too long to allow a little pain to get in her way.

Moving with him, as frantic as he was, as greedy and as wanting, Carrie cried out in ecstasy when they at last came together, and Josh buried his face in her neck.

For a long, sweaty moment, they lay wrapped in each other's arms, their skin feeling as though every nerve ending was alive.

"I never—" Josh began, but Carrie put her finger over his mouth.

"Don't say that you didn't mean to," she whispered. "Whatever you do, don't apologize to me."

Smiling, he kissed her fingertips. "I was going to say that I've never experienced anything like that before. I've never lost control like that before. Lovemaking is an art, but that was . . ."

"Need?" she whispered.

"Need and something more." Rolling off of her, he pulled her into his arms, holding her and stroking her hair.

"Josh," she whispered, but he silenced her with a kiss.

"We have to go back," he said. "The children are alone, and we'll have to get up early in the morning to catch—" He broke off as though the words were too painful for him to finish.

She lay in his arms for a few moments more, then moved away from him and began to dress, her torn dress making it difficult for her to pull the pieces together. Josh's fingers brushed hers away. "Allow me," he said, and as expertly as any lady's maid, he dressed her, his hands touching her as much as possible.

When they started walking back to the house, they were silent, but then Josh slipped his hand into hers. Carrie at first tried to pull away from him. How could they do what they had just done, then Josh talk of her leaving in the next breath?

At the house, the children laughed at their torn clothing and the red faces of the adults. The kids were in high spirits after what Carrie had done to their Uncle Hiram. Gleefully, they reported that Hiram had left in a rage and had said some terrible things about Carrie and about his stupid brother who had married someone like Carrie. Flinging her arms around Carrie's waist, Dallas hugged her and told her she loved her.

Not able to bear the thought of having to leave tomorrow, Carrie ran to the bedroom to change clothes. She almost wished she could leave today instead of tomorrow, almost wished she could get her parting over with.

When she had composed herself again, she went back into the parlor where Josh and Tem were washing dishes.

"We could show you how," Tem said to Carrie with great sincerity in his voice.

Dallas stood beside Carrie, her little shoulders straight. "I don't think I want to learn either. I don't want to be a farmer's wife. I want to be a great actress."

That made Carrie laugh and pick the child up. "If you were an actress, you'd have dreadful people for companions," she said. "And you'd have to travel all the time and you'd never be accepted into the best homes. No, it's better that you marry some nice man and have babies."

Dallas made a face. "I should like for men to give me roses."

"If you marry the right man, he'll give you roses."

"*If* he can afford them," Josh said angrily, then threw down the dishcloth and left the house.

"*Now* what did I say?" Carrie moaned. She would have thought that their intimacy would have made them closer, but with Josh it just seemed to make him angry.

Josh disappeared for the rest of the afternoon, and Carrie was left alone with the children. At least he thinks that I can take care of them, she thought. He doesn't think that I'm going to burn the house down.

In the late afternoon, she and the children sat outside on the porch, where Carrie told them stories about Maine and her brothers. She had every intention of telling them that she was leaving in the morning, but she couldn't seem to say the words.

An hour after sundown, Josh returned, hugged his children to him and told them to get washed and get into bed, that it was late.

Gloomily, Carrie got out of her chair and looked about her. Now she could smell roses, whereas before she came, the only smell surrounding the house was horse manure. Trying not to think of tomorrow, she went back into the house, and when the children kissed her goodnight, she had to work very hard not to burst into tears.

Dallas was nearly up the ladder when she looked back at her father. "Are you coming to bed soon?"

"I'm not sleeping with you tonight," Josh said. "I'm sleeping in the big bed."

"With Carrie?" Dallas asked.

"With Carrie," Josh said, as though it were the most common thing in the world.

When the children were out of sight, Josh turned to her.

"I'm not sure . . ." she began, but she didn't know what else to say. Should she say she wasn't sure they should spend the night together? Was she afraid that she'd fall more in love with him and his family if they spent a whole night together? It wasn't possible to love them more than she already did. Was she afraid that she'd cry more when she left them? Couldn't happen. If she spent the night with Josh, would he want her to stay in the morning?

She looked across the room at his eyes, dark eyes hot with desire for her and all thoughts left her mind. She opened her arms to him. "Josh," she whispered.

Moving swiftly toward her, he swept her into his arms and carried her into the bedroom.

Chapter Eleven

When Carrie awoke the next morning, the sun was already up, and she immediately felt a bit of panic. She should already be out of bed and dressed, but then, smiling, she lay back against the pillows and thought about last night. Josh's hands had been all over her. He had hands like a musician's that wanted to touch all of her, caress her. And he had kissed her and showed her how to kiss him.

They had made love all night. They had made love with enthusiasm the first time on the riverbank, but in bed they'd taken their time and looked at each other and touched each other. Carrie had been fascinated by Josh's body, at the strength of it, at the play of muscle under his dark skin. She asked him about scars here and there, and sometimes he'd answer her and sometimes he refused. After a while she realized that he'd tell her anything about himself up to the age of sixteen, but after that he kept his life a secret.

Touching her and looking at her as he made love to her body, he didn't ask her any questions, and Carrie tried not to think that it was because he thought he knew all there was to know about her. For one night she was content to live in the present, to not question what was going to happen in the future.

At one point during the night she had said, "Josh, I love you." But he hadn't said anything, merely held her to him tightly, as though he were afraid to let her go.

Now, Carrie was stretching luxuriously when the bedroom door burst open. Josh was standing there, dressed and as stern looking as she'd ever seen him. "What is it?" she asked. "Are the children all right?"

"I have taken the children to my brother's house. Your trunks are loaded and ready to go, and I've hired a driver who will take the wagon back to Maine for you. You have to get dressed so we can go." With that he shut the door again.

Was this the man she'd spent the night with? Was this the man she'd said she loved?

Getting out of bed—her marriage bed—she began to dress, but her hands shook on the buttons. Last night had changed nothing, and he wasn't going to allow her to say good-bye to the children. But then, what could she have said, that she *wanted* to go? And she couldn't tell them that their father was forcing her to go, because she didn't want the children angry at their father. Altogether, maybe her leaving this way was better. If she had to say good-bye, she would have only cried and she would never be able to explain something she didn't understand herself.

When she was dressed, her toiletries in her bag, she went outside, where Josh was on the wagon seat, and sitting in the back was a man who tipped his hat to her. Josh's horse was tied to the back of the wagon—not his beautiful stallion, for that had gone back to his brother, but his old workhorse. When he saw her, Josh came around to help her onto the seat, but he didn't speak to her.

Once they were on their way, she spoke. "Is there anything I can say to make you change your mind?"

"Nothing," he said flatly. "Nothing at all. You deserve more than I can give you. You deserve—"

"Don't you *dare* tell me what I deserve and don't deserve," she said in fury. "I know what I *want*."

His face set rigidly, Josh stopped speaking.

Carrie held onto the wagon bed and thought that if he could be silent, so could she. But it wasn't easy to stop her thoughts, thoughts of last night and of the days she had spent with Josh and his children.

"Tell Dallas I will write," Carrie said softly. "Tell her I will send her more books and tell Tem I will send him things about the sea. He wants to see the sea. He says that he wants to be a sailor, and I'm sure Dallas will grow out of wanting to be an actress. All little girls want to be actresses until they grow up so I don't think you have to worry about her. She's a good child. She's the best child. And so is Tem. He won't have reason to get into trouble again now that I'm gone. Tell him that if he ever sees his Wild Girl again to thank her for me and tell her—"

She stopped babbling, because tears were beginning to close her throat. When they reached the stage depot, Josh helped her down. She searched his face, but she could see no sign of grief or of reluctance on his part. He may as well have been delivering one of his wormy corn crops to the corn merchant as sending his wife off to never see her again.

"You don't care, do you?" she hissed at him. "You had your fun, and that's all you wanted. You knew what you wanted from me the first moment you saw me and you got that, and now you can send me away without feeling anything."

"You're right," he said, giving her a lascivious smile. "From the first moment I saw you, I wanted my hands on your shapely little body. It took me a while to manage it, but I did, and now that you're going I can go back to the happy existence I had before you came."

If she'd just heard his words, she'd not have believed them, but his face made her know that he wasn't lying. No one on earth could look as uncaring as he did and be lying.

She slapped him. Slapped him hard, and he made no attempt to stop her. In fact, she thought he might stand there and allow her to slap him repeatedly.

She turned away while she still had some dignity left. "Go on, go back to your miserable little farm. I don't need you here with me. I don't *want* you here. I don't want to ever see you again."

She didn't hear him move, but she knew when he left, and it was as though a part of her was taken away when he moved. She had to grab the wheel of the wagon to keep herself from running to him and begging him to take her with him. She could imagine herself grabbing his stirrup and pleading with him to allow her to stay.

Pride, she thought. She must have some pride. The Montgomerys had always been proud. But Carrie didn't feel very proud right now. What she did feel was lost and alone and homeless.

When she heard Josh's horse, in spite of herself, she turned to look up at him, sitting tall and straight on his horse. For just a second, she thought she saw pain on his face. Pain and misery just as deep as she felt. She took a step toward him.

But then Josh's face changed back to that insolent look of unconcern, and he tugged at his hat brim. "Good day, Miss Montgomery," he said. "I enjoyed your visit immensely." He then winked at her.

It was the wink that made Carrie turn away and made her shoulders straighten, and when he rode away, she didn't look back at him.

"Canceled?" Carrie asked. "The stage is canceled for today?"

"Broke a wheel," the depot manager said. "A rider just came in and told us. Anyway, the driver's dead drunk. Not that that would keep him from drivin', but, even drunk, he can't drive a coach that's got only three wheels."

"No, I don't imagine he can. How long do you think it will be before the next stage arrives?"

"A week or so," the man said without concern.

Carrie turned away from the man at the window of the stage depot. A week? Or so?

Sitting down on the dusty bench in the depot, she wondered what she was going to do now. She could check into that dreadful little place Eternity called a hotel.

And do what? she wondered.

She hadn't said anything to Josh, but she was very, very low on money. She had brought quite a bit with her to Eternity, but with one thing and another, she had spent nearly all of it. Of course, she didn't regret any of the money she'd spent, for she was glad that the children now had a nice place to live, but she couldn't spend day after day in a hotel, no matter how cheap it was.

Opening her change purse, she counted coins and bills. Ten dollars and twenty cents. That's all she had after she'd paid for her stage ticket home.

Money, she thought. That's what Josh was always talking about, as though money were the most important thing in the world. Over and over she'd told him that there were more important things in life than money, but he'd never believed her.

Leaning back against the bench, she closed her eyes. How was she going to live in this town for a whole week with no money to speak of? How could she buy food and lodging? She needed to wire her father to send her money. Right away she saw difficulties with that. First of all, there was no telegraph this far west and a letter would take weeks, if not months. Maybe she could go to the bank and borrow money. With what as collateral? Twenty-two trunks full of used clothing and other assorted goods?

She grimaced. Wouldn't Josh smirk at that? The next time he came into town he'd hear how Miss Carrie Montgomery had had no money so she'd used her father's name and conjured money out of the air. He'd smirk and say that he'd been right, that she was useless: Take away her father and she was nothing.

"I can make it on my own," she said aloud.

"You say something', Mrs. Greene?"

Carrie smiled. "Not a word." She stood up. "Do you know anywhere around here where I can get a job?"

The man seemed to think that was a great joke. "A job? In this town? The most money that's ever been spent in this town was spent by you last week. There's nothin' here for anybody. That's why people are leavin' ever' day."

Encouraging news, Carrie thought. Smiling at the man, she thanked him, then left the depot. Once she was outside, she looked up at the sun and pulled on her kid gloves. What could she do to make money? How could she earn a living until the stage did bother to run? Looking at the stack of trunks in the wagon and at the driver asleep in the shade under it, she knew that she wasn't yet ready to go home and admit to her family that she'd been a failure, that she'd made a horse's ass of herself over some man and he'd rejected her. She didn't yet want to go home and cry herself into a stupor. She could hear her brothers telling her that she always had been spoiled—by her other brothers, not by the one lecturing her, of course—and she could see the tears on her mother's face and the sadness on her father's. Then, of course, she'd have to give an accounting of the money she'd spent to her oldest brother. He wouldn't chastise her as the others did. No, she'd just be a disappointment to her eldest brother—and that would be by far worse than all the others.

She pulled on her glove harder. No, she wasn't yet ready to go home with her tail between her legs.

Chapter Twelve

There were six carriages in front of the new ladies' dress shop rather fancifully called Paris in the Desert, and the combined cost of the carriages surpassed the gross national product of all of Eternity. But no one in town was complaining that the carriages were blocking the street, for the customers at the dress shop often stopped in the mercantile store and made a few purchases or even went to the hardware store to buy something. And of course the horses had to be fed and watered so the stableman wasn't complaining. And the saloon entertained the husbands of the women who were in the dress shop. Six female residents of Eternity had opened two restaurants that were doing a brisk business at lunch, and the hotel had already started adding on a wing to accommodate the new business. Two other women from Eternity had gone in together and opened a hat shop they called The Left Bank across the street from the dress shop. Boardwalks were being laid down to keep the owners of the carriages' feet out of the mud.

Inside Paris in the Desert, Mrs. Joshua Greene oversaw all six of her customers without showing the least bit of tension. All of the women were very wealthy and used to getting individual attention when they entered a shop, and at first they had made it known that they didn't appreciate having to share Carrie with other women.

But Carrie knew how to handle women who were feeling neglected. She fed some of them, sat others down with the best gossip Eternity had to offer, and to others she handed books. Carrie was adept at guessing who needed what.

"Horrid color on you," Carrie said to the customer modeling an expensive silk gown in front of her. "And that neckline makes you look ten years older. No, no, that dress won't do for you at all."

"But I like it," the woman wailed, then straightened and put her shoulders back. "I like this dress and my husband likes it and I shall buy it."

Everyone in the shop looked up, waiting to see what would happen. Carrie had to give in, for the woman was the customer and wasn't the customer always right?

Carrie smiled sweetly at the woman. "You'll not buy it from me, then, for I'll not have you telling people that *I* allowed one of my customers to go out into the world looking like an old woman. *My* customers leave here looking their very best. Now, would you please remove that dress and return it to me?"

The woman had terrorized shopkeepers in four states, and she wasn't going to admit defeat easily. She smiled in a superior way at Carrie. "Possession is nine-tenths of the law." Putting her nose in the air, she started toward the door. "I shall, of course, pay you, Mrs. Greene." She had her hand on the door before she felt the back of her dress give way, and, with eyes wide in astonishment, she whirled around.

Carrie was smiling at her, a large pair of shears in her hand. "So sorry," she said, "but I'm afraid the dress is ruined." Carrie held up a large piece of expensive silk that she had cut from the back of the dress.

The customer was torn between rage and tears as she stood at the door, not knowing what to do.

"Why don't you come back here and look at some lovely peach-colored silk that I have in stock? The peach will go so well with your clear, pale complexion, and I can see you with white egret feathers in your hair. You will stop crowds." When the woman didn't move, Carrie took her firmly by the arm and led her to what she and her three saleswomen privately called the Recovery Room.

"See to her," Carrie said to her assistant as she gave a sigh as she looked down at the fabric she held. Another dress ruined and she'd have to bear the expense of it. Stupid woman, she thought. No taste at all, none whatsoever. Carrie saw it as her duty to save the women from themselves, and, also, she had to maintain her own reputation. She'd never get any more business if "her" ladies were seen looking less than their best.

Carrie looked back at the five women sitting in the front room, each patiently waiting her turn to be told what to wear, and she sighed again. Sometimes the responsibility of it all was nearly too much for her.

"I'm going to get the mail," she said. "You babysit for a while, but if Mrs. Miller gives you any trouble about that white dress, tell her to wait for me." Carrie smiled. "But after having seen what happens to women who cross me, I think she'll be docile enough. I'll be back in—" Pausing, she looked outside at the late autumn sunshine. "I'll be back when I get back."

Joshua Greene and his children rode into town, all three of them mounted on his old workhorse. It had been weeks since any of them had left the grounds of the farm, weeks since they had had any contact with people other than themselves. Josh's brother Hiram hadn't come to visit since his new sister-in-law had poured food over him. Three times people from Eternity had come to the farm, but each time Josh had run them off, because he hadn't felt like talking to anyone. The day after Carrie had gone, he'd left a note for Mrs. Emmerling saying that her services would no longer be needed. She'd cooked a great deal of food that day and left it for him and the children, and she'd also refunded the money Carrie had paid her for the rest of the month.

When the food that Mrs. Emmerling had cooked ran out, Josh again tried to cook the meals for himself and his children. The first time the children ate his burned meal, he prepared himself for their comments, but they didn't say anything. They ate what he put in front of them and said nothing at all.

In fact, they'd said nothing six weeks ago when he'd told them that Carrie was gone. He'd had that long, long ride back from the stage depot to think of reasons to give his children about why Carrie had gone, and he'd prepared himself for a scene of the most awful proportions. He had been prepared for hysterics and tears, but he wasn't ready for the quiet resignation of his children. After informing them that Carrie had returned to Maine, he had braced himself for the ensuing storm.

But the children had just nodded at him as though it was something they had expected. They were like two wise old people who had seen everything and knew that nothing good was going to come to them in this life. He wanted to explain to them that he'd sent Carrie away for their sakes, that he knew she'd grow tired of playing housewife and then she and that absurd little dog of hers would leave them. He wanted to tell the children that it was better that they had given Carrie only a week's worth of love rather than months' worth. And he'd wanted to tell them that Carrie was a fairy princess who had come into their lives for just a short time and that she wasn't real. He wanted to tell the children that they'd forget her in no time.

But in the weeks that followed, neither he nor the children could forget her. Not that they talked about her. Not even Dallas asked questions about why Carrie had gone, and Josh tried to tell himself that it would soon be as though Carrie had never entered their lives. When they were alone again, the family settled back into the routine they had established before Miss Carrie Montgomery had seen the photograph of them.

But no matter how much Josh told himself that they'd forget her and that soon everything would be as it was, he knew that he was lying to himself. Nothing was the same. Nothing at all. Not he nor the children nor the farm was as it once was.

It wasn't just that they missed her. It wasn't just that the very sight of the house with its roses outside and in made them think of Carrie. It was that she had changed the way they looked at their lives. For a while she had made them happy. She had made them laugh and smile and sing and tell stories and laugh some more.

At first Josh tried to recreate Carrie within his own house, forcing himself to pretend that he wasn't aching for her and trying to make pleasant, entertaining conversation at the dinner table. The children also made valiant efforts to be cheerful, but it didn't work. One night Josh tried asking the children to pretend to be animals, but he found himself criticizing their performances rather than enjoying them, so soon the children sat down, their eyes downcast, and said they were tired and didn't want to pretend anymore.

He and Tem went to the cornfield, and he did his best to try to make the corn grow, but he threw down his hoe. "The goddamn plants *know* I hate them," he said. Tem solemnly nodded in agreement.

Josh tried going fishing with his children, but there wasn't much joy in the outing, no one to tease them and challenge them, no one to make a game of the day.

On the previous evening everything had come to a head. He and the children were eating a meal of fried ham and canned beans when they heard a dog barking outside. They should have known that it wasn't Carrie's dog, for it was the deep voice of a large dog, but that fact didn't seem to register with any of them. Without looking at each other, without a word spoken between them, the three of them leaped from the table and made for the door all at the same time. Since the door wasn't big enough for the three of them, they began pushing each other. Dallas bit her brother's shoulder, and Josh nearly knocked his son down in his hurry to get outside, but then Josh had enough presence of mind to realize what he was doing, so he picked up a child in each arm and went through the door.

The dog ran away at the sight of the three fused people coming at him at once. It was a big, scrawny farm dog and not at all like Choo-choo.

Putting his children down, Josh sat on the porch step and looked out at the moonlit yard. As always, the three of them kept to their policy of not saying a word about Carrie, but it was Dallas who began to softly sob.

Without saying a word, Josh pulled her onto his lap and stroked her hair. Beside them Tem began to sob too, and Josh knew that Tem would rather die than allow anyone to see him in tears, so he knew how much pain his son was feeling. Josh put his arm around Tem.

"Why did she leave?" Tem whispered.

"Because I'm stupid and a fool and have no sense," Josh said softly.

Dallas nodded against his chest, and tears came to Josh's eyes too. It always amazed him at how much his children loved him. He had sent away a woman they had grown to love very much, but not once had they even questioned him. They loved him enough to believe that what he did was right, and they were willing to accept his decision no matter what it did to them. They loved him with complete trust.

Josh sniffed and wiped the back of his hand across his eyes. Carrie had said that she loved him. Did she love him enough to come back to him?

Josh hugged Tem. "Think she'd forgive me?"

It took the children a moment to understand what their father had said, then they looked at each other, smiled, leaped off the porch and began to dance about the yard. Josh hadn't seen them with this much energy in six weeks.

"I take it you *do* think she'll forgive me," Josh said sarcastically.

"She loves you," Dallas said.

Josh laughed, for his daughter made it sound as though she couldn't understand *why* Carrie loved Josh. "Maybe if I wrote her a letter and explained—"

At that the children stopped dancing and looked at their father. The next moment they were pushing him into the house, where Dallas fetched pen, ink, and paper, while Tem, his hands behind his back, looking very much like his father, began to tell his father what to write. "First of all, you have to tell her you love her, then you have to tell her you think she's the best in the world. Tell her you like her . . . her name. Tell her you like her dresses and her hair. Tell her she can fish better than you. Tell her that you're sure she is a better farmer than you."

Josh lifted one eyebrow. "Anything else?"

The children didn't seem to realize that their father was being sarcastic, or if they did, they ignored him. "Tell her about the food we have to eat," Dallas said as though that one fact would make Carrie take pity on them and return.

His hands still behind his back, still looking like a miniature version of his father, Tem looked down at the floor with a frown and began to pace. "Tell her she makes us laugh. Tell her that if she'll come back, she can sleep in the morning if she wants to. Carrie likes to sleep late. Tell her I won't do anything dumb like run away again." He looked up at his father, and his face was as serious as any adult's. "Tell her you're sorry for all the mean things you said to her and that if she'll come back you'll treat her like a queen and you won't argue with her and you'll give her the big bed all by herself."

Josh smiled at that. "She, uh, likes sharing with me."

Dallas gave a snort. "You kick and you're too big and you snore sometimes."

"Don't tell her you snore," Tem ordered.

Both children stopped and looked at Josh as though waiting for something, and it took him a moment to understand. Picking up the pen, he began to write. "Anything else I should tell her?"

"Tell her she doesn't have to see Uncle Hiram," Dallas said. "I don't like him anyway."

Tem took a deep breath. "Tell Carrie about Mother. Tell her about *you*."

Putting down the pen, he looked at his children for a moment then opened his arms to them, hugged them, and kissed their foreheads. "I will write everything you've said and more. I'll tell her how we miss her and . . . love her and want her back with us. And I'll tell her all about me."

Tem looked up with questioning eyes.

"Everything," Josh promised. "After she hears about me, she may not want me. She may want to stay back in Maine with her family."

Dallas looked as though she were going to cry again. "Tell her she can kiss you all she wants."

Josh laughed. "I'll be very glad to tell her that. Now, I want the two of you to go to bed. And don't look at me like that, I swear that I'll write the letter."

"Can we read it?" Tem asked.

"No you may not. This is *my* letter and it's private."

"You won't forget to tell her that—" Dallas began.

"I don't want one more order from either of you two runts. Now go to bed so I can work on this. And stop looking at me like that. I'm perfectly capable of writing a letter by myself."

The children didn't say another word as they went up the ladder to the loft, but Josh thought he heard Tem whisper, "He hasn't done anything else very well without us."

Josh resisted the urge to defend himself, but what stopped him was that what Tem had said was correct. Smiling, he looked back at the paper.

Last night he had written the letter to Carrie and now he and the children were on their way into town to mail it. This morning Tem had found his father asleep, his head on the table, a many-paged letter beneath his arm, and when Tem had tried to sneak the letter out from under his father, Josh woke.

"What time is it?" Josh asked, rubbing his stubble-covered face.

"Late. Are you going to mail the letter today?"

Josh smiled at the pleading look on his son's face. "*We* will mail it today. All three of us will go into town. The corn can't get worse than it is already. Go on, get dressed and help Dallas while I shave."

So now they were riding into town, but it was a town that they barely recognized. The last time Josh had been to Eternity—with Carrie—it had been nothing more than dirt streets, usually filled with people leaving town. Now there were rich carriages and men in suits such as he'd not seen since coming West.

"Is this Heaven?" Dallas asked from her seat in front of her father.

For a moment Josh thought he'd made a wrong turn and was in another town, Denver perhaps, but he recognized too many things for it to be anywhere else.

When they reached the mercantile store, where the post office was, Josh stopped. Tem dismounted, then Josh got down and helped Dallas to the ground. All three of them were speechless as they looked about at the activity in the usually dead little town.

"What is going on in this town? The last time I was here, this place was dead," Josh said to the storekeeper as soon as they were inside.

Before anyone could give Josh an answer—and they had plenty to say to the husband of the town heroine when he hadn't so much as been to visit her—Dallas gave a squeal.

Turning, Josh saw Carrie standing in the doorway. He couldn't believe it, but she was prettier than he remembered, and he wanted to run to her, to take her in his arms. But after the first moment when she'd seemed to look at him with love, she gave him a look as though he were something that she'd found growing on her face cream.

The next moment she had her arms open to the children, who ran to her as though it had been only yesterday that they'd seen her last. They didn't seem to feel the least bit of shyness or doubt that Carrie still loved them. Josh watched his son unabashedly kissing Carrie's firm, pink cheek and hugging her with no reserve. Dallas had, quite simply, wrapped her legs about Carrie's waist and was seated on top of her wide skirt and didn't look as though she ever meant to leave her perch.

The children and Carrie started talking at once, Choo-choo running and barking around them like an annoying gnat, and Josh felt some hurt that the children were telling her things that they hadn't told him. They told her what they had thought about and done while she was gone. Tem told Carrie that he had been searching for the Wild Girl—something that Josh hadn't known.

"And Papa has missed you every day. He wrote you a letter," Dallas said.

"Oh? Did he?" Carrie said, looking over Tem's head to Josh. "I have received nothing from him."

"We came here today to mail it," Tem said.

Carrie looked down and smiled at him. She didn't know it was possible to miss people as much as she had missed these children. Every hour of every day she had wondered what they were doing, and every time she missed them, she thought about shooting Joshua Greene. Or maybe stabbing him. Or keelhauling him. Or spending three weeks in bed with him.

When she looked back at Josh, her mouth was set in a firm line.

He walked toward her. "I'd like to talk to you," Josh said softly.

"Really? Do you want to talk to me as much as you did the day you left me at the depot?"

"Carrie, please," he said.

But Carrie wasn't going to give in to him. With Dallas still on her hip, she swept past him and went to the store clerk. "Anything for me?"

The clerk was looking from Josh to Carrie and back again as he handed Carrie a letter and one to Josh. Taking her letter, she started to move away.

Josh took Dallas and set her to the floor. "Out," was all he said to the children, and they left the store.

Carrie started to follow them, but Josh blocked her way.

"I said I want to talk to you."

"We don't always get what we want in this life, do you? I wanted to live with you and your children. Heaven only knows why I should choose a mulehead like you when you won't listen to a word I say, but I did and I lived to regret it. Now, would you please move out of my way?"

"No, Carrie. I have something to say and you're going to listen to me."

When he wouldn't move, she decided to pretend he wasn't there, so she opened her letter and began to read it. "There's nothing you can say," she said. "You discarded me once, and I won't be—" She broke off as she realized what her letter said. She looked up at Josh in horror, then the next moment, everything became black. As she fainted, Josh caught her in his arms.

Chapter Thirteen

When Carrie awoke, she was stretched out on a sofa in a pretty little parlor that she had never seen before. She started to sit up.

"Ssh, be still and drink this," Josh said, his hand behind her head, a glass of brandy to her lips. He was sitting on a chair facing her.

Carrie took a drink, then at Josh's urging, lay back down. "What happened?" she whispered. "And where am I?" Looking at him, she narrowed her eyes. "And what are *you* doing here?"

Josh smiled at her. "I'm very glad to see that you're feeling better."

"I was until I saw you," she said, but there wasn't much conviction in her voice. More than anything in the world she wanted to feel his arms around her. She had started her dress shop and she'd done well at it, but the truth was she hated it. What she really wanted was to be home with Josh and the kids.

Josh saw that gleam in her eyes. "You'd never make an actress, you know," he said in the softest, silkiest voice she'd ever heard. "Your face is too readable."

"Don't you come near me!" she said, as he bent forward and kissed the corner of her mouth.

"I plan to come a great deal closer to you than this. Carrie, my love, I came to tell you that I love you, love you with all my heart, and I'd ask you to marry me if I hadn't already had that privilege."

She wanted to punish him, wanted to play hard-to-get, wanted to make him feel as miserable as he'd made her feel. Instead, she put her hands over her face and began to cry.

Josh looked at her in consternation as he handed her a hand-kerchief. "I thought you'd like the idea." When she kept crying, he took her damp hands in his. "Carrie, there isn't someone else, is there? I thought, no, I hoped that when I saw that you were still here that maybe you had stayed because . . . well, because you . . ."

Sniffing, she looked at him. "I stayed because I didn't have enough money to get home."

At that Josh began to laugh, and Carrie joined him. As he was laughing, he took her head in his hands and began kissing her face. "Tell me there's no one else. Tell me. Oh, God, Carrie, I've missed you. I think you took my soul away when you left. How could anyone come to love somebody so much in so few days?"

He was leaning over her, almost on top of her, and kissing all of her skin that he could reach. "I fell in love with you from a photo-graph," she said softly as he kissed her lips.

Behind them, the parlor door opened. "I just wanted to see how— Oh, excuse me," said the storekeeper as he closed the door again.

Josh looked at Carrie and smiled. "We'd better get you home. I'll finish this tonight."

Carrie, dazed with happiness, began to sit up, but then put her hand to her forehead. Instantly, Josh pushed her back down and held the glass to her lips again.

"You're not well," Josh said.

Carrie smiled at him, for he made it sound as though she were about to die at any second. "I'm—" Carrie cut herself off as she saw her letter lying on a table, and she remembered what had so upset her to make her faint. Her eyes widened; she was speech-less.

Frowning, Josh picked up the letter. After Carrie had fainted and he'd carried her to the storekeeper's house, while the man's wife was passing smelling salts under Carrie's nose, Josh had read the letter. For the life of him he couldn't see what was in the letter to upset her enough to make her faint. One of her precious, per-fect, unreproachable, rich brothers was coming to visit her.

Carrie drained the brandy, then the water and lay back against the pillows. "When does he say he's coming?" she asked softly.

Josh scanned the letter. "October the twelfth." He looked up at her. "That's tomorrow."

Carrie looked as though she were going to faint again so Josh poured more brandy and handed it to her.

"Look on the bright side," Josh said, smiling. "The stage hasn't run on time in all the years it's been coming to Eternity so there's no reason to believe your brother will be here for weeks yet."

Carrie's voice was glum. "If my brother 'Ring says that he's going to be here on the twelfth of October, then that's when he'll be here. If he has to *carry* the stage, he'll be here when he says he will."

"Would you mind telling me why the impending visit of one of your perfect brothers makes you turn the color of rice powder?"

"And what do *you* know about rice powder? And, besides that, how do you know so much about corsets and other parts of women's garments? And, furthermore, I hate you for leaving me alone for six weeks and two days while you made up your mind whether you loved me or not. If I'd taken the stage back to Maine, I could have been killed by Indians by now for all you knew. I could—"

He kissed her to make her be quiet. "You are not going to get around me by starting an argument. What has upset you about your brother?"

"I shouldn't tell you anything. You've never yet told me anything about yourself." Crossing her arms over her chest, she set her mouth in a thin line.

"But then you're not a secretive person, are you?"

She glared at him. "Is that the same as not being mysterious?"

"Carrie, you are stalling."

Carrie dropped her arms. "All right," she said. "It's not just *any* of my brothers who's coming, it's 'Ring. It's my eldest brother. It's my *perfect* brother."

Josh looked at her as though she'd explained nothing. "As far as I can tell, you consider each of your brothers to be the very essence of all the manly skills."

Carrie took a deep breath. How to describe 'Ring to someone who'd never met him? " 'Ring is *actually* perfect. My other brothers, well, they have flaws." At the way Josh lifted his eyebrows in mock disbelief, Carrie made a face at him. After he'd kissed her three times, he sat back on his chair and waited for her to continue.

" 'Ring never lies, cheats, or as far as anyone can tell, has any human weaknesses. He can do anything better than anyone else. The only bad thing that can be said about him is that he's my ugliest brother." This made Carrie smile. " 'Ring isn't human."

Josh rolled his eyes. "Why should the appearance of this angel-on-earth make you unhappy?"

Carrie put her hands over her face. "I don't know. He won't like what I've done. I'm sure he's very upset if Mother has told him about the papers I had Father sign." Sniffling into Josh's handkerchief, she told him the entire story of how she'd sneaked the proxy documents into a pile of business papers her father was signing.

Josh was aghast. "And when you told your parents what you had done, they didn't just destroy the papers and lock you in your room?"

Carrie blew her nose. "Oh, no, of course not. My parents and my brothers always give me what I want. Only 'Ring . . ." She started crying again.

Josh took a few moments to digest this glimpse into her family. The spoiled baby, always given anything she wanted. If she wanted to travel alone across the country into the wilds of Colorado because she'd illegally obtained a signature on some papers so she could marry a man she'd never met, then that was all right with them. Whatever their darling wanted. And look at what had happened, Josh thought. Carrie had come out smelling like a rose. She had a man and two children who loved her as much as they loved sunshine and air.

"Why are you looking at me like that?"

"I think perhaps your brother 'Ring has the right idea about you."

"That's a horrible thing to say! You sound like 'Ring. He's always telling Father to send me to a nunnery, and we're not even Catholic."

Josh coughed to cover a laugh, but Carrie wasn't fooled. She started to get off the couch, vowing to never speak to him again.

Pulling her onto his lap, he began to kiss her. She was rigid at first, but then relaxed against him. "All right, sweetheart, tell me what you're afraid of." When she didn't answer right away, he paused in stroking her hair. "It's me, isn't it? You don't want him to know your husband is a poor farmer who can't even give you—"

"Shut up!" she screamed in his face as she got off his lap. "I am sick unto death of hearing about money. This has nothing to do with money. I have lots of money."

"Your family's money," Josh said grimly.

"For your information, I have money *I* have made." She stopped shouting at his look of disbelief. "Did you by chance happen to notice any difference in this town since the last time you were here? And you don't have to tell me you haven't been here in weeks because I know. Everyone in town has told me how you and those poor, darling children—which I might add you don't deserve—have become hermits. Tell me, did you?"

"Which question am I to answer? About the town or the children?"

She ground her teeth; he was teasing her. After turning her back to him, she looked back at him with a smug smile. "You've said that I'm useless. You said that because I can't cook and have no ambition to learn to clean, but you know what I *can* do?"

"Yes," he said in a way that made Carrie blush and lose her train of thought.

"I can . . . oh yes, I can make money."

"Out of tin? Or do you use a spell cast with frogs' tongues and such?"

"No, much simpler than that. I made it by *working*. If you laugh at me again, Joshua Greene, I swear on my family's name that I'll never go to bed with you again."

Josh didn't laugh. In fact, with such a punishment facing him, he didn't feel any inclination to laugh—none at all.

Taking her seat again, Carrie told him about opening her store. She told of staying in Eternity's nasty little hotel after he left her at the stage depot and how she'd spent two days doing nothing but writing letters. She wrote to the wife of every important man in Denver. The people of Eternity supplied her with the names and vague addresses of anyone they'd ever heard of in Denver who had any money.

"What did you write to these women?" Josh asked, genuinely curious.

Carrie told him that she'd written to the women that her brothers had recently returned from Paris and brought back far too many clothes for her to wear. And, furthermore, her brothers were such blockheads that they had brought her clothes that were in the very widest range of sizes imaginable, as well as in every color that could be found in Paris.

"A cry of help if ever I heard one," Josh said, but he was definitely not laughing at her.

She told the rest of her story quickly, telling of her first customers, of hiring seamstresses, of not allowing the idiot women to wear what was unflattering to them. "You should have seen them. Two-hundred-pound women in white chiffon ruffles and thin, bosomless women in black. I began to supplement the fronts of the gowns with cotton. You know, 'For what God has,' etc., etc."

"No, I don't think I do know."

"'For what God has forgotten, He supplied cotton,'" Carrie quoted.

Josh didn't laugh, but he had to drink brandy to keep from doing so. "What is the name of this shop?"

"Paris in the Desert."

Josh's mouthful of brandy went spewing out across Carrie.

After brushing the front of herself off, she narrowed her eyes at him. "Are you laughing at me?"

"No, my love, not at all. Paris in the Desert is an excellent choice of name. It goes with Choo-choo very well."

She was looking at him hard, but she couldn't tell if he was being serious or not. She finished her story by telling how the increasing business of her shop had helped the economy of the entire town.

When she'd finished, she looked at Josh in triumph. She was expecting praise from him, but instead, he looked gloomy.

"What is wrong now? Haven't I proven to you that I'm not useless?"

"You can even earn money," he said miserably. "What's your brother going to say to your being married to a man who can't seem to earn a decent living? A man who can't support his wife?"

"My brother doesn't expect me to marry for money. His wife had no great fortune when he met her so why does my husband have to be rich?" Carrie thought that sometimes talking to Josh was like talking to a block of wood.

"You don't understand. But I imagine your brother will. Isn't that why you're worried about his visit?"

"No. 'Ring will have a great deal to say about my . . . well, he'll see the way I got Father to sign the papers as dishonest.

Then there's the possibility that our marriage isn't quite legal because Father didn't know what he was signing and I'm not twenty-one yet. And 'Ring will be upset about you and me living together for a few days then my living in town all alone, unprotected, uncared for, while my husband stays at his farm. 'Ring is an old-fashioned man who believes that a man and wife should live together."

Josh smiled. He couldn't make her understand what it meant to a man to not be able to support his wife, but at the same time he knew he was testing her. In three years he could leave the farm, and when he could get away from the farm, he could again earn his own living.

He pulled Carrie back onto his lap. "If your brother is worried about our not being married properly, then we'll just have to get married again. I'm sorry I missed the first one, but this time we can have a wedding night." Holding her face in his hand, he kissed her. "I am beginning to think that you really do love me. If you can love me as I am now, perhaps you can love me later."

"What does that mean?" After one look at his face, she turned away in disgust. "Oh, yes, secrets again. When are you going to love me enough to tell me all about yourself?"

"As a matter of fact, I already have," Josh said as he reached into his coat pocket and pulled out the letter he had spent the night writing. As he withdrew it, the letter that had come in the mail to him fell to the floor, and Carrie picked it up. "I spent all night last night writing this to you," he said. "I was going to send it to Maine."

Carrie reached out to take it, but he pulled it back.

"I can tell you everything in there now."

"I'd like to read it. Do you make undying declarations of love to me in the letter?"

"Yes," he said, his eyes soft. "What is that?"

Looking down at the letter she held, she saw that it had no return address. "It's addressed to you."

Teasingly, Josh put the letter he'd written to her on a table out of her reach. "Perhaps I'd better read my own mail first. Maybe it's from a female admirer." Still smiling, he ran the letter under his nose.

Josh had meant to tease Carrie, but as he smelled the letter, he turned pale.

"Josh, are you all right?"

More color left his face. Getting off his lap, Carrie went to refill his brandy glass. At this rate, both of them were going to be drunk.

After Josh put the brandy back in one gulp, he held out the glass for her to refill, and after she'd done so, he downed that too before he opened the letter with trembling hands.

He took only seconds to read it. Carrie had never seen a man faint before, but she thought she was seeing one now. Picking up his arm, she put it around her shoulders and helped him to the couch.

"Josh!" she cried, beginning to shake him. Smelling salts were on the table, and she held them under his nose.

He turned his head away so he was facing the couch back.

"Josh, what's wrong?" He didn't answer her, but just kept staring at the back of the couch, looking as though his life were over.

Picking up the letter from where it had fallen to the floor, Carrie read it.

My Darling Joshua,
  Just one more paper to sign, then you are free. I shall bring it to you on the thirteenth of October. How are our dear, dear children?

                                                    With all my love,
                                                    Nora

P.S. Won't you reconsider, or is the life of a farmer agreeing with you?

When Carrie finished reading the letter—three times—she too was trembling. "Who—" She cleared her throat. "Who is Nora?"

Very slowly, Josh turned toward her, then sat up. "It seems that she is still my wife," he said softly.

Gaping at him, Carrie stood stock still. Her family and others had told her that life was difficult, but she'd never believed them. Whenever anyone told her that life was hard, she'd told them that life was what you made of it. She said that people either chose to be happy or sad, and she always had examples of poor people who had one misfortune after another in their families yet they were happy, and others who were rich and had everything to be glad about yet were miserable. One day, when Carrie was about sixteen and was spouting this great wisdom, her mother had told her that happy people had never really truly been in love. She said that love was about two thirds joy and one third the most awful pain on earth. The pain of love beat death all to bits. At the time, Carrie thought her mother was not very bright, but now she understood exactly what her mother meant.

Carrie straightened her shoulders. "How opportune for me. My brother is coming tomorrow, and he can take me back to Warbrooke with him."

Josh was off the couch in seconds, his hands on her shoulders. "I thought the divorce was final. I thought it was final a year ago. God knows I paid enough to get rid of her!"

Carrie gave him a cold look. "And I thought you were a widower. Of course you never thought enough of me to tell me any different. Would you get out of my way? I need to get back to my shop." She looked him up and down. "Not all of us are business failures, you know."

At that Josh dropped his hands from her shoulders, because at the moment he couldn't think of anything else to say. Stepping back, he allowed her to leave the room.

Chapter Fourteen

Looking in the mirror, Carrie pinched her cheeks, wishing she could put some of the redness from her nose on her cheeks. She dabbed more powder on her nose. 'Ring wasn't going to like her wearing powder, and he wasn't going to like her red eyes, either. But most of all, he wasn't going to like what she had to tell him. He was going to be angry at her.

Carrie could see tears forming in her eyes again. How much water could a body excrete? She'd cried all night and all morning.

After she'd left Josh yesterday, she'd gone back to her shop, planning to lose herself in her work. That's what her brothers always did when they were upset about something, but it hadn't worked for Carrie. Maybe it was that running a shipping company was more important than choosing dresses for women, but Carrie hadn't been able to think of anything except that her husband was married to someone else. She hadn't even known that his wife was still alive. He may love her, but he didn't trust her enough to tell her anything about himself.

Two hours after she'd left Josh yesterday, Tem and Dallas had come to her shop and wanted to see her. Carrie had tried to dry her eyes so the children wouldn't see that she'd been crying, but they had noticed immediately.

Tem asked her if she'd read their father's letter. Thinking only of the letter from Nora, Carrie said that she had indeed read it, and because of the letter, she was going to have to leave Colorado forever.

When the children left her store, they had seemed like old people, tired, weary old people who had seen too much misery in their lives.

After the children had gone, Carrie went to the tiny house she rented at the back of her store and cried herself into a fitful sleep. As for the women in her store, those who worked for her and her customers, she couldn't have cared less.

Now, this morning, she had to meet her brother's stage, and the last person on earth she wanted to see was her brother 'Ring. Maybe he wouldn't say, I told you so, but she'd see it in his eyes. He'd always thought she was flighty and too indulged by her family, and she was proving him right.

When Carrie put her bonnet on, she didn't even bother to tie the ribbon in a jaunty little bow as she usually did, for she didn't really care what she looked like.

When she walked to the depot, she didn't look at the people who called hello to her or answer them. All she wanted to do was get this over with, to see her brother and have him arrange for her to go back to Maine. Where I'll once again be the baby of the family, she thought. The little girl they all think of as their toy, a place where I'll no longer have my own little family or a man who loves just me. Of course she hadn't had that when she thought she did.

She arrived at the depot thirty minutes before the time the stage was due, and the depot manager laughed when he saw her. "That stage ain't been on time in years and it ain't gonna be today. I've heard they had Indian trouble. Probably be days before it's here."

Carrie didn't even look at him. "My brother will see that it's here on time," she said tiredly as she sat down on the bench.

This proclamation set the man into howls of laughter, and he left the building, no doubt to tell his story to the rest of the townspeople.

He wasn't out of the door two minutes before Josh entered the building.

"My goodness," Carrie said, "if it isn't Nora's husband." She turned away to look at the wall.

Sitting down by her, Josh took her hand in his, but Carrie snatched it away.

He grabbed her shoulders and turned her to face him. "Carrie,

I've learned something from you: You never admit defeat. Never."

"Sometimes you have to." She tried to pull away from him, but he wouldn't let her go.

"I didn't tell you about Nora because I thought she was out of my life. It's that simple. You read the letter. I thought the divorce was final, because I thought all the papers were signed. I thought that I had given her enough that even she was satisfied."

"What else did you give her? All of your love?"

"Nora didn't want love. She wanted money, so I gave her every penny I had. And when I'd sold everything, including my clothes, in order to get rid of her and get my children, she still wanted more."

"She wanted you," Carrie said.

Josh smiled at her. "You are the only woman who wants me. You want me in spite of my bad temper, in spite of my hopelessness at farming. You want me and my children and whatever else I have, not what I can give you—except maybe enough love to fill the earth."

"Shut up," she said softly, because she'd started crying again.

"Carrie, I'm sorry about everything that's happened. I'm sorry for misjudging you and thinking you were an idiot." He smiled at her look of protest. "Can you blame me? You're much too pretty for any man to think you have a brain. And it's been my experience that pretty girls think only of themselves."

"Is your wife pretty?"

"My ex-wife. No, Nora's not exactly pretty." He untied the ribbon of her bonnet under her chin and retied it so the bow was nice. "I don't love Nora. I'm not sure I ever did."

"But she's the mother of your children."

"I didn't hate her."

At that Carrie started to get up, but he pulled her back to the seat. "What matters is now. I love you and I want you to marry me and I want you to stay with me and the kids. Forever. That's what you've wanted since you first saw us, isn't it?"

Carrie's eyes were betraying her again. "I don't think I like you. You lied to me."

"I didn't lie. I thought the divorce was final. The letter yesterday was as much a shock to me as it was to you."

When she didn't say anything, he pulled her into his arms, but it took her a moment to relax against him. "My brother . . ."

He stroked her hair. "Leave your brother to me."

"You don't know him. He'll be very upset when he hears that I'm married to a married man."

"Not to mention that you're going to have his baby," Josh said softly.

Carrie didn't breathe for a moment. She didn't need to ask how he'd found out, since she'd fainted three times in the last week and she had an idea that half of the town was talking about why she'd fainted. "Do you want me for the baby?"

"Oh, yes, of course. The baby is the only reason I want you. Didn't you realize that I'm collecting kids? I do so well with them. In my company, all children laugh their lives away. It couldn't possibly be that I want you because the mere thought of going on living without you makes me miserable. Carrie," he whispered, "please don't leave me."

She hugged him back then, and he kissed her, kissed her softly and with yearning.

"When your brother gets here, whenever the stage arrives, to-day or tomorrow or whenever—" He put his fingertip over her lips to keep her from speaking. "You leave everything to me. I'll make him think we're the happiest couple in the world and that nothing has ever been wrong between us. Who knows, maybe the stage won't arrive for three days yet. By that time Nora will have come and gone, we'll have been married, and everything will be fine—except for my corn crop."

"My brother won't care about your wormy old corn if I'm happy and—" She looked at the watch pinned to her bosom. "The stage is due in ten minutes. It will be here in ten minutes, and my brother will be on it."

Josh gave her a patronizing smile. "All right then, if he is, I'll deal with him. If he wants us to remarry, then we'll stall him until Nora gives me the paper and my divorce is final. Twenty-four hours at the most." He put his hand under her chin so she looked up at him. "Can you forgive me? About Nora? I didn't want to tell you that I'd failed at my first marriage. You can't blame me for that, can you? I figure the corn made me look enough like a failure."

"You're not a failure."

He kissed her. "You don't know what that means to me. For the first time since I got saddled with that damned farm, when I look in your eyes, I don't feel like a failure."

"I knew you needed me."

"I was too stupid to know it," he said and bent to kiss her again, but Carrie's head came up as she listened.

"That's the stage." Disentangling herself from him, she got up and went outside.

Sitting where he was on the bench, Josh smiled at her fondly. She was so trusting, so believing in other people, and now she honestly believed that the stage was going to arrive on the dot of four o'clock.

When the sound of the approaching wagon came closer, Josh went outside. Carrie was standing at the end of the platform, where she could see everything should the stage indeed arrive.

Josh looked toward the direction of the noise, and coming toward them was indeed what looked like a stagecoach. He glanced down at Carrie's watch. "They'll never make it. It's two minutes to four, and they're a long way off yet."

" 'Ring will make it," Carrie said without a great deal of interest.

By this time most of the citizenry of Eternity was leaving the shops and streets to see what looked like the phenomenon of the stage being on time. Looking over Carrie's head, Josh watched with growing fascination as the driver cracked his whip over his horses. He could see the man standing in the box now, could hear him shouting to the horses, and could almost hear the deep breathing of the horses as they ran full gallop toward the platform at the stage depot. Usually, the driver, almost always drunk, ambled into town at little more than a walk, not caring when he arrived.

"I think they're going to make it," Josh said under his breath.

"Yes, of course," Carrie answered. "Four o'clock on the dot."

Josh's eyes widened in disbelief as the stage drew into sight. If he wasn't mistaken, those were arrows sticking out of the roof. Looking about at the ever-increasing crowd of people, he saw that they were pointing.

At four o'clock exactly, precisely, on the nose, the big stagecoach came screeching to a halt beside the depot platform. There were not only arrows sticking out of the roof, there were bullet holes all over one side of the coach. Tied to the back of the stage was a very fine riding horse.

"What happened?" everyone yelled at the driver at once.

Josh didn't think he'd ever seen a more tired-looking man than that driver. He was usually drunk, but today he was too sober, for there were black circles under his eyes, he hadn't shaved in a week, and the left corner of his mouth was twitching.

"What didn't happen?" the driver said as he unsteadily got down from the box. "We was attacked by thieves; some drunk cowboys was being chased by Indians, and the whole kit and caboodle attacked us. We run into a herd of stampeding buffalo. There ain't nothin' that didn't happen to us."

The driver was now beginning to enjoy his audience, and he warmed to his story. "But we got a crazy man on board. Name of Montgomery."

Carrie gave Josh an I-told-you-so look.

The driver continued. "That man said he had a schedule to keep, said he'd set a date and he meant to be in Eternity on that date. I tell you, the man is crazy. We was travelin' about a hundred miles an hour, give or take a bit, and he climbed out of the coach window, got on his horse, and singlehandedly kept them buffaloes off a the coach. He wouldn't let me slow down for him to get back inside, either. When them cowboys attacked us, he shot their hats off. The Indians thought that was so funny they quit shootin' at us. I tell you, the man is crazy."

By this time the driver had dismounted, pulled the steps down, and opened the door to the coach. At long last, the passengers began to disembark. They were a mess: dirty, frightened looking, the women in tears. They looked as though they'd been placed inside a small barrel and dragged from Maine to Colorado.

The two women, shaking, their clothes torn, fell from the coach into the arms of townspeople. One woman's hairpiece had fallen over her ear, giving her a lumpy-looking head.

Three men got out of the coach, and they didn't look any less frightened than the women. One man had a bloody cut in his coat sleeve, another had three holes in his hat. The third man tried to light a cigar, but his hand shook so badly he couldn't get the match to the tip of the cigar. When one of the townspeople walked up to him with an offer of help, he said, "I need a drink."

"Which one is he?" Josh asked Carrie, surprised that she wasn't going forward to greet any of the men. She didn't answer him, but kept looking at the stage.

After the others were off, another man stepped down. He was tall, over six feet, well built, and extremely handsome, and he was wearing a black suit that Josh knew had cost a great deal. Instead of being nervous and frightened as the other people were, this man looked rested and utterly calm, as though he'd just returned from a Sunday stroll instead of the ordeal of the stage, and there wasn't so much as a hint of dust on him.

As Josh watched, the man stepped onto the platform and smiled at the people around him. One of the women who had been on the stage looked at him and started crying, burying her face in the shoulder of an older woman. The man reached into his inside coat pocket, withdrew a slim cigar, and, with a very steady hand, struck a match and lit it. As he took a deep draw, he seemed to be oblivious to the way a hundred or so townspeople were staring at him in fascination, then flicked an imaginary speck of dust off his shoulder.

"Guess which one is 'Ring?" Carrie said in a heavy voice.

Reassuringly, Josh slipped his hand into hers.

As though he'd known all along that they were there, 'Ring turned toward his sister.

"Hello, sweetheart," he said quietly, and Carrie ran to him.

'Ring caught his little sister in his strong arms and hugged her fiercely while the townspeople watched. If this man, this half-monster, half-hero was known by Carrie, then they were ready to accept him. After all, Carrie was providing jobs for them.

"Let me look at you," 'Ring said, setting her down. He was probably twice as big as she was, and one of his big hands caressed her cheek.

Josh had never experienced jealousy before. He'd always believed in people living their own lives, and he'd never tried to tell anyone, man, woman, or child, what they should do. But then Josh knew he'd never really been in love before. Right now he couldn't stand this man touching Carrie, and it didn't matter that he was her brother.

Moving next to Carrie, he folded her arm in his in a way of ownership.

Carrie looked at her husband. 'Ring was a bit taller than Josh, but he wasn't built better than Josh, and Carrie thought that Josh was about a thousand times handsomer than her brother.

'Ring looked at the two of them, at the way Josh held Carrie's arm, at the way Josh's mouth was set, as though he were ready to do battle with 'Ring if 'Ring so much as touched a hair on Carrie's head again. He saw the way Carrie's eyes looked at Josh, as though he were the bravest, finest man in the world, and 'Ring knew all that he'd wanted to know. He'd traveled all the way from Maine to see if his sister loved this man and if he loved her, and now he had his answer. For his part, he could have stepped back on the stage and gone home to his own wife and children.

'Ring smiled at his little sister, and Carrie gave him a tremulous smile in return. It was that smile that let 'Ring know that something was wrong, for Carrie had never been able to keep a secret. He'd tried his best to teach her to play poker, but when she had a good hand, she was delighted and showed it. But 'Ring had an idea that nothing serious was wrong. After all, what was important was that the two of them loved each other, and he could see that they did. They were standing together as though they thought 'Ring was an evil force who was going to try to break them apart.

"Let me introduce myself," Josh said, extending his hand to 'Ring. "Joshua Greene."

As 'Ring shook his brother-in-law's hand, he realized that he'd seen him before, but couldn't remember where. "Have we met before?"

"I'm sure we haven't," Josh said smoothly.

He can play poker, 'Ring thought. You'd never know what cards this man held. Not by the merest flicker of his eyes would he give away a secret. He'd let people know only what he wanted them to know.

"Perhaps not," 'Ring said in a tone that he hoped was as smooth, but he doubted that it was. "Is there somewhere I can get a bath?" 'Ring asked as he turned to Carrie.

"Of course. I have reserved you a room at the hotel, but it's not what you're used to."

'Ring would have kissed his sister's cheek and laughed at her nervousness, but Josh was hovering over her like a bird of prey. 'Ring wondered if he acted in the same proprietary way with his own wife.

"I'm sure that I'll manage," 'Ring said. "Perhaps this evening we could dine together, and tomorrow I'd like to see these children of yours."

Carrie's stomach was beginning to hurt. She couldn't stand the suspense any longer. "Why are you here, 'Ring? I'm not going back no matter what you say."

'Ring wouldn't have thought it possible, but Josh moved closer to her. "Is that what you thought? That I came all the way out here to make you go back with me?"

"I thought maybe because of the papers, well, you know . . ."

"The ones you tricked Father into signing?"

Carrie looked at her shoe.

'Ring looked at Josh. Where had he seen the man before? "What an ogre you must think me. I came because, yes, your marriage was illegal, but Mother wanted to know if you're happy. She also sent her own wedding dress to you and asks that you be remarried in it, and she wants a photograph of her daughter and new son-in-law. I hoped there would be no problems with that so I took the liberty of arranging for the ceremony to take place tomorrow afternoon. I chose pink roses for flowers. I hope that's all right. I do need to return home as soon as possible."

"Yes," Carrie said hesitantly. "I think that's possible."

"Good," 'Ring said, picking up his bag the driver had thrown from the top of the coach. "Shall we go?" he asked, sweeping his arm aside so Carrie could lead him to the hotel.

"I'll say this for him," Josh said. "The man's got—"

"Don't say it," Carrie groaned. "He's got my life in his hands is what he's got. Knowing 'Ring he has power of attorney from my father, and he is my legal guardian. I sure hope your—" she swallowed, "your wife shows up early tomorrow so we can get married when 'Ring thinks we should."

Chapter Fifteen

"**H**e's going to make me go back with him," Carrie said gloomily. She and Josh were in 'Ring's hotel room, waiting while 'Ring bathed.

"Would you mind not saying that again? It's beginning to bother me. What do you think he's going to do? Wrap you in a blanket and kidnap you? That's what he'll have to do if he means to take you away from me, and even at that, I'd come after you."

Sitting on the sofa, Carrie looked at the worn, dusty carpet. "We just have to make him believe everything is all right. We can't let him know there are any problems between us."

"There aren't any problems between us."

Carrie glared at him. "Merely that you have a wife and I am carrying a child conceived in sin. You don't know 'Ring as I do. He has a high moral character, and he would be horrified if he found out the truth."

Josh groaned. "I think you've misjudged your brother. I think he's all too human."

"Ha! If 'Ring has any human emotions, he keeps them hidden."

Josh laughed at that in an arrogant way. "The man doesn't hide his emotions very well at all. He dotes on you. It's my guess that he may be the softest of your brothers when it comes to you. Your brother would give you anything you wanted; he'd do anything for you. If you wanted to marry a chimney sweep, he'd be happy for you."

"You don't know anything!" Carrie snapped. " 'Ring is—"

"I am what, my dear sister?" 'Ring asked as he entered the

room. He was freshly bathed and had on a perfectly pressed dinner suit, while she and Josh looked rumpled and dusty.

"You are my very dearest brother," Carrie said, standing on tiptoe to kiss his freshly shaved cheek.

" *'A goodly apple rotten at the heart. O, what a goodly outside falsehood hath!' '*" 'Ring quoted.

"What is that?"

"Shakespeare, which you'd know if you'd bothered to finish school. Shall we go down to dinner?"

Carrie and Josh led the way, 'Ring behind them. Last night Carrie had sent one of her employees to the hotel to arrange the best that the Eternity Hotel had to offer, and now Carrie wondered what it was going to be.

A table for three had been set in a windowed alcove of the dining room, and if Carrie had not been so nervous, she would have laughed at what she saw. Instead of the waiters wearing their usual clothes—by the look of them, what they'd dragged from under their beds—tonight they were wearing suits, most of them, by the look of the fit, borrowed. They were carrying napkins over their arms in the French manner, except that the napkins were none too clean and hadn't been ironed.

As soon as they were seated, the waiter picked up 'Ring's wine glass, started to pour him some wine, saw that there was something in the glass, blew it out, then poured the wine. Carrie could see pieces of cork floating on the top of the wine and little flaky bits in the bottom of the glass. She held her breath while 'Ring took a sip.

She expected him to do what he did at home: declare the vintage unfit to drink.

Instead, he smiled at the waiter. " *'Good wine is a good familiar creature if it be well used.' '*"

The waiter, who helped in the stables when no one was staying at the hotel, had no idea what 'Ring was saying, but he went away smiling. Soon bowl after bowl of food was placed on the table before them.

Carrie pushed her food around her plate.

"What do you do for a living, Mr. Greene?" 'Ring asked.

Looking at Josh, Carrie held her breath. It was one thing to tell Josh that her brother wouldn't care that Josh had no money, but then again, men were odd about money. She hoped Josh would have sense enough to, well, make his farm sound a bit better than it was.

"I raise worms," Josh said. "Fields of them."

Carrie gave a sound very much like a whimper.

"I see," 'Ring said. "Anything else?"

"A few beetles, a rather nice crop of weeds, but corn worms are my specialty. Nice fat green ones. They eat every ear of corn I grow."

" *'O thou weed, who art so lovely fair and smell'st so sweet that the sense aches at thee, would thou hadst ne'er been born!'* " 'Ring said.

Carrie ignored 'Ring's poetry spouting. " 'Ring, it's not true that Josh grows only weeds and worms, at least it's not the whole truth. Josh can do many things very well."

Both men turned to her, both of them with identical looks of interest on their faces.

"Pray tell me what I can do, my dear," Josh said.

Carrie narrowed her eyes at him. He was taking this as a joke. When they were dealing with Josh's brother it had been serious business, but now that her own somewhat difficult brother was here it could be treated like a joke. "He loves his children very much and he loves me and I love him."

Josh smiled at 'Ring. "She has no reason to love me, she just does."

'Ring smiled back. " *'I have no other but a woman's reason: I think him so, because I think him so.'* "

"Exactly," Josh said and seemed extremely pleased with 'Ring. "More of this fine brew, brother-in-law?"

'Ring held his glass aloft. " *'O thou invisible spirit of wine! If thou hast no name to be known by, let us call thee devil!'* "

"What is wrong with you, 'Ring!" Carrie snapped. "Can't you say anything but that awful poetry?"

'Ring gave an exaggerated look of self-pity. " *'She speaks poniards, and every word stabs: if her breath were as terrible as her terminations, there were no living near her; she would infect to the north star.'* "

"Stop it!" Carrie said and banged her fist on the table. "What in the world is wrong with you?"

'Ring shook his head a bit, as though to clear it. "I don't know. Ever since I stepped off the stage, every Shakespearian phrase I've ever heard has been running through my head. In the bath I was trying to do all of Hamlet."

"You can do them at home," she said fiercely. "Right now I'd like to spend time with you and my husband and not with some two-bit stage player."

'Ring opened his mouth, looked as though he were going to quote something again, but closed it. Then, with a serious look, he said, "You were telling me about your husband. About the worms, I believe."

"And the weeds," Josh added.

Carrie sat across the table and looked at both of them. She had no idea what was going on, but she felt like getting up and leaving them there alone. They both wore the same smug, self-satisfied look that only men can put on, as though they were superior merely because they had been born men.

Reaching across the table, 'Ring squeezed his sister's hand. "I apologize. I think I have my poetry under control now. Tell me about yourself and what you've been doing."

"I was telling you about Josh. About his farm." For all that she'd said that 'Ring wouldn't care about Josh's farm, the truth was she was a bit worried that 'Ring would find the place a little bit ragged. "And about Josh." Her face lit up. "Josh can read a story aloud as well as Maddie can sing."

'Ring looked at Josh with new respect. "Can you now? That's saying a great deal."

"Who is Maddie?" Josh asked.

"She's 'Ring's wife and to the world she's known as LaReina."

It was Josh's turn to look at 'Ring with respect, for LaReina was one of the world's greatest opera singers. "My congratulations on your choice and on the honor of having such a woman for a wife. I've heard her sing many times. In Paris and Vienna and Rome. I've gone to hear her whenever possible."

"I didn't know you'd been to all of those places," Carrie said, but Josh ignored her.

"Thank you," 'Ring said. "She's a wonderful woman and—" He broke off as his eyes widened. "You can *read* aloud . . . You're—"

With one very swift gesture, Josh flung his arm out and knocked 'Ring's wine glass over, effectively stopping 'Ring from saying what he'd started to. As Carrie was looking at the mess on the table, she missed seeing the way her husband looked at 'Ring with eyes that begged him to say no more.

After Carrie finished trying to mop up the spilled wine, she didn't know what had happened, but she knew that something had. It was as though both men had joined some secret club that excluded her. It was as though, in the space of a few seconds, they had become the best of friends. For the rest of the long dinner, they talked to each other, only now and then acknowledging Carrie's presence. They talked of all the cities they had seen, plays they had attended, and 'Ring's wife's singing. They talked of people they both knew, of hotels and food and wine.

Carrie sat silent through the meal, ignored and smoldering at the way they treated her: as though she were much too young and untraveled to be of interest to them.

At long last the two men decided it was time to retire. "I shall see both of you tomorrow," 'Ring said. "Shall we say at your farm at noon? The wedding is set for five o'clock. That will give me time to meet these children of yours. Tell me," he said to Josh, "are they anything like you?"

Carrie felt that her brother was asking Josh a question that had a different meaning from what she was hearing.

"They are like me with one exception: They have more talent."

That seemed to amuse 'Ring a great deal.

By the time she and Josh said goodnight to 'Ring, Carrie wasn't speaking to either man.

As Josh took her arm, he was musing over something to himself and didn't seem to realize that Carrie was angry at him. Nor did he seem to notice that she wasn't speaking to him.

"I brought Hiram's wagon," he said. "It's at the stables. I assume you are going home with me."

Carrie's first thought was to tell him that she was staying at her shop in town, but she wanted to see the children again, and she wanted to tell them that she was staying in Eternity after all. She might never speak to their father again, but she was going to marry him tomorrow—if his *wife* gave him a divorce, that is.

Josh went to the stables, got the wagon, helped her onto the seat, then talked to her all the way home. He told her what a fine fellow her brother was, how educated, how wise, how cultured.

"I guess that's because he knows all the people *you* know, has been to all the places *you* have been. Places that I didn't even know you'd seen." Carrie's voice rang with sarcasm.

Josh didn't seem to hear her derision, but kept on talking about 'Ring and what a great guy he was. A man's man. "A man like him can handle a horse, a gun, a line of Shakespeare, and a woman all at once."

At that particular line, Carrie said she thought she was going to throw up.

"Is it the baby?" Josh asked, concerned, starting to halt the horses.

"No, it's you."

Smiling, he flicked the reins of the horses.

Before going to Josh's house, they stopped at Hiram's big, sturdy, perfectly clean, perfectly dull farmhouse—not a flower in sight—to pick up the children. Carrie stayed on the wagon while Josh went in to get them, carrying a sleeping Dallas in his arms, a drowsy Tem following. Carrie took Dallas, and Tem climbed onto the seat, snuggling against Carrie.

"Are you going to stay or leave?" Tem asked, yawning.

"Stay," Carrie answered.

Tem nodded as though to acknowledge that this was the latest decision, but that it might change in the next minute.

At home Josh took the children up the ladder to the loft, then came back down to the first floor. Yawning, he walked to the bedroom.

Carrie met him at the door. "What are you doing?"

"Going to bed."

"Not in this room, you're not," she said firmly.

Josh sighed. "Carrie, love, this is ridiculous. I'm tired and I don't want to have to share that tiny bed with Dallas. Have pity on me."

"You are *not* spending the night with me. You and I aren't married. In fact, legally, you are married to another woman. If you and I slept together, we'd be committing adultery."

"But I was married to her before when we spent the night together."

"But then I didn't know anything."

Moving closer to her, the sleepy look left his eyes, and his voice lowered to a silky tone of seduction. "Carrie, my love, I just want a place to sleep. You can't deny a man that, can you?"

"Are you tired from raising worms all day or from talking to my brother and ignoring me all evening?"

"Carrie, honey," he said, pleading and reaching out to caress her cheek.

"Don't you touch me!" she said and slammed the bedroom door in his face.

Upstairs, when Josh climbed in the narrow bed with his daughter, Dallas sleepily said, "I *told* you Carrie wanted the big bed by herself."

The next morning Carrie was sound asleep when Josh allowed the children in the room to wake her up. But instead of jumping on the bed as they usually did, they climbed in with her and Choo-choo, and soon all of them were sleeping together in a heap.

Josh stood in the doorway drinking a cup of the world's worst coffee and looked at his family with love—well, maybe he didn't love the dog, but even that creature was growing on him.

Last night at dinner, contrary to what Carrie thought, he had been very aware of her anger. He probably shouldn't have indulged himself so, but her jealousy had felt so very good. He'd had women jealous when he'd given his attention to others, but those women had meant nothing to him. Those women had not loved him, not loved the man, but had loved who they thought he was. Several women in his past had tried to get to Josh through his children, but his children were very astute: They had universally hated all the women.

But now, looking at Carrie and the kids, not being able to tell where one person began and the other ended, he knew how very much he loved her. And she was right: He and his children needed her.

He smiled at the lot of them. Everything was going to be all right now. He knew it. All he had to do was deal with Nora, and then he'd be free.

As though thinking of her conjured her, Choo-choo jumped out from under the covers and began to bark frantically. Outside was the sound of an approaching carriage, and as Josh turned toward the front door, he grimaced. It couldn't be Nora already, could it?

At Choo-choo's bark, Carrie came awake slowly, and for the first few moments she wasn't sure where she was.

Tem raised his head. "Who's that?" They could hear the carriage as it stopped in front of the house; a man was yelling at the horses.

"I hope it isn't Uncle Hiram," Dallas said. "We'll tell him Carrie is here, and he'll be afraid and run away."

Laughing, Carrie began to tickle the child, while Tem went outside, but came back in seconds, his face pale. "It's Mother," he whispered.

Carrie sat up straight in bed. She had thought of this woman as Josh's wife, but not as the children's mother. Would they be so glad to see her that they'd forget about her, Carrie? Carrie chastised herself for even thinking such a terrible thought. This woman was the children's mother, and of course they loved her.

"Go on, go see her," Carrie urged.

But Dallas sat down on Carrie's lap, while Tem stayed by the door.

At that moment the front door to the house burst open, and even though Carrie couldn't see the woman, she could feel her presence, for the woman's spirit seemed to fill the little house.

"Where are they?" she called. "Where are my darling babies?"

Before Carrie could say anything, before she could tell Tem to close the bedroom door so the woman wouldn't see her sitting in bed with her hair mussed and wearing only a nightgown, Nora swept into the room.

She was large. She was tall and big boned and had a dramatically colored face: white skin, dark eyes, red lips, black hair. She wore an expensive dress of black and red brocade, her waist corseted down to what Carrie's practiced eye knew was no more than twenty inches. Above her waist was a bosom that most women would have given a few, or more, years of their lives to possess. Josh had said that his wife wasn't exactly pretty. No, this woman wasn't pretty. What she was, was beautiful. Stunning. A woman to make men stop in their tracks. A woman to inspire poems and songs written about her.

As Carrie was staring at this woman in speechless wonder, Tem had moved closer to her, and she put her arm around him as she hugged Dallas on her lap. For once, even Choo-choo was quiet.

"My goodness, what a very . . . domestic scene. Tell me, Josh, do all your new . . . ladies sleep with you *and* our children?"

Carrie wanted to defend herself, but what could she say, that she was this woman's husband's wife?

The children just looked at their mother silently.

"Come, darlings, and give your mother a kiss."

Obediently, silently, the children went to their mother. Bending, Nora allowed each child in turn to kiss her lovely cheek. But she didn't hug the children or touch them in any other way.

"And who is your little friend?" Nora asked Tem, nodding to Carrie.

"She's our new . . . I mean she and Papa are married."

"Are they? How very interesting." Turning, she looked at Josh who was standing behind her. "Darling, it looks as though you have *two* wives. I may not know a great deal about the law, but I don't think that's legal."

"Perhaps we should allow Carrie to get dressed," Josh said as he led his beautiful, ravishing, divine wife from the room.

Carrie dressed in her riding clothes, and when she was ready, she went into the parlor. Josh and his wife were sitting at the table, heads bent close together.

Pulling away, Nora looked Carrie up and down in appraisal. "Aren't you the cutest little thing? She's darling, Josh, wherever did you find her?"

"In the tadpole pond," Carrie said through her teeth and started toward the front door.

Josh caught her, held her arms to her sides, and led her back to the table. Still holding her, he pushed her onto the chair. "Tem!" he snapped. "Get Carrie some coffee."

When he'd placed the coffee before Carrie, Josh said, "Carrie, my love, my one and only love, I'd like you to meet Nora."

"Your wife," Carrie said flatly and tried to get up, but Josh held her shoulders.

"Why Joshua, darling, I do believe the little thing is angry at you. You did tell her about me, didn't you?"

"And how could I have accurately described you?" Josh's voice dripped acid.

Nora seemed to take that as a compliment as she gave a suggestive little laugh. "Of course you couldn't describe me, darling, but many men have tried." She turned back to Carrie. "She looks awfully small to be on the stage."

"She isn't on the stage," Josh snapped. "She's a wife and mother and nothing else."

"How very . . . interesting," Nora said, making no doubt as to what she thought of Carrie's life's work.

"I can run a shop," Carrie snapped, because Josh made her

sound as though she stood over a laundry tub all day and hadn't a thought except how clean her floors were.

"A shop?" Nora said, one eyebrow raised.

"She buys dresses," Josh supplied, again making Carrie sound insignificant.

Carrie started to get up, but Josh held her down.

"Nora, just give me the paper to sign and get out of here. There's nothing here for you."

At that Nora began to cry rather prettily into a lace handkerchief. "Josh, how could you be so unkind to me? I only came as an excuse to see my children once more. I miss them so much. I miss the sound of their footsteps in the night. I even miss the way Dallas used to wake up with bad dreams. I miss their voices. I miss—" She was crying too hard to go on.

In spite of herself, Carrie stretched her hand across the table to take Nora's. Carrie had known the children only a short time, but she thought she'd die if she had to leave them. What must this woman be feeling to have her children taken from her? And why had Josh done something so cruel to a woman he'd once loved?

Josh caught Carrie's hand before she could touch Nora.

"Your timing is off," Josh said. "You're getting lazy."

To Carrie's consternation, Nora's face changed from misery to a smile in an instant. "But, darling, I don't have you to rehearse with. How can I be good without the Great Templeton beside me?"

Carrie turned to look up at Josh, but he was looking at Nora.

"I want the paper," Josh said.

Nora leaned forward, her arms propped on the table. Her gown was very low cut, not what any decent woman would wear before sundown, and it was obvious that she had no need to supplement her bosom with cotton. "I lost it, darling," she purred. "I lost it down the front of my gown."

Looking up at Josh, Carrie saw that he was looking down the front of his wife's dress as though he meant to search for the paper. Carrie got up, left the house, and went to the shed that Josh euphemistically called a barn. She was throwing a saddle on Josh's old workhorse when he entered.

"Carrie," he began.

"Don't you say a word to me. Not one single word. There is *nothing* you can say, darling—" She sneered the last word. "There isn't anything you can say to me. You have lied to me for the last time."

"Tem," he said softly. "Dallas."

Putting her head against the saddle for a moment, tears came to her eyes. "How dare you use the children to get what you want from me." She tried to pull the cinch on the horse, but her vision was too blurry to see.

Josh came to stand beside her, brushed her hands away, tightened the cinch, then stood to one side. "You're free to leave. I won't try to stop you. If it doesn't matter to you that I love you and that my children love you and that we've already made another child who will grow up without a father, then leave. I will make no effort to stop you."

Carrie started to mount the horse. She put her foot in the stirrup, but then, turning, she flew at Josh, hitting him on the chest with her fists. "I hate you, hate you, hate you! Do you understand me? I hate you as much as I love you."

When her first fury was past, Josh pulled her into his arms and held her while she cried.

"She's so beautiful," Carrie said. "She's the most beautiful woman I've ever seen."

"Rather like a coral snake. Beautiful and deadly."

"You don't really think that or you wouldn't have married her."

"I was nineteen years old when I married her, how was I supposed to have any sense?"

"I'm only twenty," Carrie sobbed. "Does that make me stupid?"

"Of course not. *You* have the good sense to be in love with *me*."

Carrie hiccuped a laugh between her tears.

"That's better. Now, I want you to come over here and sit down. I think it's time we had a talk."

"Talk? You're going to talk to me? Talk to the woman you profess to love? You couldn't be going to tell me what everyone else in the world seems to know about you, could you? Your . . . wife, your children, your brother, even my own brother—they all know. Don't look at me like that. For all that you seem to think that I'm stupid, I'm not. 'Ring wouldn't have taken to you last night as he did if he hadn't known something about you."

Josh pulled her to stretch out beside him on a pile of straw, his arm under her shoulders. "Where should I begin?"

"Why ask me? I don't know enough to tell you where you

should begin. Besides, are you sure you have time to talk to me? Won't your adorable, mysterious, overweight *wife* want you to go searching for the divorce paper? Not that you'll need much encouragement. Perhaps we could tie the rope we rescued Tem with around your waist and you can go diving for the papers. All I ask is that *I* be allowed to tie the knots."

Josh put his hand over his mouth so she wouldn't see his smile. "Nora is busy with Eric. You didn't see him, did you? Six foot. Blond. Adoring. Ten years her junior."

"She's older than you, isn't she?" It was the happiest thought Carrie'd had since Nora had entered the bedroom.

"Much," Josh said. "Now, do you want me to tell you about myself or do you want to continue being catty about Nora?"

Carrie had to take a moment to decide. "Listen," she said.

"My parents were two-bit actors, not very good, although I think my father would have been better if he hadn't drunk half a gallon of anything with alcohol in it every day of his adult life. Anyway, I was raised in dressing rooms and in dingy hotel rooms until I was eight. Then my father died and—"

"How? How did your father die?"

"Fell off a boardwalk into the street and was run over by a beer wagon. It was the way he would have wanted to go."

Carrie could hear that there was no love in Josh's voice for his father.

"My mother was past her prime as an actress or as anything else by then—she had a heavy hand with the whisky too. She tried to make it in the theater as an actress, but she couldn't even get bit parts. So, when I was ten, she answered an ad in the newspaper and traveled to Eternity, Colorado, and married a lonely widower, Mr. Elliot Greene, who had a little house in town and a grown son."

"Hiram?"

"The one and only." Josh's mouth tightened. "Hiram was always an overbearing, pompous ass, but he'd had all his father's attention for years and he resented me greatly."

Pausing, Josh smiled. "I came to love Mr. Greene. He was a kind and gentle man, and he continued to take care of me after my mother died two years after their marriage. But he died when I was sixteen and that self-important son of his inherited everything. Immediately after the funeral, Hiram told me that if I didn't obey him, he'd throw me out on my ear. I saved him the trouble. I left the house about four hours later."

"And what did you do?"

"The only thing I knew how to do: I went on the stage."

He paused as though Carrie were supposed to figure out more of the story on her own. It was then that she remembered something that Nora had said. "The Great Templeton," Carrie said.

Looking at Josh, she saw the little smile on his face. "Joshua Templeton," she said. "I've heard of you."

"Oh?" Josh said, one eyebrow raised. It was a smug look as though to say, Of course you've heard of me, the whole world has. She didn't like that look.

"An actor?" she said as she looked down her nose at him.

"A Shakespearian actor. The best actor in the world. The greatest—"

At his bragging, Carrie started to get up, but he pulled her back down beside him.

"I thought you'd be pleased," he said.

She took a deep breath. "All this time I thought you'd done something dreadful. I thought you'd been in jail for robbing people. I couldn't believe you were a murderer. And all it was, was that you're an actor." She said the last word the way she'd say, bug.

"Not just any actor." Josh sounded hurt and disbelieving. "I'm Joshua Templeton. THE Joshua Templeton."

"*I* am Carrie Montgomery. THE Carrie Montgomery."

Josh laughed.

"Would you mind telling me why you've felt the need to keep this from me? Why have you lied to me about your name and about what you've done in your past?"

"I thought it might make a difference."

Carrie took a moment to figure that out. "You vain peacock. You thought that if I knew you were a famous man, I might want you for that reason. How insulting to me."

When she started to get up again, Josh pulled her back down and began kissing her. "But then I didn't know you. I've never met anyone like you. Most women are impressed by the outward trappings of a man."

"You have met a sorry lot of women."

He laughed. "That I have. A very sorry lot. But then, the sorry lot and I were happy. They got the famous man they wanted and I got—"

"Do *not* tell me what you got from them."

Laughing again, he rolled off of her. "Here, I want to show you something." Digging around under the straw and under some rotting horse harness, he pulled out a small black trunk with the initials JT on it. He unbuckled it, opened it, and withdrew a packet from which he pulled out papers and handed them to her. They were photographs of the world-famous Joshua Templeton in the guise of Hamlet and Othello and Petruchio. There were shots of him in evening dress, and in another he was holding a sword and looking at the camera with a rakish gleam in his eye.

After looking at the photos for a few minutes, Carrie handed them back to him.

"Well?" he said eagerly. For so long now he'd wanted to tell her about himself, tell her that he wasn't a failure in his chosen profession. He wanted her to know that maybe he wasn't any good at farming, but he was very, very good at something.

"I don't like that man," Carrie said softly.

For a moment Josh couldn't speak. Women all over the world liked Joshua Templeton. Hadn't he proven that? From coast to coast in America and throughout most of Europe, he'd proven himself to be irresistible to women of every size, age, color, and marital state.

"I don't want to hurt your feelings," Carrie said politely, "but that man isn't real. You know, I remember now that Euphonia had some pictures of that man—you, I guess—in her house. All the girls swooned over him, you, but I didn't."

"You liked the sad but smiling man in the photo with his children," Josh said in wonder.

Carrie smiled at him. "That man has a soul. This man—" She pointed to the carefully posed studio pictures. "This man has no soul. There's nothing in his eyes."

At that Josh began to laugh as he hugged her to him. "I was afraid that if you found out about me, it would change your feelings for me. On the day you arrived, when I first saw you, all I thought of was your beautiful little body, but I told myself I couldn't touch you. I was sure you'd return home the moment you saw the dump where I was living." He smiled. "My experience with making women fall in love with you involves champagne and presents in black velvet boxes."

"Oh? And how long did this 'love' last?"

"Until I got her clothes off." He pulled her back into his arms when she tried to get away.

Carrie was trying to hold her body rigid, but he was kissing her neck. "It wasn't really love, was it? Tell me about her."

"Who?" Josh was moving down to her shoulder.

Carrie pushed him away. "Her! The big one in the house. The woman you stood up with in a church and swore to love and honor for the rest of your life. *That* one."

"Mmmmmm. Nora. Well, you can see why I fell for her." The moment he said it, he knew it was wrong, and he had to hold Carrie to him. "I *had* to marry her. She got pregnant."

"Got pregnant? All by her oversized self? She should watch what she drinks or get out of the way when the stork flies by."

"All right. I was eighteen when I met her. I'd had a bit of success on the stage and she was an established actress."

"Swept little you off your feet, no doubt."

Josh couldn't keep from laughing. "I was infatuated with her. I married her and Tem was born, then—"

"Tem!" Carrie said. "What is his name?"

"Joshua Templeton the Second."

"We thought you'd misspelled his name on the back of the photo. Go on, you were drooling down the front of Nora's sagging chest."

"After Tem was born, I went on the road and Nora stayed home with the baby." He paused and all laughter left his voice. "Carrie, I've done some things I'm not proud of. I was horribly unfaithful to my wife—as she was to me—but I have always loved my children. I didn't love any of the women I, well, took to bed, not even Nora, but I loved Tem from the moment I saw him. When I was traveling, I wrote him every week, even when he was an infant. When he was old enough to walk, I wrote him every day. I sent him presents, I thought about him, I—"

He stopped, embarrassed by this display of real emotion. There was a great deal of difference between what he showed to an audience and what he was showing now. His voice lowered. "I never let anyone know about Tem. Oh, they knew I had a son, but they didn't know what I felt about him."

"What about Dallas?"

Josh sighed. "I knew Nora was unfaithful, but I didn't care. She's the type of woman that all you want from her is to get your hands on those—" He cleared his throat. "I had no desire to live with her. I sent her money and assumed she was taking care of Tem. I assumed she loved him as much as I did. But then I was playing in Hamlet in Dallas, and I saw her in bed with another man. I didn't think that was good for Tem and I told her I wanted a divorce."

He didn't say anything for a moment.

"I assume she talked you out of the divorce," Carrie said, her voice dripping sarcasm.

"Yes, she did. Dallas was born nine months later and given that absurd name to remind me of when and where she was conceived. I put up with Nora for two years after Dallas was born, then I realized I had to get rid of her." He smiled. "The oddest thing. When I lost my desire for Nora I realized what a really bad actress she was."

"A condemnation if ever I heard one."

"Up until then, I'd believed Nora when she said she was taking care of the children and was being a good mother to them." Josh gave a snort. "I thought it would be so easy to get a divorce. She had cause and to be divorced for infidelity certainly didn't hurt my reputation any, and I gave Nora all the money I had saved over the years—seeing the poverty my parents lived in has made me spend less than I make—and asked only for the custody of my children. Nora was more than willing to trade the kids for money. It should have been very simple. I'd already hired an excellent French governess to take care of the children while I was on the stage."

"Why wasn't it simple? Why are you living on your brother's farm and killing corn?"

Josh gave an ironic laugh. "My own towering vanity. A vanity that surpassed everything that meant anything in life to me. A vanity that nearly cost me my children."

Carrie took his hand in hers. "Tell me what happened."

"A judge gave me what I asked for." Josh gave a grim smile of remembrance. "You should have seen me that day in the court-room when I was to plead with the judge to give me custody of my children. It was probably the most brilliant performance of my life. I planned it all very carefully. After all, I was the Great Templeton, and I was to argue my own case. How could I possibly lose? I wore a black cape lined with red satin and carried a silver-headed cane."

Josh looked up at the rafters of the shed. " 'The best laid plans,' etc. etc." He sighed. "In return for the judge giving me my children I was planning to honor him and the rest of the courtroom with a private, one-time-only performance by the great Shakespearian actor. Fool that I was, I went into the courtroom thinking I was doing them a favor."

Pausing, his voice grew soft. "I had to put on a show because I couldn't allow anyone to see how I really felt, that I was scared to my very bones of losing my children."

"What did you ask the judge for?" Carrie urged.

"I talked for over an hour. You should have seen my audience —for that's how I saw the spectators in the courtroom. I had them in the palm of my hand. I made them laugh; I made them cry. I frightened them; I soothed them. They were mine. I told them how much I loved my children, how I'd do *anything* in the world for them. I said that I would give up all my worldly goods in order to have them. I said I'd even go so far as to give up the stage for them. By this time I'd made them realize that if the world lost me as an actor, the world would suffer a great deal. I went on to say that I'd go so far as to farm the land like a peasant of old if I could but have my children. I think it was at this point that I flipped my satin-lined cape so the audience could try to picture *me* as a farmer.

"When I'd finished, I received a standing ovation from the audience and I was sure I'd won my case. The judge said he'd never heard such an eloquent plea in his life and he had but one question for me: Did I even know anyone who owned a farm. I, with a slight bow, told him that my brother was a member of that worthy profession. The judge said such a speech as mine should be rewarded, so he was going to give me exactly what I'd asked for. All my worldly goods were to be put up for sale at auction, with the exception of one suit, and all the money was to be put into trust for my children. I was to refrain from going on the stage for a period of four years, during which time I was to live on and work my brother's farm with my children. If I could make it through four years, then the children would be mine. The judge, after giving his sentence, gave me a little smile and said he thought I was going to miss my red cape, that I used it so well.

"Later my attorney informed me that the judge's wife had run off with an actor two years before and that his uncles, aunts, and cousins were farmers. I'd managed to insult the man on every level."

Josh sighed. "So that's what I did. I moved back to Eternity, took my stepfather's name in the hope that no one would recognize me, and tried to become a farmer."

"So," Carrie said, "you have to live on your brother's farm and be a normal person for four years. No applause. No footlights. No adoring young ladies begging you for your autograph. Nothing but people who love you and see you as you are, warts and all."

Josh smiled. "Lots of warts."

"A few. But at least they're not hidden under greasepaint."

Josh began nuzzling her neck. "Right now I wish I didn't have anything at all on, greasepaint, clothes, not anything."

Responding to him, Carrie slipped her arms around his neck and kissed him with weeks' worth of pent-up desire.

"Papa! Papa!" Dallas yelled as she came running into the shed. "There's a man here, and he wants to see you."

Josh's brain was a little foggy as he pulled away from Carrie. "Who is it?"

"I don't know," Dallas whispered loudly, "but I think he's God."

Carrie and Josh looked at each other. " 'Ring," they said in unison.

Chapter Sixteen

Carrie and Josh were still brushing straw off of each other as they walked back to the house.

"He's going to make me go back with him," Carrie mumbled. "As soon as he meets that fat woman you married, he's going to make me leave with him."

Josh tightened his grip on her arm. "I do wish you would give me a little more credit and your brother less. I can handle this."

"By fishing for the papers down Nora's pond?" Carrie said nastily.

"One does what one must," Josh said, then had to hold Carrie to him. "Good morning, brother," Josh called to 'Ring, who was kneeling to speak to the children.

"I have three little boys of my own," 'Ring was saying to Tem as he rubbed Choo-choo's ears. "You'll have to come and visit them and sail on a boat."

"And I'll teach them to ride a horse," Tem said, but since all three of his new cousins by marriage were younger than he was, he didn't think much of them.

Standing, 'Ring handed Carrie a large box that she knew contained her mother's wedding dress.

In the next moment, Nora came out of the house, her big blond Eric following behind her like Choo-choo followed Carrie.

"Oh, no," Josh said, hurrying forward, but Carrie pulled him back.

"If you think that my brother is stupid enough to fall for something like that painted, fat, overblown—" She broke off because

'Ring was kissing Nora's bejeweled hand and looking at her as though she were the most delicious thing he'd ever seen.

"You were saying . . ." Josh said.

Her nose in the air, Carrie swept past him, and when she reached her brother, she put herself between him and Nora. "How kind of you to stop by, Mrs.—" She broke off, not knowing what to call the hideous woman.

"West," Nora said, looking over Carrie's head to 'Ring. "Nora West is my professional name."

"I saw you as Juliet," 'Ring said. "You were divine."

"Must have had a mule skinner to play Romeo," Carrie muttered before looking up at her brother and batting her eyelashes. "You must have been a child to have seen her when she was young enough to play Juliet."

Grabbing Carrie's arm, Josh pulled her toward the house. "Food," he said. "Carrie has to make lunch for everyone."

Once Josh and Carrie were inside, he turned on her. "Can't you contain yourself for even a few hours? At least until I get the paper from her?"

"You expect me to be *nice* to the woman who is married to *my* husband?"

"Just for a few hours."

Carrie gave a nasty little laugh. "Maybe you are a professional liar, but I'm not."

Josh rubbed his eyes in exasperation then laughed. "I cannot believe my own vanity in thinking that my being a renowned actor would change your feelings for me. Alas, the Great Templeton has been reduced to 'a professional liar.' " He drew her into his arms. "Do you think I'll ever be able to impress you? After my sentence is up and I go back on stage, are you going to come to see me? Will you swoon over my performances?"

She closed her eyes in ecstasy as he kissed her neck. "I think I might like for you to quote some of 'Ring's poetry just to me."

He touched her cheek. " '*See, how she leans her cheek upon her hand! O, that I were a glove upon that hand, that I might touch that cheek!* ' "

She smiled at him. "I'm not sure I'll like hearing you say such things to other women, even women as old and as fat as she is."

"It won't be real, Carrie," he said softly. "I am a liar with them, but I won't be a liar with you."

She smiled at him and he kissed her.

"What a cozy little scene," Nora said from the doorway. "Of course, Joshua, darling, it's not as though I haven't seen you kiss hundreds of other women, both on stage and off."

Josh released Carrie. "I want the paper, Nora, and I want it now."

"I've told you where it is," she purred at him.

Josh kept his eyes off Nora's magnificent bosom, for he knew that Carrie was watching him. "What do you want?"

"Why, I want you, of course. I've missed you."

Catching Carrie's hand in his, Josh squeezed it. "You want me and half a dozen other men. I don't have any money, you know that, so what else could you want?"

"A bit of Warbrooke Shipping."

Josh opened his mouth to tell her that he didn't know what she was talking about, but then he began to put the pieces of the puzzle together. Carrie seemed to have limitless access to money and she came from Warbrooke, Maine. He had known she was wealthy, but he'd had no idea she was *that* wealthy. Warbrooke Shipping's motto, We Carry the World, was known everywhere, from China to India to the wilds of America and Australia.

"Josh, my love," Nora purred. "I do believe you've been away from the stage too long. Your face is as readable as a child's. So, you didn't know that she was part of Warbrooke Shipping." Smiling in triumph, Nora sat down at the table.

Josh turned to Carrie, ready to tell her what he thought of her not telling him that her family was so very, very rich, but then he smiled at her. Carrie hadn't kept that fact a secret from him; it just hadn't occurred to her that her wealth was of any consequence.

On impulse, he kissed her, not a kiss of passion, but a kiss of thanks, thanks to her for coming into his life. With her by his side, with a wife who had her feet so firmly on the ground that she didn't consider "who" her family was to be of any importance, he didn't think she'd ever allow his vanity as an actor to rule his life. Carrie would never let him forget what was *really* important in life.

Having no idea what Josh was thinking as he looked at her with so much love in his eyes, Carrie smiled and stepped closer to him.

"How did you find out about Warbrooke Shipping?" Josh asked Nora, stalling for time while he tried to figure out what to do. He could not, under any conditions, allow Carrie's family to buy his freedom.

"Your dear brother Hiram. Really, Josh, you shouldn't treat that man so badly. He has given you this darling farm." Nora looked around the house with a sneer. "I would never have believed you could have lived this way. Tem says you cook."

As Josh held Carrie's hand and looked at his former wife, he wondered how he'd ever thought her beautiful. Maybe he'd been drunk. "So Hiram told you I had married into wealth."

"Yes. It seems your little—" She looked Carrie up and down. "Your little mistress did something to displease Hiram and he investigated her." She looked up at Josh. "Did you know that her adorable brother has spent the morning buying large pieces of Eternity?"

Josh looked at Carrie in question, but she just shrugged. " 'Ring does that wherever he goes."

Josh blinked a couple of times at her nonchalance, both at her acceptance of the amount of money her family had and of her brother's buying habits. Everyone needed a hobby.

"I want fifty grand," Nora said. "When you put fifty thousand dollars in my hands, the paper is yours." After giving them both a smile, she left the house.

Carrie gave a sigh. "An odious woman. Really odious. I am disappointed in you for marrying someone like her."

"That's odd," Josh said sarcastically. "Most second wives like the first wives. Where are you going?"

"To tell 'Ring I need fifty thousand dollars," Carrie said.

Josh caught her arm. "Just like that? You're going to ask your brother for that fabulous amount of money? What are you going to tell him you need it for? To purchase a divorce paper? Yesterday and this morning all you've talked about is how 'Ring is of such high moral character that he'll be furious if he finds out we're not actually married."

"Then I won't tell him."

"You'll just ask him for fifty thousand, and he'll give it to you with no questions as to why you want it?"

"Of course. Families help each other. Money doesn't matter. Your being married to someone else is much more important than money."

At that Josh had to sit down at the table and put his face in his hands. He'd never met anyone with the philosophy of life that Carrie had. He wanted to rage at her that she was too naive to realize that money meant *everything*, that people lied, cheated, stole, and killed for money. He'd like to be able to tell her that she didn't understand because she'd never had to earn money, had never had the responsibility of having to support herself, much less a family. But she'd left him for a mere six weeks, and during that time, she'd not only supported herself, she'd changed the economy of an entire town.

"Carrie," he said softly. "I've never met people like your family. If money isn't important to you Montgomerys, what is?"

"Oh, money is very important to us. It's just that love is more important. Love and money in that order. We'll give up money for love, but not love for money. But then, money isn't usually a problem for my family. Our major talents seem to be marrying well and earning money."

Laughing at what she'd said, he stood and hugged her. "Well, my talents lie elsewhere. And one of my talents is that I do take care of my own family. Maybe at times I don't do it as well as I should, but I take care of them. You are *not* going to ask your brother for a dime. You're not going to depend on him to get you out of this. This is my problem and I'll solve it. Do you understand me?"

"But it would be so easy to have 'Ring write her a check. Then—"

He kissed her to silence. "Do you want to tell your brother the truth about us? That you're carrying my child and we're not married?"

Carrie sighed. "No, I don't. Oh, Josh, I don't understand it. Everyone else in my family has such easy love affairs. 'Ring says that when he and his wife met they fell in love at first sight and they had no problems at all." She gave Josh a hurt look. "You didn't even know that you loved me when you first saw me."

Josh laughed. "True, I didn't, so how about if I spend the rest of my life trying to make it up to you?" Pulling her into his arms, he kissed her. "You love me, but do you trust me enough to solve our problems?"

"Of course I trust you."

"Then do what I tell you, no questions asked."

"But—"

He kissed her again. "I take care of my own family, understand? You're not a Montgomery anymore, you're a Templeton." Carrie smiled. "I like that better than Greene. Carrie Templeton." As she looked up at Josh, she knew it wasn't going to be easy to prevent herself from going to 'Ring. All her life she'd gone to her brothers or father when she needed anything. "All right," she said at last, kissing him again. "I'll do what you say."

Chapter Seventeen

Carrie knew that the most difficult thing she'd ever done in her life was to lie to her brother. 'Ring had arranged for the wedding to take place at five o'clock that day, and when 'Ring made plans, he expected them to take place. Only his wife was able to laugh at his schedules and get away with it. As for Carrie, if 'Ring told her there was to be a meeting at six in the morning, she would be at that meeting and on time.

Now she had to lie to him. She had to tell him that she couldn't be remarried until the next morning at ten. The worst part of lying was that she didn't know what was going to happen between today and tomorrow. She didn't know what Josh had in mind to do about Nora and the unsigned paper. Carrie had visions of Josh wrestling with Nora to get the paper, and above all, she was sure that 'Ring would find out about Josh being married to another woman. Would he do something primitive like draw a gun on Josh? Her brothers had often hit men who had been too forward with their precious little sister, so what would 'Ring do if he found out a man had impregnated his sister while not being married to her? Oh, how she wished her perfect older brother had experienced problems and obstacles in his own marriage.

She was shaking when she went outside to tell 'Ring that the wedding would have to be postponed.

To her utter bewilderment, 'Ring smiled at her, then offered to ride back into town with Nora and Eric. He was disgustingly pleased with Nora and asked her if she'd perform a few scenes from *Romeo and Juliet* for him during the short journey.

Nora preened and, to Carrie's way of thinking, made a fool of herself in front of the three men. Carrie knew it might be her imagination, but it seemed to her that all of them were looking at Nora with big eyes. Carrie kicked Josh's shin, then smiled at him when he yelped in pain.

When the carriage was out of sight, with 'Ring riding beside it on his horse, Josh turned to Carrie. "Could you rustle us up some food? The kids and I have some work to do."

"Rustle—?" Carrie began. "Food? I am being sent to the kitchen? What are you three going to do? I want to participate."

Josh kissed her cheek in an absentminded way. "What I have planned is for actors—professional liars, as it were. You, my dear, couldn't lie well enough to convince a chicken."

"I just lied to my brother!" She was insulted by what he was saying.

"Yes, you did, and he didn't believe a word you said."

"Of course he did. If he hadn't believed me, he wouldn't have gone away. He would—"

"I think you underestimate your brother. I don't think he's the stern moralist you think he is. In fact, I think he's enjoying everything, and it's my guess that tonight he'll flatter Nora enough that he gets most of the story from her. Nora is very susceptible to flattery."

"You should talk," Carrie said under her breath.

Josh pretended he hadn't heard her. There were disadvantages to living with someone who knew so much about you, about the real you, not the person you wanted the world to think you were. "Now, make us something to eat while I talk to the kids."

"Is Carrie going to cook eggs?" Dallas asked, sounding as though she might cry.

Josh ushered his children outside.

"Just follow my lead and say nothing, you understand?" Josh said to Carrie. Carrie, Josh, and the children were standing outside Nora's room in the hotel, and it was about six o'clock, an hour after she and Josh were to have been married.

"D'uh," Carrie said, mocking an idiot. "I think I can do that." She was still smarting over the fact that Josh had felt it safe to tell two children what he was planning, but he had left her out.

Winking at her, he knocked on the door.

Nora, wearing a red silk gown that was—how could this be

possible?—lower than the one she'd worn during the day, opened the door.

Carrie was still gaping at Nora's dress as Josh pulled her into the room, the children close behind them, and shut the door.

"You win, Nora," he said.

She smiled. "So, you have the fifty thousand?"

"No, I don't have it, at least I don't have that much money to give to you. I plan to keep every penny for myself."

For a second Nora looked puzzled, then recovered herself. "But, darling, no money, no paper. You'll never get your divorce if I don't get the money, and you'll never get to marry your little heiress." She made it sound as though the only reason Josh would want to marry Carrie was for her money.

Josh put his arm around Carrie's shoulders. "You know, Nora, I've been on my brother's farm for one whole year now, and I can tell you that it's been hell. I have to get up before dawn and spend the day hoeing weeds or burning fields or other disgusting things. I've hated every minute of it."

"Of course you have, darling. I knew you would. Don't you remember how hard I laughed when I heard the judge's sentence?"

"Well, you were right, therefore I've decided to give up farming."

Nora raised one eyebrow. "But the judge said the children would be taken from you if you didn't live on Hiram's farm for four years."

"That's another thing," Josh said. "Come out here, you brats," he said.

Carrie looked at him in disbelief as he grabbed an arm of each child and pulled them forward. Carrie's disbelief intensified as she looked at the children. Minutes before, while standing outside the door, they had been clean and presentable, but now their hair was mussed, there was a streak of dirt on Dallas's dress, and they both had tears running down their cheeks.

"When I told the judge I wanted them, I had no idea what I was saying. I guess I thought raising children would be easy, but they're brats. They take all my time, they whine and complain, and they're dirty little creatures. So, Nora, my dear, they are yours."

Josh pushed the children toward Nora.

Thank heaven Carrie was in too great a state of shock to say anything.

"Papa," Dallas screamed. "No, no, we want to stay with you. We'll be good, we promise."

"Josh, you can't mean—" Nora began.

"Of course I can. The judge said that the children would go to you if I defaulted on my sentence, and I am going to default. I'm going back to the stage where I belong."

"B . . . but what about her?" Nora asked, looking at Carrie. "What about the little love of your life?"

Before Josh could open his mouth, Carrie spoke up. She wasn't going to be left out of this. "We are going to live in sin," she said brightly. "We decided that sin was much more exciting than boring old marriage." She gave Josh an adoring look. "As soon as we're free of the children we're going . . . Where was it, dear?"

"Venice," Josh said, and there was admiration in his eyes.

"Yes, Venice. We shall use the thousands I receive from Warbrooke Shipping and go to Venice. Or would you rather go to Paris first? I do need some new clothes."

"Wherever you want, my dearest." Josh kissed her hand.

Josh turned back to Nora. "You see, my dear, it doesn't matter if you and I are married or not. I have Carrie and her money and I no longer have the burden of those brats. *Au revoir.*" With that, he tucked Carrie's arm in his and started for the door.

Behind them Dallas screamed, "Papa, don't leave us. Please, please don't leave us. We'll do anything if you'll let us stay with you. Anything."

Josh had to hold Carrie's arm firmly to keep her from turning back to the child. When they were outside the door, Carrie looked at Josh. "Is Dallas all right?" she whispered.

"No," Josh replied. "She has a serious case of overacting, and I plan to talk to her about it. No child of mine is going to get away with that." He smiled at Carrie. "You were excellent. Maybe we'll make a liar out of you yet."

"Josh," Carrie said slowly, "the children *were* acting, weren't they? And you were, too, weren't you? You're not going to leave them with her, are you?"

He looked at her. "What do you think?"

"I think you'd kill before you gave them up."

Smiling, he kissed her hand. "Let's go get something to eat. I missed lunch." His eyes were twinkling, because it was Carrie who had served the inedible lunch.

In spite of Josh's reassurances, Carrie was still nervous. She picked at her food at dinner and, later, when Josh took her to her dress shop, she wasn't interested in it. Her employees had a hundred questions to ask her, but Carrie couldn't think of the answers. Instead, she turned to Josh and said, "What if she wants to keep them?"

"You don't know Nora."

"Not as well as you do," she snapped at him. "And at one time you thought she was a good mother."

"I was younger and dumber," he answered, trying to make her smile, or make her angry—anything but as scared as she was. Even when he told her that he wasn't going to allow her to name their child, what with her propensity for names like Choo-choo and Paris in the Desert, he got no reaction from her.

When they went back to the farm, it was dark, and Josh told Carrie he was sleeping with her. The truth of the matter was, he wanted to hold her, wanted to be near the woman he loved tonight.

"You just gave your children away and you expect me to sleep with you?" Carrie said.

He kissed her hand, trying, and succeeding, to sound lighthearted. "At last my acting has received a compliment from you."

She glared at him. "You don't touch me until you get those children back." When she slammed the bedroom door in his face, she heard a sound from him that was half whimper, half smug laughter. And there was something else in the sound that almost made her open the door again, but she didn't.

For the first time in her life, Carrie didn't sleep for the whole night. When dawn came creeping over the horizon, she dragged herself out of bed and, holding Choo-choo, she went into the parlor. Josh was already sitting at the table, and he was wearing the clothes he'd worn the day before.

"You haven't been to bed, have you?" she said, sitting across from him.

When he looked up at her, there was no falseness in his eyes. "I couldn't help remembering how good a liar Nora is. And how spiteful. She might want to keep the kids just to repay me. She might—" Breaking off, he looked down at his empty coffee cup.

When Carrie reached out and took his hand in hers, Josh got out of the chair and went to kneel before her, his head in her lap. She stroked his hair.

"I'm afraid, Carrie," he said softly. "I can't lose them. When I came up with my little plan, it seemed so foolproof, but now I don't know. If Nora told a court how I'd given the children back to her and told them what I said, I think the judge—any judge—would take the children away from me. What will I do without them? You and the kids are the only things in my life that mean anything to me."

She kissed his head and wanted to reassure him, but she was as afraid as he was. "Tell me what you have planned."

When he lifted his head, he turned away from her so she wouldn't see him wipe away tears and said, "They're to come to the church at ten o'clock. By then they're to have made Nora's life such hell that she'll be glad to give me the paper just so she can get rid of them."

"Then we'll have to go on the assumption that your children are as good at acting as you are. They are the children of the Great Templeton, you know."

Josh managed to smile at her. "Come on, let's see what we can find to eat and then let's go. We have to trust the children."

Carrie nodded and tried to keep Josh from seeing the way her hands were shaking.

It was cold in the church, Carrie thought, but it wasn't as cold as she felt. Her hands were clammy, yet she was sweating. It was five minutes after ten, and there was no sign of the children. 'Ring, sitting in the first pew in the otherwise empty church, looked at his pocket watch for the third time, and the minister had already said that he had another wedding in an hour.

But Josh and Carrie had said that they couldn't be married without the children there, and they meant it. Josh took Carrie's hand, and his was as cold as hers. Even Choo-choo, hiding under Carrie's old-fashioned dress, was quiet.

After Josh looked at her once and saw the fear on her face under her veil, he couldn't meet her eyes again. Too many thoughts were going through his head. Had Nora seen through the whole scam and taken the children away with her? Was she going to hold out until she got her Warbrooke money? Dallas was only five years old, yet Josh had asked her to be mean to her own mother. Could the child do that? *Should* she do that?

Round and round Josh's thoughts went. Had he been so clever that he'd lost his children? Due to his reputation with women, the judge had been reluctant to give Josh custody of his children, so if Nora went to a judge and testified to what Josh had said to her last evening, about the children being brats and his not wanting them, no court in the world would give the children to Josh.

He squeezed Carrie's hand harder.

Standing up, 'Ring walked up behind them. "It's twenty minutes after," he said to his sister. "Is there something you'd like to tell me?"

"No," Carrie said, but her voice squeaked. "I mean . . ."

"I'm sure Nora will bring the children soon," Josh said. "She is an old friend of theirs and—"

He broke off at the commotion at the back of the church.

Nora entered, and for the first time since Josh had known her, Nora looked awful. Her dress was dirty, her hair hanging about her shoulders; there were dark circles of sleeplessness under her eyes, and worse, she looked her age.

Dragging Tem and Dallas behind her by their wrists, she marched to the front of the church, practically threw the children into the first pew, then held out a paper and pen to Josh. Her face was past rage as she looked at him.

Josh had to stick the pen in his mouth to dampen the ink, then held the paper on his hand as he signed it. When he was done, he put the paper inside his coat pocket and looked at the woman who used to be his wife.

Nora opened her mouth to speak, but could say nothing. Turning on her heel, she stomped out of the church.

Very calmly, Carrie and Josh turned back to the minister. "You may begin," Josh said.

"Dearly beloved, we are gathered here today in the sight of—"

Carrie turned to Josh as he looked at her, and in the next minute the two of them exploded in laughter. In unison they turned to the dirty, scruffy children who were sitting on the pew, legs swinging, and wearing expressions of being extremely pleased with themselves. Bending, Carrie and Josh opened their arms to them.

While the minister and 'Ring watched, the four of them hugged and kissed each other and laughed uproariously at some private joke.

Josh was the first one to recover himself. He took Tem's hand and Carrie's, while she took Dallas's hand. "You may begin again," Josh said. "You may marry *all* of us."

"Hooray!" Dallas yelled, and the children said, "I will" and "I do" with the adults, and at the end of the ceremony, everyone kissed everyone else excessively.

Dear Readers,

Two weeks ago I finished a very special book. I don't say that about all my books because the truth is, being a writer is rather like playing a never-ending game of Russian roulette. You never know what's going to happen when you start a book, and as far as I can tell, there's no way to predict the outcome. You can research for months, plot for months and when you write, the book just plain doesn't have any sparkle. Once I spent six weeks traveling all over western America doing research for a novel about mountain men, then spent three months reading and plotting, but when I started writing the book, the hero and heroine didn't like each other. Not romance-novel didn't like, but genuinely cared nothing about each other. After a hundred and fifty pages, I threw the thing out—along with all that research—and started from scratch again.

But every so often my Guardian Angel seems to say, "Let's give Jude a break," and when she does that I get a super book, a book that takes over my mind, my body, every fiber of my being. *SWEET LIAR*, the book I just completed, was just such a book.

One day about a year ago, all day long I kept thinking about my grandmother, whom I loved very much, and that night on television there was a show about a man's search for his grandmother, who had disappeared. The next day my editor called and said her grandmother had died the day before. These three things happening in the course of twenty-four hours made me think of a story of a young woman whose grandmother had left her family years before.

Over the next few months I continued to work on *Eternity*, but I also made lots of notes on my grandmother story. Then in April of 1991, I went to New York for a month to research my grandmother story, which I was now calling *SWEET LIAR,* and to see my friends. Ordinarily I am the most unsocial creature in the world. At home in Santa Fe I go out so seldom that I have my secretary start my car for me once a week so the battery won't run down, but in New York, I go out to lunches and teas and movies—just like a normal person.

The difference on this trip was that suddenly I didn't want to see anyone. I stayed in my rented apartment for the whole month, doing nothing but thinking about *SWEET LIAR*—and for the next six months I thought of nothing else but this book.

Sometimes I don't talk about my books, but with this one I never shut up. If anyone had the misfortune to call me and ask how I was doing it would be ten minutes before I quit telling them about *SWEET LIAR.*

I was so wrapped up in this book and its characters that I cried for the entire last two weeks of writing it. I think the love story in *SWEET LIAR* is the most poignant, the most meaningful, the most personal one I've ever written. During the last three days of writing I didn't sleep or eat much, I just typed and cried. I don't know if the author bawling through the end of her book is a recommendation or not, but I can attest to the fact that the book is indeed involving.

Last of all, I want to tell you that *SWEET LIAR* has a contemporary setting. Throughout my career I've found that each of my stories demands its own special time and place. From its conception, *SWEET LIAR* cried out to be set in the present day. When I wrote *A Knight in Shining Armor* I thoroughly enjoyed working on the contemporary sections and so I was delighted to get the chance to write a novel set entirely in the modern world—a modern world with the fairy tale still in it.

I loved everything about this book: the hero, the heroine, the story. And writing it was a great deal of fun (yes, even the parts where I cried were, in their own way, fun). I got to write about my beloved New York City, and I got to visit a few characters from some of my earlier books.

On the day I finished the book, 14 August 1991, I went to my secretary's office and told her I was done. She said I looked awful, but by then I hadn't eaten or slept for nearly three days (no, I did not lose a single ounce. I guess my Guardian Angel is only willing to do so much) and I was shaky. After she read the book she said the story was worth whatever I had to go through to write it.

I hope you, the reader, will like my story and will like my Michael Taggert as much as Samantha and I do.